*Los Angeles Times* Bestseller

A *New York Times Book Review* Editor's Choice

A *San Francisco Chronicle* Best Book of 2012

## PRAISE FOR

# PANORAMA CITY

"Antoine Wilson's delightful *Panorama City* is a transcript of 10 tapes recorded over one long night in the hospital by Oppen Porter, a 28-year-old, 6'6" 'slow absorber' who fears he won't live until morning, laying out for his unborn son an account of his life . . . With very dry wit, a cockeyed tolerance for human foibles and a goofy idealism, Oppen painstakingly records his journey, helped along the way by bus drivers, a pretty police officer, a collector of abandoned shopping carts, and Carmen, the Mexican prostitute who's carrying his child. Long before the last tape begins, readers will have grown to love Wilson's earnest, well-meaning protagonist, who just wants to learn what it means to be a man of the world." —Shelf Awareness

"Charming and oddball . . . A bracingly humane story whose narrator's wisdom and forbearance make you see the world afresh . . . A delightful performance, a winning and warm story whose success can be credited to Wilson's canny and often piercing use of Oppen's sensibility . . . Like Oppen, the reader concludes his story feeling something akin to joy."
—Adam Ross, *New York Times Book Review*

"Clever and wisely funny." —Elissa Schappell, *Vanity Fair*

"In his second novel, Antoine Wilson brings much comedic grace and a sure feel for Southern California. In spots, *Panorama City* is laugh-aloud funny, building toward a slapstick climax that the Marx Brothers might have relished . . . [*Panorama City* is] worth cheering for taking a route rare in serious contemporary fiction: finding a way to a happy ending." —*Cleveland Plain Dealer*

"A gift . . . An astonishing narrative that offers the pleasures of irony without the sting . . . Nowhere in [Oppen's] purview is there blame or regret. He travels from innocence to experience without falling into disillusionment. The great triumph of the book is that Oppen matures without spoiling. He comes to affirm the integrity of his innocence, which is its own wisdom."
—*Los Angeles Review of Books*

"A crisp comic novel . . . Recalls some of the best of the mid-century South, New Orleans specifically, *The Moviegoer* and *A Confederacy of Dunces* particularly. Those books never mistook time spent seeing through a cracked idea for a loss of urgency . . . Wilson's [novel] is a trot and a treat." —*San Francisco Chronicle*

"As enjoyable a comic novel as I have read all year, a coming-of-age story that vividly captures the modern world through innocent eyes." —Largehearted Boy

"Idiosyncratic . . . Charming . . . Indelible." —Flavorwire

"Fresh and flawlessly crafted as well as charmingly genuine . . . Untouched by cynicism, Oppen's interpretation of the world around him evokes both the sublime and the ridiculous . . . framing a classic coming-of-age story in an unexpected way." — *Publishers Weekly*, starred review

"This is a book you will hold in your head all day long, a book you will look forward to when you get home from work, a book you will still be savoring as you drift into sleep. *Panorama City* is often very funny. It is filled with joy and wonder, and a sort of goodness you had stopped believing might be even possible. Antoine Wilson's sentences are like diamond necklaces but his greatest treasure is his human heart."
—Peter Carey, author of *Parrot and Olivier in America*

"Candid and perceptive . . . Readers who enjoyed Mark Haddon and Greg Olear will appreciate Wilson's authorial voice . . . A funny, heartfelt, and genuine novel."
—*Booklist*

"God bless Oppen Porter! His innocence and lack of pretense are our good fortune and our delight. Under his observation, our follies and schemes and manias go up in the brightest, funniest, heart-rending flames. This is precisely (and artfully) because he does not judge them. *Panorama City* is charming, absurd, very funny, and best of all, humane through and through."
—Paul Harding, author of *Tinkers*

"This funny and wise novel reminds us that the best fiction often treads the subtle line between tragedy and comedy. With ears keenly tuned to the music of language, and a limpid mind slyly hidden behind a persistent soliloquist, Antoine Wilson has written an intricate novel that makes us laugh and cry."
—Yiyun Li, author of *Gold Boy, Emerald Girl*

# PANORAMA CITY

Also by Antoine Wilson

*The Interloper*

# PANORAMA CITY

Antoine Wilson

Mariner Books
Houghton Mifflin Harcourt
Boston New York

First Mariner Books edition 2013



www.hmhbooks.com

Portions of this novel have appeared in a different form in the magazine *A Public Space*.

*Library of Congress Cataloging-in-Publication Data*
Wilson, Antoine.
Panorama city / Antoine Wilson.
p. cm.
ISBN 978-0-547-87512-5 ISBN 978-0-544-10627-7 (pbk.)
I. Title.
PS3623.I5778P36 2012
813'.54—DC23
2012014832

Printed in the United States of America
DOC 10 9 8 7 6 5 4 3 2 1

*To Léonide,*
*and to the memory of his grandfather,*
*William E. Wilson, M.D.*

# PART ONE

## TAPE I, SIDES A & B

# MAYOR

If you set aside love and friendship and the bonds of family, luck, religion, and spirituality, the desire to better mankind, and music and art, and hunting and fishing and farming, self-importance, and public and private transportation from buses to bicycles, if you set all that aside money is what makes the world go around. Or so it is said. If I wasn't dying prematurely, if I wasn't dying right now, if I was going to live to ripeness or rottenness instead of meeting the terminus bolted together and wrapped in plaster in the Madera Community Hospital, if I had all the time in the world, as they say, I would talk to you first of all about the joys of cycling or the life of the mind, but seeing as I could die any minute, just yesterday Dr. Singh himself said that I was lucky to be alive, I was unconscious and so didn't hear it myself, Carmen told me, I'll get down to so-called brass tacks.

First of all, ignore common advice such as a fool and his money are soon parted. Parting with money is half the pleasure, and earning it is the other half, there is no pleasure in holding on to it, that only stiffens the vitality, especially in large amounts, though the world will advise you otherwise, being full of people who would make plaster statues of us. Second, I haven't made knowledge of my life yet, I'm only twenty-eight years old, when you get to be my age you'll know how young that is, and if you're a man of the world by then I salute you, the road isn't wide or straight. Everything you need to know is contained in my experience somewhere, that's my philosophy, but I'm afraid you're going to have to make the knowledge out of it yourself. The world operates according to a mysterious logic, Juan-George, I want to illustrate some of its intricacies, so that you can stand on the shoulders of giants, not, as Paul Renfro used to say, the shoulders of ants.

For the first twenty-seven years of my life nothing happened to me. I rode my bicycle into town every day from our patch of wilderness, I rode into Madera and asked my friends if they had any work for me, everyone called me Mayor, even Tony Adinolfi, who was the real mayor, called me Mayor. Then came my so-called mistake. On the day in question I was working a construction job in Madera, or rather it was a demolition job, I was carting wheelbarrows of drywall out of a house, it is a strange thing to remove the walls from the inside of a house. At some point I noticed that my bicycle, this was my blue-flake three-speed Schwinn with the leather saddlebags, a fine machine that made the softest burring sound along the asphalt roads of

Madera County, I noticed it was missing. It had happened before, it was fine with me, except this time whoever took it didn't return it to the job site by the end of the working day and so I had to head home on foot. The construction guys were going to a bar, and I avoid bars, when you're six and a half feet tall, drunk people always want to fight you or try to take your binoculars. Our patch of wilderness was some miles outside town on a road that didn't lead anywhere good, there was never anybody to hitch a ride from. I walked with my hands clasped behind my back, you should always walk with your hands behind your back unless you are carrying something. People who walk with their arms swinging look like apes, my philosophy.

I noticed some gnats zigzagging over a culvert, a nearby tree let some sunlight through, it carved a cube of light out of the shade, the gnats seemed to like having it to themselves. I was watching the gnats when a vehicle appeared on the road, coming the opposite way, it was the Alvarez brothers' pickup. Hector and Mike were two of my oldest friends, still are. Whenever we saw each other on that road we played a game called chicken, but usually I was on my bike, usually it was me and my bike that ended up in the ditch. This time Mike saw me in the road and even though I was on foot he steered that truck toward me and gunned the engine. He drove straight at me, he stayed on course until Hector's grin turned into a look of terror, Mike's stayed a grin, and I leaped into the ditch just in time to avoid getting hit. I dusted myself off, Greg Yerkovich and some girls were laughing in the back. Once Greg saw that I was okay, once he saw that I'd gotten up just fine, he flipped me the bird, which was our traditional hello and goodbye gesture. He tapped the back window and Mike spun the tires, gravel pinging the wheel wells like crazy. Then they were gone, leaving behind only the smell of burning oil, that head gasket was done for. I just kept on walking home. We had been playing chicken so long it had become a matter of routine, I mean no matter what happened I always ended up in the ditch, there was no real game to it, I was always the chicken.

It was getting late, the sun was dipping behind me so that my shadow grew larger and larger in front of me until it became one with the general darkness. Eventually I saw the house, or I saw the blue glow of the television in the front window, the roof was a black line dividing it from the stars. I don't like watching television, you're always bouncing around from one person to the next, back and forth and looking at everything from all angles, I don't know how anybody can watch television, it seems like they made it for hummingbirds, but your grandfather George loved television, especially when he stopped leaving the house, he was always trying to convince me to watch television, he said it was my ticket to the world, he always talked about me knowing something of the world, he said you can go everywhere with television from the comfort of your own chair. I've never been able to watch more than five minutes without getting a headache. I should be clear that it was his body that decided to stop leaving the house, he was only a passenger in his body, his words. After he stopped leaving the house he watched a lot of television and worked on a Letter to the Editor, and I brought groceries and supplies home on my bicycle. I became a sort of caretaker to your grandfather, though I never thought about it that way until he was gone and people began to worry that he wasn't going to be around to take care of me. As usual, they had it backwards.

I walked toward the glowing light of the television and tripped over something in the tall grass, namely my bicycle. Everything was in working order, the grass was wet but the bicycle was dry, meaning it hadn't been sitting there long, so I knew who had taken it from the construction site, mystery solved, and as I rolled it to the porch I thought about what I would say to the Alvarez brothers, starting with they should check to see if I'm still in town before going through the trouble of returning my bicycle to the house, which was why I was distracted, which was why my thoughts were turned inward as they say when I walked into the house and saw your grandfather George's chair empty with only his impression in it, like an invisible man. He was, or his body was, lying on the floor, the side of his face was on the carpet, one arm was under him and the other was straight out to the side. I touched him to make sure he wasn't sleeping but it was obvious his body lacked what Scott Valdez of the Lighthouse Christian Fellowship later called a soul, the visible form of a soul being muscle tone. I got a spoon from the kitchen to be sure, held it under his nose, no fog. I left the spoon right there on the floor and went upstairs to my room. I crawled under my blankets and breathed my own air for a while, which Dr. Armando Rosenkleig later called an impressively effective homespun technique for processing feelings, his words.

When I went downstairs again my head was a black box. Many people have tried to explain my actions to me since that night and I have come to realize that what I did was surprising and even shocking to some people, but I need you to know that I was only respecting his wishes. Your grandfather had always wanted to be buried on our patch of wilderness, it was his wish to be put into the earth next to Ajax and Atlas, hunting dogs he called them, though they had never hunted a day in their lives. He used to take me outside when he was still going outside and he'd stomp his good foot and say that whatever those cretins did to this great world of ours he would be right here rotting away, stomp stomp, and there was nothing they could do about that. He was wrong, at first, but then he was right, which is better than the other way around. I had many feelings, I was overwhelmed with feelings, of course, but my actions came from duty and love and respect, not from feelings, or any hidden motive, or, obviously, but it must be mentioned in light of what came after, anything criminal. My mistake was simple, my mistake was not picking up the telephone, my mistake was picking up a shovel instead of a telephone in a moment of blind grief, or so Officer Mary put it while advocating on my behalf, her words. In fact there was no mistake, his wishes were respected, then and eventually, if they hadn't second guessed me, your grandfather wouldn't have had to move around so much after he died. Also in fact I did not pick up a shovel but went out to the garage, the night air smelled like manure and almonds, I went out to the garage, which was full of wine making equipment and wood and tools, and I set about making a suitable box, a coffin, for your grandfather's final rest, there was nothing hasty about it, I wasn't overcome by anything.

I am handy with wood, it is one of my qualities, and so I was able to make a suitable box out of scrap plywood reinforced with some better pieces from the wood set aside for grapevine stakes. Your grandfather's dream, or more accurately your grandfather and grandmother's dream, had been to make a vineyard there. I dragged him across the living room and into the kitchen, one of his loafers slid off at the threshold, I returned it to his foot. I went upstairs and got his Rotary pins and pinned them to his shirt, he hadn't attended a meeting in ages but he always took good care of the pins. I'm not going to describe the struggle it was to get him into the box or to get the box, which was then a coffin, into the hole, which was then a grave. I had to dig out a ramp and slide it down the incline, I dug all night to make that grave, stopping only to breathe my own air in my bed when I needed what Dr. Rosenkleig would later call emotional management. I don't want to subject you to the feelings I had when I combed his hair and kissed his forehead before laying the plywood on top, I can only tell you that I didn't want to say goodbye, I wasn't ready. Hammering the same nail into the same wood with the same hammer feels different when you're building a suitable box than when you're securing the lid on a coffin. Your grandfather had more wisdom and knowledge in him than anyone I had ever met, now it was all gone, all that was left was his Letter to the Editor, which he had been writing for some time at his typewriter onto a continuous piece of computer paper we had bought at a discount auction back when he was still going out. The paper came out of one box, got covered in words, far too many for me to read, my gift has always been gab, and into another box, page after page of words, covering who knows how many topics and subjects, the whole of it preserved in that box, he kept meaning to send it, but then the next day's *Bee* would arrive and a whole new set of offenses, his words, would come to his attention. I pulled some flowers from around the yard, the sun was lightening the horizon, I picked a handful of flowers and threw them onto the coffin, there was some comfort in that. I said a few words in my head, I didn't say them out loud, I thought about all of the words other people might say, I had never been to a funeral before, I kept it simple, I said goodbye to your grandfather, then I replaced the dirt. When I was done I went around the house and sat on the front steps and thought about what would make a dignified marker for his grave.

[*Hissing sound.*] When your mother, that was your mother, that was Carmen, when she sits in her chair all the air goes out through tiny holes in the stitching. Last night whenever she got up for the bathroom, which was often, you push on her bladder, she says you like to keep her moving, whenever she came back and sat in the chair, hissing snakes and punctured tires invaded my dreams, it was not restful sleep, I dreamed that the air was going out of my life. This afternoon I asked her to fetch from the house this cassette recorder and the only cassettes I own, both gifts from Scott Valdez of the Lighthouse Fellowship down in Panorama City, and at first it looked like the cassettes weren't going to work, but Felix the orderly showed us how to put medical tape over the tabs so we could record over them, he did only one, he crossed himself after, he said Carmen would have to do the rest, he couldn't be a party to recording over the word of God. Your mother laughed and said it would be the least of her sins, and Felix repeated that he didn't want to be involved. You'll be able to find the word of God anywhere if you're so inclined,

Juan-George, hotel rooms for instance, just don't expect him to make sense. She's shaking her head at me now, the fluorescent lights are gleaming off her golden smile, or off some of her teeth, which are gold and some regular, she has nothing but tenderness in her eyes, your unluckiness in never meeting your father will be made up for by having her for a mother. She's still shaking her head at me, the smile is gone.

Dawn broke, I watched the house's shadow shrink toward me as the sun rose in the sky. The postman pulled up in a cloud of dust. Wilfredo drove his own truck with a postal service magnet on the side, the post office van gave him lumbar pain and motion sickness, especially on rural roads, his words. He drove up on the wrong side of the road and his arm was like a blimp delivering the mail from his window to the box, I mean his arm was fat but moved with fluidity. He kept his steering wheel almost flat like a bus driver to accommodate his belly. He was the busiest person I knew in Madera, driving around with mail to deliver and business to attend to, but he always made a point to take the time out to talk with me and your grandfather, usually he and I talked about bicycles, Wilfredo had been a champion bicycle racer before the glandular problems. I waved for him to stop a second and made my way over to the mailbox, I asked him if he knew anything about marking a grave, which didn't seem momentous but was probably the beginning of the end of my life as Mayor. He left the truck in the road with the door open, his seat was covered with a wood bead mat and the cushion underneath was like the edge of a pancake. I had seen him out of his truck only once, it was at a grocery store in town, he was in the produce section leaning on the lettuce fridge, sweating.

When Wilfredo walked his whole body moved from side to side like he was still pedaling for the championship. We went around to the back of the house. I had left the dirty shovel leaning against the wall, Wilfredo's eyes were glued to it, he avoided looking at the ground, he would only peek at the dirt for a second and then his eyes would go back to the shovel. He pulled a cloth out of his back pocket and wiped his forehead and upper lip and asked whether it had been an accident or natural causes. I told him how I had found your grandfather, I told him about the empty chair and the television, and your grandfather's body on the floor, and the lack of muscle tone. After which he seemed relieved, he said that an accidental death would have been a big problem. Even so he said that life was about to become more difficult for me, and he was sorry to have to be a part of that. I felt it in my guts, I didn't have the words for it, which is rare, I usually have the words for everything, I felt that Wilfredo and I were never going to talk about bicycles again.

Wilfredo said he had to get going, he was late on his route, he had to get the mail to people. I watched him walk back to his truck, his body twisting from side to side. I sat at the kitchen table and I noticed there were flies all over the fly strip, they had met their fates. I took down the fly strip. I opened the windows at the front of the house and the back of the house so flies could pass through unimpeded, though I didn't think of the word *unimpeded*, I hadn't yet met Paul Renfro who taught me that word. It struck me that Wilfredo had run away. He had run away like a child. Pay attention in school, Juan-George, anyone will tell you that's good advice, but they don't say that you should pay attention to your classmates most of all. How they act is how they will act when they grow up, only they'll be able to disguise it better, pay attention in school and you will be able to see through the disguises. Wilfredo had run away like a boy in the school yard, which surprised me when I realized it, he and your grandfather had always been friendly. I couldn't understand why Wilfredo wouldn't apply himself to the problem of marking your grandfather's grave in a dignified way. I pictured him on his route, delivering the mail, continuing on, but I couldn't picture it clearly, and when I can't picture something clearly I know it isn't going to come to pass.

# CHANGES

The police had questions for me, which I answered truthfully, which is a fine strategy for talking to police, though it can confuse them. The big question of course was whether I had buried your grandfather in the yard, and when I said yes and showed them the disturbed earth, there were no more questions after that, everyone just looked at the ground, nobody knew what to do, that was the first time somebody used the word *mistake*, I told them there was no mistake, this had been in accord with your grandfather's wishes, but when the police all agree on something there's no convincing them otherwise. A scrawny policeman with a shaved head asked me to sit at the kitchen table while things got sorted out. Some flies had come in and buzzed around the kitchen, I couldn't blame them, the sun was blazing. I sat at the table and looked at your grandfather's Letter to the Editor still there in the corner of the room, still running through the typewriter, and I wondered what offenses the *Fresno Bee* had committed that day. I wondered too when everyone was going to leave so that I could ride my bicycle into Madera and find some work.

I don't need to tell you that I can be a slow absorber, I've always been a slow absorber, but it's better than the opposite, your grandfather used to say, which is to be a quick absorber, or sucker. The police and authorities milled around the house, measuring things and talking out of earshot, none of them stood near me. Then Community Service Officer Mary, who wore a police uniform but wasn't exactly a police officer, her words, finally got fed up with all of this pussyfooting, also her words, and sat down across from me, she lay her palms flat on the kitchen table, like the way a psychic puts her hands on the table, of course I had never seen a psychic, I wouldn't meet a psychic until much later, Officer Mary looked at me with sympathetic eyes, I couldn't imagine her arresting anyone, maybe that was why she wasn't exactly a police officer, her shirt was too big, her shoulders drooped like her bones were soft.

Everyone has a different way of coping with death, her words. That made sense to me, everyone is different. Then her voice changed, she was quoting someone, she said that for this situation there were some general practices outlined in the law. She explained that despite the fact that my father, your grandfather, had been buried according to his wishes, despite the fact that it had been his wish to be buried on our piece of land next to his beloved hunting dogs Ajax and Atlas, despite the fact that what I had done seemed perfectly reasonable to her, even honorable, the authorities, the Madera City and Madera County authorities, had decided that the method and location of burial were not satisfactory. By then everyone had gathered, they stood around the kitchen, they tried to look like they weren't listening but they were listening. Mary explained that because of general practices outlined in the law, they were going to have to move my father, your grandfather, to one of the cemeteries in town. If it was up to her she would let him rest where he was, she didn't want to move him any more than I did, but it was not up to her, she hoped I could understand. I asked if I could first talk with whoever it was who did want to move him, whoever it was who wanted to unbury and rebury my father, I asked if I could talk to that person for just a moment. I scanned the room very deliberately, looking everyone in the eye, but no one stepped forward. She said that it wasn't like that, nobody really wanted to unbury him, if it was up to them they would just leave him be, her words. I suggested they should leave him be, then, and leave me be as well. I excused myself and stood and walked through the group of police and authorities, my hands joined behind my back, I climbed the stairs slowly, one after the other, I waited for someone to stop me but no one did. Everything is permitted until it isn't, your grandfather's words.

In my room, the shades were up, it was bright in there, I could see what a mess I'd made of my sheets, there was dirt everywhere, I couldn't bear to clean up, I didn't even remove my shoes, I crawled under the sheets, sheets dirty with the dirt of what should have been your grandfather's final resting place, and I covered myself, and I breathed my own air. Muffled voices rose through the floor, through my bed, through my pillow, to my ears, they were arguing, I couldn't make out the words. After a while the voices mellowed into regular talk and after another while the house was quiet. When I could no longer breathe my own air, I made a little vent at the side of the sheet and breathed the air in my room. I made the vent as small as I could, exposing only my mouth, but bringing my face close to the vent I could sense the light changing, the day's end approaching, time marching forward with no regard to anything, I did not want to see that, I wanted to see nothing, I only wanted to breathe and be left alone. Soon my stomach gurgled and growled, my stomach demanded I go downstairs, which I did, a hungry stomach is not to be ignored, it's the stomach that carries the feet, not as you would expect the other way around.

The light had gone orange, the light shot through the house from back to front, the sun was setting over town. It was cool downstairs, the house smelled like outside, like sour grapes and roasting almonds. I remembered I'd left everything open to let the flies pass through. I stepped into the kitchen and saw a figure in the corner, in the shadows, sitting at your grandfather's typewriter. I had not forgotten that he was dead but some part of my brain had put two and two together based on yesterday's picture of the world, and so for an instant I thought it was him. Even after I knew it couldn't be him, it took me another little while to figure out it was Community Service Officer Mary. Her shoulders gave her away, her shoulders sloped down like she'd gotten tired of holding them up, even when she had sat down across from me, frustrated with all of the pussyfooters, her word, even then, when there had been an edge to her voice, her shoulders had a slope, her police shirt looked like it was slipping off a hanger. It was dark where she was sitting, the corner with the typewriter was hidden from the light shooting through the house, she must have been straining her eyes, she was bent over the typewriter. I said hello and she leaped from the chair, I apologized for surprising her. She apologized, too, she said that it had been a very long day, she hadn't been getting enough sleep. She said that everyone was concerned for my welfare now that I was alone, especially after what I had done, and they had asked for someone to stick around, and she had volunteered. I thanked her for her concern then explained that I was twenty-seven years old and could take care of myself, that I had taken care of my father all these years, all the years he had decided, or his body had decided, not to leave the house, that instead of taking care of two people I would now be taking care of only one, I was actually twice as safe as before. On the other hand, I told her, if she was in the mood to stick around I was always up for making a new friend. I went to the fridge and pulled open the door and there among the foodstuffs was a plate wrapped in foil. I asked Mary if she was hungry and she looked long and hard at the plate then said no thanks. I pulled the foil off the plate, it was wet underneath, I dried it with a dish towel, I flattened it out on the countertop, folded it carefully, and put it back in the drawer for later. Mary stood in the center of the kitchen and watched, she didn't stand next to me at the counter, she didn't sit at the kitchen table, she stood at the center, which in the kitchen was nowhere, her badge hanging off her loose shirt like a bat hanging in a cave. I heated the lasagna in the microwave and divided it onto two plates. Mary said that your grandfather had left that food for me, it was too important for her to eat, she had no business eating it, she hadn't even known him, she was here only by happenstance. I told her what he always used to say, which was that meals were for sharing. We ate without talking for a while, then I said I was thinking of taking the radio out of the living room, we had a radio in there, it hardly ever got used, and moving it into the kitchen. I thought it would be nice to listen to music while cooking and eating, I like just about any kind of music, it's all interesting to me. Your grandfather had always objected to background music, he objected to music playing all day long, it bothered him deeply, I could never understand it, when he listened to music, which was not often, he sat in front of the radio and gave it all his attention, he looked at it like it was the television, he didn't do anything else. I was going to be alone now, changes were coming, there were going to be all sorts of changes around here, that's what I said. Mary brought her napkin up to her face, she brought it up higher than I expected, when someone is eating and they bring their napkin up to their face, you expect them to wipe their lips, or if they have a cold maybe wipe their nose, but you don't expect the napkin to keep going. She had bony little wrists, I couldn't imagine her pointing a gun at a criminal, she wiped her eyes, one at a time, straight across. I asked her if she was all right. She said she was, she said she'd had a long day, she'd also recently changed medications, nothing serious, but at the moment everything was right on the surface, her words.

With all of this talk of my so-called mistake and Community Service Officer Mary and so on, I don't want to neglect the most important point, which was that I missed your grandfather already, I missed his goodnight kiss on my forehead, his goodnight kiss had always been like a door clicking open, the door to sleep clicking open in my head, he would kiss me on the forehead and I would fall asleep, like a magic trick. Without it, I did not know how to sleep. In the middle of the night I saw a light outside my window, a bright light that wasn't the sun. I got out of bed and looked into the front yard, the light hung there at the street, it was a foggy night, the light glowed white, I pulled on some clothes and went downstairs. Officer Mary lay on her back on the sofa, not snoring but breathing deep and loud, her hair sticking out all over the place, her badge resting on the coffee table.

I stepped through the front door into the darkness and fog. The bright light stayed where it was and I made my way toward it. All kinds of ideas went through my head, I remember thinking I had seen your grandfather at his typewriter earlier when it had only been Officer Mary, I wondered whether this light could have been a visitation, the goodnight kiss, even, that I had been missing, there seemed to be no other explanation for it. Only when I was past it, only when it wasn't blinding me any more, only then could I see that it was mounted on a tripod, there was a video camera and a tripod. The bright light was on top, there was a white van, too, with one of those dishes on a pole sticking up from the roof. I went to the front of the van and looked in the side window, two empty seats. I went to the back windows, they were tinted, it was difficult to see through them, there was a whole command center in there, switches and televisions, one of the televisions showed the morning news, or what would be the morning news if anyone was sitting at the desk, and another showed the view from the camera with the light on it, which was a view of lit-up fog with the dim outline of my house in the background. On the floor of the van was a pile of clothes, which turned out to be two people, a man and a woman, doing what men and women do, which is something no one should interrupt, I let them be, I let them go on. I went back to bed wondering why they were in front of my house. As I said, I am a slow absorber. Plus, I had never done anything newsworthy before.

* * *

I lay in bed and tried to sleep and eventually dawn came, then the sounds of machinery, then the reporter talking to the camera in front of the house, somehow her clothes were not at all wrinkled. From the bathroom window I could see a mini-excavator, they were scraping away the soil, they had come to unbury your grandfather. Officer Mary waited for me at the bottom of the stairs. She had pulled her hair into a ponytail, her shirt was wrinkled, her badge was missing, she had forgotten to reattach her badge, she looked as if all that sleep had tired her out. She said she had tried to stop them, she said they didn't really want to do it, it was the law, it was the law that made them do it, they were like a big rock at the summit of a steep hill, they had been knocked into motion. I stepped outside, I stepped out the back door. The guy who was operating the mini-excavator, I knew him, he was a friend from Madera, his name was Freddy, one of his legs was shorter than the other, I waved at him but he just lowered his head. People were arriving by the carload, there were people everywhere. The authorities pulled your grandfather's makeshift coffin, their words, out of the ground and they put it on the back of a flatbed truck, the funeral director didn't want to get his hearse dirty, the wood was caked with dirt but you could see the craftsmanship, the grapevine stakes held everything together perfectly, anyone could see the work that had gone into it. Most of Madera had come to watch and those who weren't there were seeing it on the news at home. I caught a glimpse of Wilfredo's blimplike arm hanging out of his truck window, from atop the pancake cushion and the wooden beads. Then the flatbed with the makeshift coffin headed onto the road, leaving behind two black gouges across our little patch of wilderness. People got into their vehicles and followed it into town, they made a parade into Madera. You can tell your children someday that when your grandfather died there was a parade, it was on the news.

There was a service the next day, someone had arranged a service at a church even though we had never gone to church. Only a few people showed up to that, some of them must have been regular churchgoers, I didn't recognize them. And then Carmen, your mother, your future mother, walked in. I hardly knew her, I mean we had been introduced, Rowdy and Manuel had introduced us, they were painters from Fresno, they had introduced me to your mother, in a manner of speaking, I can't get into it right now, she is staring daggers at me. I hadn't seen her since. She came straight down the pew to me but didn't sit down. She had seen the unburial on television, she said, she had recognized my name. She handed me a bouquet of flowers, she kissed me on the cheek, she said she was sorry to have heard about my loss, and sorry too that she couldn't stay for the service. Everyone in the church gave her stern looks, she wore clothing that revealed her figure, she wore short skirts and low-cut shirts, people looked down on her for that, which was ridiculous because she had a right to show off her assets, her later words, let them say what they wanted. Officer Mary and I sat in the pews, the pastor gave his sermon, it concerned the well-being of your grandfather's soul, which I did not understand, which I did not comprehend, your grandfather had never mentioned anything about having a soul. But it seemed important and it was outside the areas of my expertise, which at the time were very small areas and very few, so I listened and kneeled and bowed my head when everyone else did, I mouthed the words like I used to back in school. After the service your grandfather was put into the ground for the second time, in a manner consistent with the general practices outlined in the law, he was put into the ground next to some people called Brown and next to some other people called Kutchinski, miles away from Ajax and Atlas and our piece of wilderness. The burial attracted less of a crowd than the unburial.

Afterward, Mary and I walked to the sandwich place for lunch, it was a strange walk, I mean everything inside my head was strange, I couldn't absorb what had just happened, everything felt temporary, like I was holding my breath while getting a shot, everything felt tight and suspended, I kept waiting for the moment to be over. But outside my head, too, things were strange, I mean even taking into account my mental state, things had changed around town. Everyone knew about my so-called mistake. Bad news has wings, your grandfather's words. Nobody waved from across the street, nobody said, Hello, Mayor. No, the people who saw me, all my friends, they didn't know what to say, they didn't say anything. I had always been a target, it came with being tall, it came with being friends with everybody, it came with being called Mayor when technically I wasn't. Ever since I was a boy, my friends had found ways to trick me one way or another, always in the spirit of goodwill, it was fine with me, it had become fine with me, because I had discovered something early on, while still in grade school. Greg Yerkovich had tricked me into eating a clod of dirt, he had pulled what he called a truffle out of his lunch box, he had asked if anyone wanted it. We didn't have much money for food and I was on my way to being six and a half feet tall, so I was always hungry, and besides, I was always looking for, I am always looking for new experiences. It was shortly after biting into that dirt clod that I discovered, while breathing my own air in a janitor's closet, I discovered in my head an idea that stuck with me all through school, that saved me many trips to the blankets and closets, which was that when those boys were making fun of me, they weren't making fun of someone else. That idea gave me strength, Juan-George, most of what people call strength is just belief, is just believing that you're strong, I mean mental strength, no matter what you believe you're not going to be able to lift a car above your head. The idea that I was a shield made me into a stronger shield. After my so-called mistake, though, it stopped.

Nobody mentioned your grandfather, nobody made jokes about burying him in the yard, nobody commented on my manner of walking with my hands behind my back, nobody tried to steal my binoculars, nobody tried to convince me of anything preposterous, nobody laughed, and so for the first and only time in my life Madera felt like a lonely place.

That evening I got a call from Aunt Liz, your grandfather's sister, I hadn't seen her in years, she asked first if I was okay, if I was doing okay. Then she told me, despite the fact that I was twenty-seven years old and perfectly able to take care of myself, despite the fact that I had friends everywhere in Madera and made new ones all the time, despite the fact that I could ride my bicycle into town and find interesting work to do every day of the week, she told me that it would be best if I packed my things and left my bicycle and got on a bus and came to live with her in Panorama City. She was concerned for my well-being, she was concerned about my ability to take care of myself, she thought I should be with family in this time of need, her words, rather than in that drafty old house all alone, also her words. I got to thinking about what Madera had been like that day, I got to thinking about how things had already changed because of my so-called mistake, which got me thinking about whether I really wanted to go back to being Mayor, and I felt a shift inside me, a movement. I thought about your grandfather's radio, about my idea to move his radio into the kitchen, and

I thought about what other things I would like to change, I don't usually do much thinking about change, I am not one of those people who seeks out change, it is not one of my qualities, but if I can say anything about the shape of life, if I can give you any idea of what it is like to live a whole life, even one cut short at the Madera Community Hospital, I can say this, which is that everything stays the same for a long time, and then suddenly there comes a moment when everything changes. Aunt Liz talked for a while about keeping an eye on me, she talked about my potential, and while she talked I thought, my head was somewhere else, I thought about what it would be like to be Oppen Porter instead of Mayor, I thought about going someplace where no one had ever heard of my so-called mistake, where no one had seen me covered in algae from when I went coin hunting in the wishing well, where no one remembered the time I went over the handlebars on a scooter while trying to see if the headlight was working, I hadn't thought of sticking my hand in front, your grandfather had said it was physically clumsy but philosophically admirable, I was the type who required primary sources, his words, I wasn't going to settle for shadows in a cave. I had enjoyed being Mayor, I was a good sport, as they say, I had been a good sport, but I was done.

[*Extended beeping sound. Nurses talking.*] An automatic pump sends painkillers into my veins, without them I would be in unspeakable agonies, Dr. Singh's words. The doctors have made a plaster statue of me, but only literally, I am a rigid mass of what Dr. Singh called bonesetting, the setting process, all we can do is wait, his words, wait it out and see how you do, he said, at which point I knew he was a man to trust, because my philosophy is, my philosophy has always been, that most problems can be solved by waiting.

# PART TWO

TAPE 2, SIDES A & B;
TAPE 3, SIDES A & B

## A MAN OF THE WORLD

C: You're not dying.

O: It's just in case, I'm recording this for Juan-George just in case, just in case I die, you never know, Carmen, you never know what might happen once you get inside a hospital.

C: You're healing up.

O: My father used to point at this building and say that if you were in there, you were either coming or going.

C: *Dios mio*. So dramatic.

O: I'm wrapped in plaster and bolted together, I can't move.

C: Just don't go on and on about dying, I can't bear it. When they called me, when they told me you'd been in an accident, I nearly died myself.

O: Now that sounds dramatic.

C: I did. I felt a tightness in my chest, Oppen, I pictured my whole life without you in it, and little Juan-George, and I felt my chest go tight. I told God that if he let you live I wouldn't let you out of my sight ever again.

O: And what did God say?
C: You're here, aren't you?

If you had seen me boarding that bus to Panorama City, Juan-George, if you had been able to witness me handing over my ticket to the meticulous driver, with his meticulous mustache, handing it to him with confidence, dressed not in my usual Mayor clothes, which were work jeans and a T-shirt from a business in Madera, I wore them in rotation, people used to say that on my bicycle I was a rolling billboard, if you could have seen me wearing your grandfather's brown corduroy suit and excused the fact that it was too warm to be wearing a corduroy suit, and excused the fact that I had taken out the tailoring at the ankles and wrists so it would better fit me, which left frayed fabric there and a band of dark where the fabric hadn't for a long time been exposed, if you could have seen me and excused those facts and noticed the handsome leather suitcase I handed to the driver nonchalantly, and the fact that I'd polished my boots until they looked almost like dress shoes, and saw too that I was carrying an elegant carry-on bag, actually your grandfather's old shaving kit, containing various papers, money, and my compact binoculars, carrying it under my arm as if gravity did not apply to it, and if you'd admired the hat upon my head, which had been your grandfather's and was a real hat, not a baseball cap or fishing hat but a real proper hat, if you had seen my watch, my Rotary Club tie, my tie clip, if you had watched me say to the meticulous bus driver that I was headed to Panorama City, as if I'd been there and back a million times, if you'd seen how I bowed my head when I thanked Officer Mary for everything and shook her hand, and the way I removed my hat at precisely the moment my head entered the bus itself, you might have said, you couldn't be blamed for saying, There goes a man of the world.

Now, I'm not a small person, I'm six and a half feet tall, and so I was shocked to see how small, despite the size of the bus, how small the seats were. I scanned the rows looking for somewhere to sit, I scanned past all kinds of people, no row was empty. I sought out the littlest person, a teenage girl, and attempted to slide in next to her, but folding myself into that seat without injury would have been impossible. The driver suggested the front row, but a scrawny old man was taking up both seats. He had the look, I don't know how else to put it, his face looked like that of a newly hatched crocodile. His eyes were alive and penetrating at the same time, and his mouth seemed wider and flatter than most, he didn't have much in the way of lips, his mouth was like a straight line across his whole face, and yet you couldn't shake the sense that he was, at the very corners, smiling. Papers were spread all over the seat beside him, a disorganized pile of sketches and notes and diagrams. I had no way of knowing where he had boarded, but judging from the pleasure the bus driver took in asking him to collect his papers and make room for me he had been making a mess of his papers for many miles. He managed to stuff into what he called his briefcase, which was actually a flat cardboard box, he stuffed into that box the whole pile of papers that had been the mess on my seat, somehow that briefcase was bigger on the inside than on the outside, and then he asked the bus driver if he was happy now. The driver stated that he was. We started down the road and the little man looked straight ahead. By way of introduction I told him my name, my age, where I was from, and where I was going. He did not respond, I looked at the landscape. The front windshield was enormous, the bus ate up the road, if I let my vision narrow it felt like riding a very fast bicycle, except without the wind. All I could think about were all the bugs and birds I couldn't see, all of the plants whizzing by in a blur. I missed my bicycle already, bicycle travel was the perfect speed, traveling at this speed was pointless, you missed everything. But then I figured that if I was going to be a man of the world, I should learn to appreciate other modes of transport, I should give the bus a fair shake, and so I opened my eyes and I opened my mind and I saw something I never would have noticed on a bicycle unless I was going very, very fast down a very long hill. Because of the speed of the bus and how I was exerting no effort, the telephone wires on the side of the road, sagging between poles, went up and down with the same rhythm as my heartbeat.

* * *

The next thing I knew I was watching the Alvarez brothers and Greg Yerkovich driving down a country road like the one that led to our patch of wilderness, and they saw someone riding a bicycle, coming the other direction, it wasn't me, it was someone else riding a bicycle, someone nobody had ever seen before, a stranger. They drove their truck straight at the stranger, he saw them, he saw them coming at him, but he didn't know what to do, he didn't know he was supposed to dive into the ditch.

I jerked awake and the man next to me asked if I was okay, I said yes, it was just a dream. He seemed to be in a receptive mood now, so again I told him my name, my age, where I was from, and where I was going. Because we were in the first row, the one with the steps in front of it, if I didn't sit up straight my knees hit the metal bar separating us from the steps. He was small enough that he didn't have to sit up straight, he had room to move, he was short and narrow, he wore a tan sport jacket over a plaid shirt with a dark blue oval at the bottom of the front pocket, there was a pen in the pocket, I couldn't tell if it had exploded there or if another pen had exploded there before and this was a new pen. I was ignorant enough then not to recognize a true man of the world when I saw one. He told me he was heading down to L.A. to pick up a shipment of antioxidant cream, he engaged in a sort of rude commerce, his words, now and then, to support himself, to buy himself time for advanced thinking, his words. He explained that by using this cream several times a day, on your face, in conjunction with a special handheld light, sold separately, you could reverse the effects of aging, you could look five years younger in as little as two weeks, and if you didn't, he said, he would refund your money completely, he was offering a one hundred percent money-back guarantee. He asked me whether I found that impressive. I said that of course I did. Then he asked me if I'd like to order some. I told him I didn't want to look younger, I've never wanted to look younger. He said I was in the minority on that one. I pointed out that when you look younger, people treat you like a child. That's when he said, his words, You're a thinker, I like that. We shook hands, which was awkward, which was difficult in the bus seats, he was seated to my right, he could turn in his seat to face me and bring his right arm around, there was plenty of room for his right arm, but my right arm was trapped, the more I tried to turn toward him, the more trapped my right arm became, trapped between my body and the seat, not to mention that I could barely turn because my knees pressed against the metal bar separating us from the steps. I suppose we could have shaken left hands, but I heard somewhere, source unknown, that it is unlucky. The man introduced himself as a thinker also, his words, named Paul Renfro. At the age of two, at two years old, he told me by way of introduction, he'd seen a butterfly trapped in a cobweb and concluded that life had no intrinsic meaning. I did not know what *intrinsic* meant, he explained it, *intrinsic* was the first word I learned from Paul Renfro. As a result of his advanced development, he told me, he skipped two grades in school, he skipped ahead of those who followed conventional wisdom, which was no wisdom at all. At university, after three semesters of straight A's, he experienced the first of several total and complete breakthroughs and quit to pursue his own projects beyond the academic kabuki, his words. I mentioned earlier that one of the qualities of life is that there are periods when nothing changes for a long time and then suddenly everything changes. Well, another quality is that any event no matter how small could happen a different way and change everything that follows. Meeting Paul Renfro on the bus was one of those events, because in not finding a place to sit farther back in the bus, and in having the bus driver seat me next to Paul, I had, without even arriving in Panorama City yet, made the acquaintance of a true man of the world from whom I would learn powerful methods of thinking and countless facts not to mention hundreds of words.

While Paul talked we drove across a flat landscape, we cruised down a very large and long highway, which was almost totally flat, to the sides were foothills, golden grasses, probably a million birds and bugs, but the bus didn't bother with that stuff, that was not the stuff of a bus ride, we were stuck to the gray ribbon, eating it up mile by mile, the only bugs we saw were expired on the windshield, I imagined a bus with no windshield and no back window, the bugs could pass straight through. While he talked Paul shuffled through his briefcase, he showed me many sheets covered with his writings and diagrams, with his patents pending, his words. The bus groaned into a lower gear and started climbing, we were climbing and winding. I had been watching Paul and his papers, I hadn't noticed the hills until we were in them. Paul called it the Grapevine and said that L.A. wasn't far. He said that was the real world down there, which I did not understand until I got there and saw that it meant a place where it is impossible to make friends with everyone, there are too many people, you'd run out of time. He said that we thinkers had to stick together. That's when I got the idea to show Paul Aunt Liz's address, I showed him the card Officer Mary had made for me with Aunt Liz's address on it, I suggested he copy it down, so that when it was convenient for him he could drop by. I hadn't seen Aunt Liz in many years but I had a feeling she would want to buy what he was selling.

At the station in North Hollywood I recognized Aunt Liz immediately, she looked the same as when she had visited us in Madera years before, when she had taken over my bedroom, when she had alphabetized all of your grandfather's books, which had made him very angry, they had been sorted according to his own private system. She wore the same animal print shirt, it was a blouse I guess you'd call it, with a cheetah spot pattern on it, every time I'd seen her she was wearing some kind of wild animal print, she had the same reddish hair in the same short no-nonsense style, your grandfather's words, she wore the same shade of lipstick to match her hair. She kissed me on both cheeks, and then she looked at me approvingly, as they say, and I wondered whether it was because I looked like a man of the world. Her car was a Ford Tempo, which was the opposite of Paul Renfro's briefcase, the Tempo was much smaller on the inside than the outside. She asked me to put my leather suitcase in the trunk. Only low-class people carried their bags into the passenger compartment, only low-class people put their bags and laundry and various other things on the backseat, because their trunks were stuffed with coolant and tires and low-class junk, Aunt Liz's words. I hadn't been aware of this. In Madera people always kept things in the backseat, things were easier to reach that way, the trunk was reserved for things that were dirty, but I didn't want the people of North Hollywood to get the wrong impression, so I put my suitcase in the trunk, which was carpeted, which was spotless, which was empty except for an emergency kit and a foil blanket, and I thought, Here I am in the real world, here I am starting a new life. Back in Madera I never stopped and thought like that, I never thought, I am riding my bicycle into town, I am eating a sandwich. Already, being a man of the world was taking effect, I thought, already I am becoming more reflective, like that foil blanket. And then Aunt Liz told me to get in the car, or more accurately she asked what was taking so long.

* * *

When we got out of the parking lot and onto the streets, I saw that she sat only inches away from the steering wheel, she sat so close to the steering wheel it looked like something attached to her rather than to the car. She kept her hands together very high, both hands high on the wheel, at twelve o'clock, or more accurately at eleven-fifty-five and twelve-oh-five. We pulled onto a larger street and a short look around confirmed for me that she sat closer to the wheel than was the custom in North Hollywood. My body was crammed in the passenger seat of the Tempo, there were controls somewhere for moving the seat back, but out of respect for Aunt Liz and her way of sitting I remained where I was, I didn't want her to have to turn her head completely backward to look at me when she spoke, if she spoke I mean, she seemed very focused on driving. We drove past low-slung buildings lined up one after the other, gas stations, car dealerships, parking lots, and palm trees growing out of the sidewalks. There were signs on everything, there were signs on the trees, there were enormous billboards, shop signs, there was writing everywhere. My gift has always been gab, but even if I was a stronger reader I couldn't imagine reading all of those signs, it was like driving through a crazy book, it would take a hundred years to read it all. I asked Aunt Liz whether we were heading into town or out of town, and she said, Neither, which didn't seem possible. I remarked, I remember remarking, that the weather was pleasantly mild in North Hollywood.

Aunt Liz said that we were technically in Sherman Oaks. I asked her when we had left North Hollywood, and she said we'd been out of it for quite a while, we'd left it and gone through Valley Village, and we were, she paused, well, now we were out of Sherman Oaks, too, we'd just entered Van Nuys. I turned this over in my head, I tried to understand how we had entered a new place without ever having left the old one. I watched the city, or the cities, go by. Then Aunt Liz announced that we had arrived in Panorama City. I had been paying attention, I had been looking out the window, and I had noticed no change, from my perspective there was no difference, but apparently we had crossed a whole series of invisible lines.

Big full trees ran along Aunt Liz's street, they met above the street and kept the road in shade, they kept the street shady and cool, they leaned away from the houses toward the middle of the street, like they wanted to exclude the houses from their company, which made sense, the houses were made of dead wood, the trees were made of live wood, the living wants to be with the living, the dead with the dead. There were no more signs, there was no more language everywhere to confound the eye, which was a relief. The houses that weren't stucco were peeling, which reminded me of Madera, which reminded me of working construction in Madera, where the sun used to peel paint off all of the houses that weren't stucco. Aunt Liz's house was the only one with a wooden fence in front, the other houses had fences of chain-link or iron and brick, which I could understand from the point of view of maintenance. There were no people, no one was outside, sheets hung in windows and cars sat in front of houses, there were cars all over the place, cars and trucks, and campers, a boat, a panel truck. Many houses had rolling gates and the vehicles were jammed together inside the gates, on the lawns and on the driveways, as if each lot was its own little harbor, everything tied down for a storm, but there were no storms coming, in fact, there was hardly any weather at all. We pulled into Aunt Liz's driveway, she had no gate, there were no cars on her lawn, her lawn was green, the blades had been cut to within an inch of their lives. Two doors down, a house was painted a rich blue, or what would look like a rich blue if it was wet but dried out and peeling looked more like a rich blue under a layer of dried milk, their lawn had grown in a wild state of nature, dozens of grasses and plants fighting it out, a tiny patch of wilderness, I had to respect that, it reminded me of your grandfather, I decided to introduce myself to those people as soon as possible, they would be like-minded, I thought.

The first thing Aunt Liz did was show me my room, which had been the guest room, which had been previously reserved for guests, she said, though she didn't say when the last guests had stayed there. The carpet was peach, the linens were covered in flower patterns, and the wallpaper, too, the wallpaper was patterned with flowers and columns of winding ivy. She said she hoped it wasn't too feminine. In fact, these design features gestured admirably toward nature while also providing respite from nature's brutalities, which has been the hallmark of human habitation since the days of cave painting, all Paul Renfro's words, later. Aunt Liz said that she was exhausted, your grandfather's death, her brother's death, had come as a shock to her, it had affected her sleep, she needed to make a pot of coffee. She said she would fix me a snack, too, while waiting for the coffee to brew, but in the meanwhile I should make myself at home, I should take a few minutes to familiarize myself with my quarters, which was what she called my room.

I could see right away that the bed was too short, it would require me to hang my feet off the end or fold myself up. I had been sleeping in the same bed my whole life, or most of my life, and I had gotten used to my bed, I didn't think I could ever get used to this bed. I lay on it, I let my feet hang off. The wood at the end, what do you call it, the opposite of the headboard, the footboard, it jammed into my calves, I couldn't imagine how it would feel if I rolled over, the wood against my shins, I couldn't imagine it and I didn't want to try it. I put pillows under my calves to ease the pain of the footboard, which worked, but not for long. Finally I saw that the only way to sleep would be on my side, in a zigzag, I decided I would sleep like that temporarily, until I could cut a notch in the footboard and then build a padded platform for my feet.

Above the toilet in my bathroom was a photograph of the beach, the sun was setting and someone had been walking but all you could see were footprints, footprints going off into the distance and around the corner, out of sight. They looked like fresh footprints, they still had good hard edges, the water hadn't gotten to them, there was some writing down one side of the picture. At first I though that the photographer was following somebody, I wondered whether he caught up with them before the sun went down, I pictured him stumbling over the rocks in the dark, coming around the corner to discover that there, on the next beach over, the water had washed away all the footprints, I pictured the photographer sitting down in the sand, plopping himself down, waiting for something. A seagull or two coming over for a look. The photographer's lost the trail, he's thinking he's lost everything, and yet there's this picture, he doesn't know it yet, it's still in his camera, but he's going to come back with this beautiful picture, he thinks all is lost, but it's not, he's taken a beautiful picture, and it's going to end up on Aunt Liz's bathroom wall with some writing on it, and I'm going to see it, and it will remind me that all is not lost. I didn't have all those ideas right then, I don't usually get an idea all at once, I'm a slow absorber, I developed those ideas while looking at that picture many times, I looked at that picture every time I stood in front of the toilet, while my body was occupied and my mind was free.

[*Long beep.*] The medications are beeping again, I do not want to sleep, your mother is sleeping, she is napping now, in her chair, her hands are resting on her belly, she is making a tent for you out of her fingers. Be still, don't press on her bladder, I want to discuss something important, something she doesn't want me talking about. You won't be a grapefruit forever, you're going to want your father's advice on women. I had your grandfather's advice, which was limited, he based his advice on your grandmother, my mother, I was too young to remember her, I never knew her, the only woman in the house when I was growing up was your grandfather's words about your grandmother, my mother, words that made me wonder whether I'd ever want a woman in my life, words that gave me pause and even made me fear women, I don't need to get into that. I want you to know that without love we would be very lonely and without sex we would be the last ones here, our replacements would never show up. Your mother and I were introduced by Rowdy and Manuel, I've mentioned them already. I'd been stripping and prepping an office building with those guys, and at the end of a work day Rowdy said he had some friends in Madera that he wanted to visit, there was someone he thought I should meet, he thought we would hit it off. It was Carmen he was talking about and he was right, we hit it off, we became involved very quickly, or completely you might say, that night. We moved forward too quickly I think, that is the nature of animal attraction, as it's called, but we slowed down after that first night, we took a long break. Sometimes the shortest distance from A to Z is to be at Z in the first place, Paul Renfro's words. Your mother and I went about it backwards, in any case, the courtship came well after the consummation, which I recommend. But I don't have much time and so I'm going to get to the point, which is that the first time we were together, which was at her house, Rowdy and Manuel had taken me there, they were visiting with her roommate, I don't pretend to know what their arrangement was, the first time we were together it was clear that your mother had experience in sexual matters whereas I did not, I had just been telling Manuel and Rowdy about it a few days prior, somehow I had reached twenty-seven without having experience in sexual matters, or at least with someone else in the room, there's no shame in doing it alone, just make sure you're really alone, check for yourself, don't take anyone else's word for it, but that's a different story. At first I wondered if Rowdy and Manuel were playing a prank, they had been known to do so, I wondered because your mother was in her robe, she didn't look like she was expecting anyone, she was in her robe and heels, like she was still trying on shoes before going out. But she was beautiful in that thick pink terry robe, it went almost to the floor, your mother isn't the tallest. She didn't look surprised to see me at all, she didn't ask me to wait until she got her clothes on, she said it was nice to meet me, but her mind was somewhere else. Then I figured they must have told Carmen about me, they must have prepared her for my arrival because she was already, I'm not sure how to say this, full of desire, I guess, I didn't know what to do. She saw that, she showed me, she took over, she had a box of condoms on the nightstand like what gift ribbon comes in, I don't need to go into detail here, but while we were getting to know each other, as they say, I caught a case of the giggles. We were involved at that moment, physically, and I could tell she was not happy with my giggles, but I couldn't stop. What happened was that I had suddenly remembered a joke from my childhood. I had never understood it and so had remembered it all those years, I always remember what I don't understand, it's one of my qualities. Your grandfather had told the joke years before, to some friends who had come out to the house, I was supposed to be upstairs sleeping but I had stayed up to listen to their adult talk. The joke was: What are the three parts of an old-fashioned stove? Answer: Lifter, leg, and poker. Your grandfather and his guests, they had been drinking, all of them laughed hard and I didn't understand why until I was in the so-called heat of the moment with the woman who would become your mother, and so that's why I was suddenly consumed with giggles. Before I could explain myself she began to cry and speak in half-Spanish, half-English about how she had lost all of her beauty, about how she could no longer keep on like this, about how she couldn't take one more drunk gringo laughing at her, it wasn't worth it. I wasn't drunk and told her so, I explained that I wasn't laughing at her, in fact I thought she was beautiful, and then I told her the joke, which got her laughing, she laughed past her tears, and she didn't ever again seem like her mind was in another place, or at least not while we were intimate together, as they say. I have limited experience in all of these matters, your mother is the one with all of the experience, but she will be reluctant to talk to you about it, she is ashamed of how many suitors she had before she got away from her roommate who was destroying herself and moved out to our patch of wilderness with me. She helped me restore it, she made a proper home for us there.

While I was down in Panorama City I was faithful to your mother, at least I was faithful in body and action, there were some problems with my thoughts because of a psychic named Maria, and if your mother entertained many suitors while I was down in Panorama City, she had every right to do so, a woman must be selective in choosing a mate, future generations depend on it, Paul Renfro's advice, it was only because Fabio, who was her roommate's son, didn't pass on my complete message when I left Madera for Panorama City. He told her only that I swung by to say *adiós*, that's a direct quote, and that I was with a woman. In fact, what I had said and what he neglected to pass on was that I was going down to Panorama City to become a man of the world and that I hoped Carmen would wait for me, I hoped she would welcome me upon my return, I was planning on returning. Also, the woman I was with was Community Service Officer Mary of the Madera Police Department, a kind and pretty woman in her own right but not someone I had ever had any relations with. Enough with misunderstandings, your mother is right now shifting in her chair, I have something else to say, which is that you should in matters of love take advice from the natural world, specifically mosquitoes. When mosquitoes prepare to mate, they mate in midair, which is quite a sight, when they prepare to mate, the male changes the frequency of his wing beats, he beats his wings in time with the female's wings, the word is *synchronize*, they synchronize their wings. Most people ignore mosquitoes unless they're being bit by them, but there is more knowledge in that one natural world fact than you're likely to get in twelve years of school. When I was in school I heard all kinds of advice about sex and love and all of it turned out to be wrong. Oh, she's waking up . . . [*Soft groaning in the background.*]

Hello, *mi amor*, how was your nap, you were sleeping for a bit there. I was just telling our little *toronja* about Aunt Liz, about my first day in Panorama City.

In the kitchen, Aunt Liz made canoes out of celery and filled them with peanut butter, she called it just a little something healthy to tide us over until dinner. She said us, but she did not eat any of the celery and peanut butter. She drank her coffee with lots of cream and sugar, it was the one thing she had in common with your grandfather, both of them drank enormous amounts of coffee, it was the only thing they had in common, besides being brother and sister. She drank coffee and ate an apple, cutting one piece at a time, she offered me a piece, but I politely refused, I've always been an orange person. Once I had put a few canoes down the hatch, for which my stomach was thankful, Aunt Liz asked whether my father, your grandfather, had established any kind of routine for me in Madera. I described how I awoke in the morning, ate breakfast with your grandfather, my father, her brother, then rode my bicycle into Madera, where I would find a friend in need of assistance, which I would then offer. Or, if no one needed my help, I'd ride around and visit friends until the end of the day, they called me Mayor, everyone in Madera called me Mayor, even the real mayor, Tony Adinolfi, called me Mayor. In the evening I rode home and ate dinner with your grandfather, my father, her brother. On the weekend, I lazed around the house and walked around our little piece of land, communing with the squirrels and pollywogs, unless my friends came by, unless Mike and Hector and Greg came by, then I would hang out with them, we did all kinds of things, they were always daring me to do things, like jump off a bridge into the Madera River, which I would not do, which I did not do, which they realized was a bad idea once I walked into the water and showed them how shallow it was, better my wet jeans than someone else's broken neck any day of the week. Aunt Liz shook her head as I spoke, she shook her head and pushed her chair back from the kitchen table and walked five evenly measured steps to the coffee maker. She refilled her coffee, still shaking her head, she spoke to the coffee maker first, then she turned and spoke directly to me, That is an idiot's life, you have been living a village idiot's life. Your father, Lord rest his soul, should have been ashamed of himself, letting you comport yourself like a village idiot around Madera.

Then she said, You won't be a village idiot here. You'll be a respectable citizen, with a sense of personal responsibility, you're going to be a contributing member of society here in Panorama City. She had arranged employment for me, she explained, legitimate employment, she had certain connections and was able to immediately place me at a job, a job at which I would be expected to arrive at a certain time and depart at a certain time, and for which I would be paid in real money, not sandwiches and other flimsy expressions of backwater goodwill, all her words.

I don't think she was trying to hurt my feelings, she was angry with your grandfather, it was as if she had forgotten I was there. There would be a period of training, she told me, a short period of orientation, and then I would be a real worker, with a real job, something to be proud of. What luck, I thought, setting aside the village idiot part of her speech, our goals were aligned. I hadn't yet discovered the chasm between being a respectable citizen and being a man of the world, as far as I knew they were one and the same.

I should mention also that it wasn't just Aunt Liz talking, I was talking too, it wasn't just her ranting and raving in one long rant with me saying nothing and listening, but I can't really remember what I said, it's easier to remember what other people have said than to remember what you have said, your words are coming out of your head and their words are going into your head, it only makes sense that at the end of the day your head is full of someone else's words.

# FLOATER

For some reason Aunt Liz's idea of a respectable job was a local fast-food place that shall remain nameless, I'd rather not say the name of it, because there are thousands of it across the country and I can only speak about the one I worked in, I can only speak about my experience in our franchise, which did not blindly follow the simpleminded standards developed by the company in charge of all the restaurants but rather blazed its own trail, as Roger Macarona the manager put it. Roger had a bushy mustache, an unruly mustache, and he wore his shirt unbuttoned one button too far, which showed off his rough throat and dry Adam's apple, and where you would expect a hairy chest was a mysteriously hairless expanse, which my fellow employees spent much time speculating about. On the first day I was introduced to Melissa, who was round and black and a mother of two, Francis, who had thick glasses and was going to become a filmmaker, Ho, who was a refugee, and Wexler, who talked about cars and nothing else. Whenever Roger told my fellow employees to do something, they always said his name twice, after which he'd threaten to make them call him Doctor Macarona, he wasn't actually a doctor, but he was way the hell ahead of the rest of us in the school of life, his words, and we couldn't call him bachelor because he was married and we couldn't call him master, because Melissa was black and what kind of message would that send, his question.

That first day, that first hour, Roger sat me down in his office, which was a tiny room, which was barely larger than a closet, and looked over the paperwork Aunt Liz had filled out. He moved a pile of binders to reveal a television and VCR wedged into a bookshelf. I am followed by televisions everywhere I go, I have always been doomed that way, there is even one here in my hospital room, hanging from the ceiling. He told me I would have to watch a training video before proceeding any further. He hit play, and the screen showed two men and a woman, naked, except for the woman's shoes, she had not taken off her shoes. I had not seen anything like it before on a television but I knew, it was clear to me, they were making love, or having sex, I should say, if the words making love are reserved for the most sincere expression of that act. I was surprised at the feelings the video aroused in me, it was clear these people, these men and this woman, were trying to portray pleasure, it was obvious, from the small bit I saw, that they wanted whoever was watching to know they were having a good time, but all I felt was a sharp kind of sadness at their bodies moving on the screen, not because I could imagine their lives outside the scene, that didn't come to me until later, but because in their bodies and in their faces, in their sounds and in their motions, I could see only effort, I could see only how hard they were working, and built into that effort was the failure of that effort, because the pleasure of pleasure is that it is effortless. These people were trapped, the harder they tried, the further they were from their goal, no wonder people called TV the box. Roger just laughed. He ejected the tape and put in the proper training video. He dimmed the lights and left the room.

[*Extended beep.*] When the medications get low, the beeper goes off twice as long. I've just seen my final sunset. I've been watching the reflection of this room in the window, the bed, the lights, the pumps and screens, the sink, the chair, your mother, everything growing clearer while through the window Madera faded to darkness. Now it is black outside, the sun is down, the sun I will never get to see again is hidden under the earth, is coming around the earth, or we are turning to meet it, I won't be here. Carmen is blinking at me. [*Pause.*] Back to sleep, *mi amor.* Good. Where were we?

The training video turned out to be reassuring. I thought I would be watching something complicated that showed how to do all the jobs at the fast-food place, but the video wasn't about how to do the jobs, it was about how to think while doing the jobs, how to be, what to keep in your head. The training video was my first exposure to a fully articulated philosophy. I had not yet begun constructing my own, not on purpose at least, I had not yet had the conversation with Paul Renfro in which he revealed that the key to being a true man of the world is to develop a coherent philosophy of your own. The video itself was well made, the camera didn't bounce around all over the place and look at things from all angles at once, it stayed put. It was like being there. The setting was a fast-food place very much like but not identical to the one in Panorama City, and the video proposed two separate realities, two alternate universes, identical in almost all respects, except that in one the restaurant was disorganized, the customers were angry, the employees were squabbling, you could hear everyone's angry thoughts, and in the other the employees were smiling and being courteous and even the grumpiest customers ended up with smiles on their faces, you couldn't hear anyone's thoughts, happy music was playing instead. The focus of the video was a freckle-faced kid who behaved badly in the first universe, then politely in the second, thanks to the application of the fast-food place's five-point system, which was illustrated by a gold cartoon star, five points for five points, each one glinting as it was listed off. One, smile even if you feel bad. When people smile back you will feel better. Two, do what you can to make others feel important, especially if they are angry about something. Three, take pride in your work. Four, the company, I'm not going to name it, is a great big family. Five, the customer is always right. After watching the video I saw the kitchen area as if with new eyes. Ho walked up to me and told me Roger was going to be right back, that he'd gone to buy some parts for his boat, that I should go back into the office and wait. Ho did not smile, not in the least. So I smiled at him the broadest smile I could, and to make him feel important I said that I hoped to someday learn a few of the many skills he obviously possessed in the kitchen, and to make him feel like family I called him brother. When Roger came in, finally, a half hour later, the first thing he asked was what I had said to Ho. I repeated exactly what I'd said. Roger said that I had disturbed Ho. I explained that I was using techniques I'd learned in the video. Roger said that the only reason he'd shown me the video was so I could sign a paper saying I'd seen the video, after which he could finally give me my uniform, which he said would be paid for out of my first check. I drew my circle and scribble and he handed me my uniform, which was a shirt, an apron, and a hat. The apron had a pocket in front that was perfect for my compact binoculars. Roger said that now I was one of the troops. I thought it was interesting that he called us troops and said so. He said we were at war. I had no idea. I asked him with who? He said the customer.

I started as a floater. I did whatever needed to get done, it suited me, I have always liked having a variety of jobs, every day brings a new challenge. On that first day I cleaned up a grease spill that was not my fault and I swept the floor all around the restaurant, but my main job was to take the trays from the top of the trash cans to the back, where I fed them into a giant dishwashing machine, Francis showed me how, he demonstrated that each tray had to be lined up right so it would get clean the first time, and while he showed me he seemed almost like he was falling asleep, behind his big glasses his eyes fluttered, he showed me specifically how to line up the trays but shortly afterward he stopped lining them up right, he started sticking them in willy-nilly. When I pointed this out, he said, Fuck it, they're fucking trays, who gives a fuck, why the fuck are you smiling, what the fuck do you have to be smiling about? I said that I was honored to be learning from someone who knew the ropes around here, as they say, from someone who seemed to have mastered the ins and outs of dishwashers. Now his eyes were wide open behind his glasses. The ropes? he said. Dishwashers? he said. He picked a tray off the rack, before it went into the dishwashing machine, he picked up a tray and threw it across the room, it wasn't a big room, the tray hit the wall before it hit the floor, it made a huge clattering sound. He said that he was meant to be a filmmaker, not a dishwasher, and he could only ignore the indignity, his word, so much longer before he exploded, he had to work here in order to rent a video camera so that he could make a film so that he could go to film school so that he wouldn't have to work here anymore. He threw another tray, and could I not smile while I worked, it made him crazy, he said, throwing a third tray, it made him crazy to see my teeth and my eyebrows, he could tell the difference between a real smile and a fake one, and he could see that my smile was real, and if it had been fake he could have tolerated it, but he could imagine nothing more depressing, in these circumstances, nothing more suicide-ideation-inducing, his words, than someone actually genuinely smiling his way through this, he held up a tray and threw it. Roger the manager came in and said, What the Samhain, his word, is going on back here? And Francis said, I'm throwing trays at the wall. And Roger said, Stop it. And Francis said, I'm going on smoke break, and he walked out the back door. And Roger asked me whether Francis had shown me how to use the dishwasher, and I said yes, and he said, Hop to it then.

After washing the trays I returned them to the counter, where I watched my fellow employees work with the customers on whatever it was they wanted to eat, I saw no signs of war, I saw people who were trying to listen to their stomachs while they tried to read the menu, which was elevated above everyone and everything and which had pictures of most of the food and numbers you could choose from. I've never been much of a reader, but numbers I know, if you don't know your numbers you'll get into a mess of trouble, your grandfather's words. I did a circuit around the dining area to retrieve the trays from the top of the trash cans, for the first time I found myself among the people of Panorama City. They looked like they could have been eating at the fast-food place by the freeway in Madera, the people of Panorama City didn't look that much different from the people of Madera, except that when I looked at their faces I didn't recognize any of them, and they didn't recognize me, they didn't know to call me Mayor, they didn't know to ask me if they needed anything done around the house, they didn't say hello, they didn't say excuse me, they just moved around me like I was a dog who wouldn't get out of the road. At one point a Mexican man in a cowboy hat smiled at me and said good afternoon, his teeth were capped with silver, he reminded me of the old ranch hand Sergio Cruz from Madera and I said good afternoon, did you enjoy your meal, and he nodded. I introduced myself, I let him know that I was new in Panorama City, I let him know that I'd only been working at the fast-food place a short while, but that if he needed anything at all he shouldn't hesitate to ask, if there had been cameras they could have put it on the training video. He shook my hand, he introduced himself, his name was Alcibiades Cervantes, he'd worked on farms and *ranchos* in the area before they had been bought out and sold to real estate developers, before there had been a Panorama City at all, he lived in an old farm building right in the middle of town, he missed his horses, he thought about going back to Mexico, but the last time he had gone back so much had changed there, too, and it broke his heart to see the changes back there, even more than to see the changes here in Panorama

City, and besides, his grandchildren, they were building their lives here, they were ignorant of all the changes that had come before, but that was their job, his words, that is all of our jobs, he laughed, to be ignorant of what came before, then he said he didn't really believe that, as a matter of fact he believed the opposite. He said that the only good thing all of this civilization ever brought here was the fast-food place, he called it by name, at least now you could eat quickly and inexpensively, in the old days feeding yourself was a challenge, you were at the mercy of the weather and your animals. Of course I was talking, too, I don't remember what I said. Then Roger appeared and said excuse me to Alcibiades, not like he meant it, but like he was telling someone to get out of his way. He pulled me to the back of the restaurant and explained that customer interaction was not part of my job, my job was floater, and right now my only interaction was supposed to be with trays and the dishwasher. He explained that customers walked in with full pockets and empty stomachs and left the other way around, no monkey business.

At the bus stop, a kid with a skateboard kept stepping into the street and standing on his toes to see if the bus was coming. I mentioned something your grandfather used to say, which was that there's an art to waiting. He said why don't you get me some fries and a Coke, then laughed, he looked around for someone to laugh with him but no one did. I didn't answer him but instead reached into my pocket and pulled out my small binoculars and looked down the road to where the bus was coming from. There it was, shimmering in the heat of the road and the afternoon, about twelve blocks away, the flat face of it peeking through a tangle of traffic and wires and signs and palm trees, it was like looking through layers of grass and dirt and branches and leaf litter and seeing a ladybug on the ground. I told the kid that the bus was twelve blocks away, that it would be here soon, and he started to ask me how I could possibly know, and when he saw the binoculars he was silent.

A moment later, or maybe it was that same moment, Aunt Liz pulled up in her Tempo, she pulled to the curb in front of the bus stop, the kid had to jump out of the way. Even before I got in the car Aunt Liz asked why I was still wearing my uniform. I explained that I was taking pride in my work, and I had thought how to best convey that, not the words I used, I don't remember the words I used, and I figured keeping my uniform on while I rode the bus home was a good way, like those soldiers and sailors you see in the street. She said to get in, I folded myself into the Tempo. She had finished work early, she said, she had gone to Glendale to notarize some loan papers, she was a notary public, her job was to drive around and make sure that people were who they said they were, she was in the verifying and certifying business. Someone in Northridge had canceled on her and so she'd decided to pick me up straight from work rather than wait for me to come home via bus, she had moved up my appointment by an hour. I didn't know what she was talking about. She said she'd made an appointment with someone called Dr. Rosenkleig. I said I felt fine. She explained that Dr. Rosenkleig was a therapist, I was going to see him to talk about my feelings in the wake of my father's death, he could evaluate my feelings. She said I could talk freely with him, because he was a professional talker and listener. That made me nervous, I had always been an amateur at both.

Dr. Rosenkleig's office was not in Panorama City but just across the invisible line dividing it from Van Nuys. The office was in his house, his yard was neatly trimmed, the pebbles bordering the path were neatly aligned, the grass looked greener and healthier than the neighbors' on either side, I wondered if he and Aunt Liz shared the same gardener. The office entrance was to the right of the front door. Once you were inside, though, it was obvious you could walk straight through the office and into the house, everything was under the same roof, it was obvious to anyone with any knowledge of houses and how they are built or demolished that all he'd done was add a separate entrance to a spare bedroom. The walls were covered with certificates and plaques, they were covered completely, there wasn't room for even one more plaque. Aunt Liz dropped me off that first time and said she would be back to pick me up, she dropped me off after introducing me to Dr. Rosenkleig, whose name was Armando, who said,

Call me Armando. He didn't wear a doctor's jacket or stethoscope, he wore a thick multicolored sweater, it was not cold in his office, his sweater looked like some kind of beast that was digesting him. His hair was what they call salt and pepper, he kept his chin up high like a cat feeling the sun on his face. I wasn't sure what to say, I wasn't sure how to start our conversation, so I explained to Dr. Armando Rosenkleig that I was new in Panorama City, that I had been there only a day, that I was twenty-seven years old, and so on. Then we were quiet, he didn't say anything for a long time, I waited for him to respond. He sat on a hard wooden chair, I sat on a sofa, he took some notes on a yellow legal pad, after twenty minutes he started to look sleepy, he looked like he was having trouble not falling over sideways, his chair had no arms. He asked me why I had come to see him, and I said that Aunt Liz had brought me. He asked me why I thought Aunt Liz had brought me, and I said that she wanted me to talk about my feelings in the wake of my father's death. He asked me what my feelings were in the wake of my father's death and I didn't know what to say, it didn't seem like a question you could just answer. I was confused as to how this man could have become a professional talker and listener. I couldn't help but wonder, if you weren't a very good talker and listener, why would you become a professional at it?

* * *

Later, much later, Paul Renfro explained to me that typically people become professionals at things they have no aptitude for. People who choose to wear the mantle of professionalism wear that mantle to conceal their lack of natural ability, Paul's words. Paul told me that in his youth he knew, he knew even at age five, while other children were talking about becoming firemen or doctors or airline pilots, he knew that he would never become a professional anything, he knew even then that professionals were the greatest perpetrators of fraud in the world, that our only hope as a species lay in the hands of those who had not declared themselves professionals at anything. Someone like Dr. Rosenkleig becomes a therapist because he is fascinated by the workings of the human mind, Paul's words, and he is fascinated by the workings of the human mind because the workings of the human mind baffle him, because he has no natural aptitude for understanding the workings of the human mind.

After our session I found Aunt Liz waiting in the driveway, in her Tempo, she was waiting in the idling Tempo, she had the air-conditioning on, she had her visor mirror down and was examining her face and making small adjustments to her makeup. Dr. Rosenkleig followed me to the car, he seemed to have found a boost of energy somewhere, he smiled wide and told Aunt Liz that we were already making tremendous progress. I did not contradict him, I was pleased to hear it, but as far as I was concerned all that had happened was that I had talked in a great big circle and ended up right back where I started.

Aunt Liz made dinner that night, she made a shepherd's pie and a salad, and we ate across from each other in the kitchen, at the kitchen table, a single unlit candle between us, despite the fact that there was a proper dining table, in the dining room, with many unlit candles on it. I asked Aunt Liz why we weren't eating in the dining room and she told me it was for guests, for when we had guests over, it was for special occasions, and once I got myself established, once I began to lead a respectable life in Panorama City, one day I would move into a place of my own, and then she and I could eat at the dining room table, because then I would be a guest, but for now I was a member of the household, and I was expected to contribute as a member of the household, and I was to eat at the kitchen table just as she had always done in the period before my arrival, except of course when guests were present. I asked her why we didn't light the candle, and she said that she didn't want to clean up the wax and have to be replacing the candle all the time and besides the lights in the kitchen were soft enough. I asked her then why have a candle at all and she said that it was for atmosphere, that it made things nicer. I suggested that if the power went out it would also come in handy. She said I was missing the point. The candle, she said, was the difference between a house and a home, it made the difference. Then, changing the subject just a little, in her Aunt Liz way, she asked whether my quarters were adequate. Which was when I expressed concern about my bed, she asked if the sheets were too feminine, I said they were not, I said that the problem with my bed was the size, I could only fit on the bed, I could only get my whole body onto the mattress in a zigzag shape, lying on my side, I had slept that way the night before, in a zigzag, on my left side, but then I had been, or my body had been, overwhelmed with the urge to turn over, for the body is always seeking a sense of balance in sleep, my philosophy, and when I tried to roll over onto my right side, into a zigzag shape on my right side, I had to straighten out and position my legs on the thing opposite the headboard, the footboard, temporarily position my legs there, supporting my weight, which was very uncomfortable, so that by the time I was in a zigzag shape again on my right side I was wide awake with discomfort. This happened several times over the course of the night. I'm not a complainer, I wouldn't have said anything, except that I was concerned I wasn't going to be getting enough rest, that over the course of several nights the lack of rest would add up to a general fatigue, it had happened to me before, it had happened to me in Madera, when I had broken my arm, or rather my arm had gotten broken while playing Smear the Queer with the Alvarez brothers, I had fallen in an awkward way, and because of the cast and the way it was situated I could not roll over freely in my sleep, and as a result I suffered from what your grandfather called general fatigue, which he said was quite noticeable with me, what happened was that in addition to having less energy I was less interested in everything and less friendly, too, I wasn't myself. At the time I did not know the root cause of the general fatigue but I have since come to realize that without sleep the head gets clogged with other people's words. The head needs sleep to make everyone else's words into our own words again, it is a conversion process.

Aunt Liz pulled off her reading glasses, she wore glasses to read, she didn't need them to drive, she wore them for things that were up close, like reading books and magazines, and she always wore them while eating, too, it made her uncomfortable, she told me later, to eat blurry food. She removed her reading glasses and rubbed her temples and put her elbows up on the table. She said that this was a vexing issue, she asked if I was sure there was no way to get an adequate amount of rest with the bed, the problem was that she could not afford a new bed, she was just scraping by as it was, her words, when I arrived on the scene. I suggested that I could make some modifications to the bed, that I would be happy to modify the bed to suit my needs, that with the right tools I could modify it myself. I described the extension I had in mind, in enough detail that the method of construction was clear, that the supplies and tools needed were clear, which were a good saw, electric if possible, but otherwise a good handsaw, a hammer or nail gun and nails, or an electric driver with drywall screws, and some plywood and two-by-fours, there was no real point in trying to match the wood to the bed, it was going to be covered with padding, it was going to be covered furthermore with an extra bit of matching bedsheet, I had the whole thing planned out in my head, it was the perfect practical solution for allowing my body to stretch out completely while in a state of rest and allow free and unfettered movement. But Aunt Liz would not let me modify the bed, despite the fact that I am good with wood. I suggested sleeping on the floor, I could sleep on the floor, it is supposed to be good for the back, source unknown, but Aunt Liz wouldn't hear of it, judging by the look on her face you would have thought I was going to lie down in the street. I wondered what I was supposed to do that night, how could I ensure that I would get a good night's rest that night, I had to be at the fast-food place in the morning again, I had to be there for the breakfast shift, I wanted to show pride in my work, I wanted to be my friendly self. Usually I could nap, if I was back in Madera I would have napped, or slept until I had slept enough, and then, only then, ridden my bike into town to look for work, but in Panorama City there was no time for napping, you went from one thing to another, there were no spaces between anything.

* * *

Finally Aunt Liz said that she had an inflatable mattress somewhere, she had bought it from a catalogue on an airplane, she had never used it, she didn't think it was very big, it was smaller than my bed, but my legs and arms could dangle over the edges, probably, without too much discomfort, it would be better than sleeping on the floor, would I be willing to try it? I'm always willing to try something new, it is one of my qualities. And so my first full day in Panorama City, the most eventful day of my life up until then, the day with more events in it than any other day in twenty-seven years, came to a close with Aunt Liz and I taking turns on the foot pump, taking turns pumping up the air mattress on the floor of my quarters, until it was firm enough to support me, until the pump wouldn't put any more air into it, and then Aunt Liz and I stretching a fitted sheet over it, she wouldn't hear of me sleeping on an unmade bed, and then Aunt Liz wishing me goodnight and going off to her quarters elsewhere in the house. I brushed my teeth and washed my face, I used the toilet and stared at the picture of footsteps on the beach. I lay on the air mattress, it was a strange sensation, it was unlike any bed I had ever lay on before, wherever I put myself the air went somewhere else, so that it didn't feel like I was sleeping on top of the mattress as much as it felt like I was sleeping surrounded by cushions of air, pressing on me from below on all sides, it felt like I was suspended. I couldn't quite place the feeling, but it was a familiar feeling, there was something familiar about it, I had never slept on an air mattress before but I knew the feeling. I couldn't sleep until I figured out where I had felt this before, where I had experienced this feeling of being suspended and also pressed in from all sides, it couldn't have been from before I was born, I couldn't remember that far back, it couldn't have been from when I was a baby. It was strange, being able to remember a feeling but not being able to say what it was, and it kept me awake much of the night, it kept me awake into the wee hours of the morning, as they say, it was altogether a restful sort of feeling, it should have led me right to sleep, but the idea that some part of me, some memory, was locked away inside me was very disturbing, I could sense it trying to peek through, it was like having a word on the tip of my tongue, as they say. I tried to think of other things, to distract my mind, I tried to think about my day, about all of the new things and new people, I tried to figure out why Roger Macarona had found the sex video so funny, and why Ho had been disturbed by what I had said, and why the trays had frustrated Francis, and why the cities here were so close together that you couldn't tell them apart, and why Roger had said we were at war with the customer, and why the skateboarder kid had asked me for fries and a Coke when we weren't in the restaurant, and why Dr. Rosenkleig had become a professional speaker and listener if he wasn't good at it, and why Aunt Liz sat so close to the steering wheel when she drove, but it was no use.

## WAGE SLAVE

I was early for my second day of work, I arrived before Roger, I must admit that I was excited at the idea of Roger arriving and seeing me already there, working, a smile on my face, I pictured Roger coming in and seeing me wiping counters clean before, technically, my shift even began, and thinking, There's someone I can count on, there's a man of the world, there's a go-getter. Eventually, Melissa let me know that Roger was up at the lake for the day, tending to his boat, and that she was in charge, that she would be the one giving orders around here today. She was the boss now, she was running a tight ship here, the cat was away, her words, but he'd left a bulldog in his place, there wasn't going to be any dillydallying, not on her watch. Time is money, she said, let that be your E equals M C squared. When she talked she shook her head side to side like she was saying no, like whatever it was you wanted to ask her the answer would be no. Within an hour she was back to being the old Melissa, she was back to treating us like she treated her kids. It turned out that she'd just been establishing a pecking order, a level of respect, so that she wouldn't have to hear any back talk later on, she had learned this from raising her kids all on her own, their father had left, she'd had to be both mother and father to them, which reminded me of your grandfather, who had been both father and mother to me, which I mentioned to Melissa, which she said she could relate to. Then she informed me that in addition to my duties bussing the trays and washing the trays and returning the trays to the counter, I would have an additional duty, which was taking the trash out. This was the nature of being the floater, new duties were always being added.

Melissa showed me the special dumpster corral in the parking lot, the dumpsters were surrounded on three sides by cinder block, and by chain link in the front and on top, you had to undo a padlock to get the chain link open so you could throw trash bags in there, but people still tried to throw their trash into the dumpster and so there would always be trash piled up on top of the corral's chain-link roof, and since I was the tallest one, Melissa's reasoning, I was now in charge of removing trash from above the dumpsters and relocating it to inside the dumpsters, which didn't make much sense to me, I mean it didn't make much sense why we had a chain-link roof on the corral if all of the garbage was just going to end up in the dumpster anyway, why not leave it open, why not give everyone access to the dumpster so I wouldn't have to move their garbage? Melissa said damned if I know, her words, ask Roger.

* * *

I had been thinking about the kid with the skateboard, and how it would have been great if I'd had fries and a Coke with me and just handed them over when he asked for them, maybe I could have told him how much it cost, or asked if he wanted anything else, I don't know. I had been replaying the scene in my head, and so after my shift I brought french fries and a Coke to the bus stop, but the kid with the skateboard wasn't there, it was just a bunch of other people. I wasn't hungry or thirsty myself, so I asked everyone at the bus stop if they wanted the fries and Coke, they were fresh, they were straight from the french fry hopper, the Coke was straight from the fountain, I had brought them for someone but he was not there, would anyone like them? No one said anything, some people pretended like I wasn't even talking, but then again many of my fellow passengers didn't know English, and many of those who did know English couldn't seem to string together words in a way that made sense. I held up the bag, I held it in the air and made a gesture as if to say would anyone like this. Finally a very old woman, I had barely even noticed her sitting there, a very old woman raised her hand at me just for a moment and I gave her the bag, I said, Enjoy, compliments of, and then I said the name of the fast-food place. Now people smiled, there had been tension in the air, I hadn't meant to cause tension, but people didn't know what I was going to do with the bag, and now people smiled at me, and at the old woman, who opened the bag and ate the fries and drank the Coke, she seemed happy to have it. This freed me up to pull out my binoculars and let everyone know exactly how far away the bus was, which kept me occupied until it was time to board. Only once I was on the bus, only once I had taken my seat in the front row, only after I had introduced myself to the driver, whose name was Clarence, only once I was comfortably seated did I notice that the old woman on the bus bench hadn't boarded, she remained there, sitting on the bench, she had finished her fries and Coke, she had spread the empty fast-food place bag across her lap, she was engaged in very carefully folding it up, pressing down hard on the creases, I wondered what she was going to do with it, but then the bus pulled away from the curb and she was gone, or we were, I should say.

After Roger returned from his trip to the lake I suggested we should remove the chain-link roof from the dumpster corral, we should just let people throw their trash in there if that was where it was going to end up anyway. But Roger said it was a matter of principle, that this was a private dumpster, it was not a place for public people to throw their public trash, we couldn't just leave it open, because then everyone would throw their trash into our private dumpster. I suggested that everyone was already throwing their trash into our private dumpster, the trash was just making a rest stop on top of the dumpster corral, it was just waiting there until I moved it into the dumpster proper, which was a dirty job, which was a disgusting job considering the pieces of public trash that ended up on the chain link, the dirty diapers and plastic bags of dog business and Pepsi Gold, Melissa's words for soda bottles full of pee. We were having this discussion with Melissa present, she was standing just outside Roger's office, we couldn't all three of us fit comfortably inside, and she suggested that if there was no roof on the dumpster corral, even more people might throw their trash in our dumpster, causing it to overflow, which I thought was an excellent point, which I thought Roger should use for his side of the argument, but Roger dismissed it as a mere practical concern, not germane to our discussion, which was about the principle of the thing, his words. I tell you this because I want you to understand what people mean, Juan-George, when they say they're doing things on principle, or according to principle. Whether the dumpster was full or empty did not matter to Roger, trash sitting on top of the dumpster corral that had to be cleaned up did not matter to him either, because in all of the time I worked at the fast-food place trash was a job I kept the whole time, even after I was later promoted to french fry cook, because Harold the new floater was too short to reach the top of the dumpster corral and when we tried to get him to use a ladder he couldn't let go of the chain link itself long enough to retrieve the trash, he was scared of heights, even low ones. In all the time I worked there, I never saw Roger anywhere near the dumpsters or the trash, he did not have to physically handle any of the stinking garbage, public, private, or otherwise, he didn't ever have to get his hands dirty, as they say, and as such he had principles about the dumpster, which is the main thing you need to know about principles, they come from the heads of people very far away from what they apply to.

I received my first paycheck, I received my first official monies from my so-called respectable job. I wasn't quite sure what to do with the check, I had never received a paycheck before, I was just staring at it at the end of my shift, when Francis asked me if I wanted to head over and cash it with him. We went to a storefront a block down from the fast-food place, I had seen it before, but I hadn't been sure what kind of store it was, they didn't seem to be selling anything, and there were pictures of happy families all over it, along with cars and an airplane in the sky, I'd thought maybe it was a travel agency. It turned out to be more like a bank than anything, except that there were no desks in the main part of the room, all of the desks were behind the tellers, and all of the tellers were behind very thick windows. Francis went first, he showed me how, he cashed his check and took the cash and put it in his wallet, he said he was that much closer to getting his hands on a decent camera, he said that would be his salvation, he said once people could see what he could do with a camera he wouldn't be a wage slave any more. I cashed my check, too, then, and since it was for only one week, instead of two, and since money had been taken out for my uniform, and since there were taxes and fees involved, the number was very low, I didn't receive much cash. Francis noticed this, he noticed the disappointment on my face, he pointed at the cash and said that's why I don't walk around with a smile on my face all day, he said that's why I don't work too hard, he said that's why I just pile up as many hours as I can, who gives a rat's ass whether the trays are getting clean or the burgers are warm, his words, I'm not the one getting rich. I hadn't really thought about it that way, Juan-George, I had thought that the better job I did, the more I would be rewarded, I hadn't heard Francis's philosophy until that moment, it got me thinking, I didn't subscribe to it, I should mention, I didn't think I could actually go in there and do a bad job and let the hours pile up, as Francis seemed to be pushing, but I did have to wonder how I was going to become a man of the world with so little money in my pocket. Later, much later, after Aunt Liz discovered that I'd been cashing my checks at the check-cashing place, she went haywire and told me that their fees were outrageous, that there was no reason I should be giving those people part of my paycheck, that they were leeches, and so on, and then she signed me up at her bank, where I also had to pay fees. After my next session with Dr. Rosenkleig, after a session during which we talked about, as usual, whatever I felt like talking about, which that day was weather, bicycles, and knots your grandfather had taught me, Aunt Liz asked me what we'd covered, and when I told her, she said she couldn't believe it. She couldn't believe Dr. Rosenkleig and I had not talked about my feelings, or my father's death, or how I was adjusting to life in Panorama City, she wondered aloud what she was paying him for. Having become more curious about such matters recently, I asked Aunt Liz how much she paid Dr. Rosenkleig, I asked her how he got paid. She told me he was paid by the hour, same as me, and for a moment I felt, I don't know how to put it, a twinge of camaraderie, maybe, that Dr. Rosenkleig and I were both in the same boat, that is we were both wage slaves. Just out of curiosity, I asked Aunt Liz what his hourly rate was, she was reluctant to tell me, then she said what's the harm and came out with it. His hourly rate was substantial. In fact, I thought she had gotten the number wrong, she assured me she hadn't. I am good with numbers, I have always been good with numbers, even if words and letters elude me sometimes, so I was able to see, instantly, or nearly instantly, in my mind, that one session, fifty minutes, that is, with Dr. Rosenkleig was equivalent, financially speaking, to my entire first week's work at the fast-food place, once the fees and taxes and uniform had been taken out. I wondered why Aunt Liz had set me up with a job working at the fast-food place, I wondered why she hadn't set me up with a job as a therapist. I have always been an amateur at talking and listening, but how hard could it be to turn professional, there wasn't any equipment involved.

* * *

That night, while sleeping on my inflatable bed, my head combined and shuffled all of the words that had gone into it that day, and while brushing my teeth the next morning I put two and two together, so to speak. No matter what we achieved or did not achieve in our therapy sessions, Dr. Rosenkleig got paid the same, he got paid by the hour, he got paid for his time no matter what he did with it, which explained his long pauses, which explained why he stopped so often to consider everything. The slower he thought, the more he got paid for each individual idea.

And then a knock at the door changed everything, or a knock at the door would have changed everything if Aunt Liz hadn't answered. I'd been in my quarters all afternoon, considering the different ways I could modify the bed so it might conform to my body type, ways that Aunt Liz would not object to, I was trying to solve that thorny riddle when I heard the knock. I came out to Aunt Liz poking her eye at the peephole. She waved me over to stand behind her, she wanted to display to whoever was at the door that there was a strong and able man in her home, she wanted to employ my guard dog capabilities, her words from a few days earlier when she was talking about how nice it was to have a young man around her home, meaning me. There was another knock, and once I was in place she opened the door and gave the visitor an icy Can I help you? I was behind the door at first, so I couldn't see who it was, but the voice was familiar, I had heard it before, the voice said that he hoped he wasn't disturbing her but he was looking for a friend of his, an Oppen Porter, we'd become acquainted, he said, on the bus down through the Central Valley. By then I stood next to Aunt Liz, watching Paul Renfro teeter uncertainly on the front steps. He did not look good, I admit, he did not look respectable in any way, he did not look even as good as he had on the bus, he appeared to be wearing the exact same clothes except dirtier. I told him how nice it was to see him, I told him I'd gotten a job at the fast-food place, I told him I was settling in quite nicely, all things considered, then I asked how he was, I invited him in, I could see that he was exhausted, I could see that he needed us, that he needed our support. Which was not what happened, of course, because at the moment I invited Paul in, Aunt Liz uninvited him, she apologized insincerely, she apologized in that way that people begin with the word *sorry* and then spend the whole rest of their breath erasing it, ending with, in this case, a declaration that Paul, she called him Mr. Renfro in a way that was somehow less respectful than just calling him Paul, a declaration that Mr. Renfro was not welcome in her home or on the premises of her home, then she apologized again, this time on my behalf, stating that I had not understood the nature of the invitation, that essentially I hadn't meant to invite him here, that I was not always capable of making the most reasonable choices, which in fact was the whole reason I was living with her. Surely a man of Mr. Renfro's stature, again every word that came out sounded like its opposite, could understand the delicacy of the situation. What choice did Paul Renfro have? He made a half bow, she closed the door in his face.

I understand now that Aunt Liz could sense, just from Paul's presence, that she was dealing with someone who possessed vast intellectual powers, that her citing his shabbiness and strangeness was just a smokescreen, that when it came right down to it she didn't want to get in any kind of argument with his superior mind. Aunt Liz said that I had to be more judicious, that was the word she used, about who and how and when I spoke with people, and more careful about making friends, especially in Panorama City, people were not to be trusted. She repeated to me the phrase This is not Madera, again and again. And as sorry as it made her to say it, her words, Panorama City was no longer the haven it had been when she'd first moved there, before all of the elements arrived. But she was going to stay the course, she said, decent people would be back soon. Which made no sense to me, Juan-George, I could see already that Panorama City was full of decent people. Only the people in the milky blue house would turn out less than decent, or decent in their own way, but not of like mind, which is only to say that there are many different reasons for letting a lawn grow in a wild state of nature, not all of them philosophically sound.

* * *

C: Your Aunt Liz is right, you know, about the people down there. When Juan-George listens to these tapes, I want him to know that. I want you to know that, my little *toronja*.

O: I was there, I was there for forty days and the people were decent. I mean there were a few exceptions, of course, there are always exceptions, but I can say with some certainty, and with experience, it was my experience that everyone I met and made friends with in Panorama City was decent.

C: Listen, Juan-George, take it with a grain of salt, your father's always giving people the benefit of the doubt.

O: It's true I don't judge a book by its cover.

C: Panorama City is gangs, drugs, lowlifes. Stay in Madera, it's safe here, it's families here.

O: I can only say what my experience was.

C: I don't know why your Aunt Liz stays there. She's crazy to stay there, Oppen.

O: She was a generous host.

## A CAREER IN SALES

A few days later, I was on top of the fast-food place dumpster corral, I was pulling a broken television off the chain-link roof of the dumpster corral, it had appeared since the last time I'd been up there, I am doomed to be haunted by televisions, at least this one was broken, I was up top when a large maroon Mercedes-Benz pulled up, Paul Renfro at the wheel. You should have seen him, he looked like the king of the neighborhood, talk about a man of the world, he was wearing a white button-up shirt and a red bow tie, and when he got out of the car I could see he was wearing fancy black pants too. His shoes weren't fancy, his shoes were plain running shoes that looked like he'd painted them black, they looked ratty, in fact. I was going to ask him about the shoes, but he told me we didn't have a lot of time, he wanted to talk with me, he had a proposition. He explained that he'd borrowed the car from his job, the people who had dropped it off were elderly, they were in for a long lunch, their situation was leisurely compared to ours. Paul pointed at the dumpster corral and said that this was typical of what society did these days with thinkers, with real thinkers, he said, not those hiding under piles of professional paper, but real thinkers, no wonder the world was short of us. To put food in our mouths we take out the trash and park other people's cars, his words, even while we single-handedly shove history forward. A prophet is not recognized in his own land, Jesus himself complained about it, Paul's words. He asked me whether the drive-thru microphone was always on, I did not know, so we moved to the outdoor dining table behind the restaurant, the lone table on a square of concrete next to a patch of grass, out of earshot, out of microphone shot, of the drive-thru. Paul asked me whether I wanted to work at the fast-food place for the rest of my life, whether I wanted to be absorbed into the mass of anonymous nonthinkers. I hadn't thought about it that way, I had been focused on the philosophy of the training video, I was trying to live by it, I was trying my best to be a part of the great big family that was the fast-food place, I told Paul that Aunt Liz and I were looking for the same thing, that we were both interested in my becoming a man of the world, and part of that idea was working at the fast-food place, and part of working at the fast-food place was what was on the training video. Paul's eyebrows went up. He said that nonthinkers have always treated the thinkers like this, always, and the thinkers have always taken it, the thinkers have always locked themselves up and starved themselves to death and only a hundred years later do their papers appear and everyone realizes they were unrecognized geniuses, his words, this has always been so but it doesn't have to be. In Paul's estimation there was no reason we couldn't build a solid financial base to enable us to think some advanced thoughts in comfort for once, without all of this car parking and garbage clearing nonsense. Which made sense to me, after all I wasn't doing any advanced thinking on top of the fast-food place dumpster corral.

They say, Juan-George, and by the time you listen to this you will have heard them say, that the journey of a thousand miles begins with a single step. And when they say it, they mean that you can't spend all of your time thinking about your far-off destination, that you have to start somewhere, that if you don't take a single step first you'll never get anywhere. They're encouraging you to act, to stop thinking about the big stuff and just get going, they're having faith in you, they're having faith that you'll get there, wherever there is, and saying that you should have faith too. But one thing they don't say is that the journey of a thousand miles usually begins with a single step in the wrong direction.

That night I waited until Aunt Liz had taken her sleeping pills and gone to sleep professionally. I changed out of my pajamas and into street clothes and set out. Following the directions Paul gave me, he had drawn me a little map on a fast-food place bag, I took the bus to his penthouse apartment in North Hollywood. I took Paul's elevator to the fifth floor, which was as high as it went. Stairs at the end of the hall led to a door marked with some words and a picture of a ringing alarm, which did not ring when I pushed it open and onto the massive roof patio. I wasn't impressed with the building or the neighborhood. Sometimes people hold grudges against their own homes, is the best way I can put it. Paul's penthouse was a big patio, he explained to me that he was remodeling the apartment and so had torn the whole thing down, he was renting a room in an apartment downstairs, which was shelter fit for a king, he said, for a deposed king, a temporarily deposed king, while he worked on plans to rebuild the penthouse itself. The patio was crowded with containers for Paul's experiments. The heat of the day had settled into the warmth of night and Paul offered me a beer from a cooler. We unfolded a couple of aluminum lawn chairs and sat. The excited and enthusiastic Paul Renfro of the fast-food place's lone outdoor table had transformed into a contemplative, gazing-at-the-stars Paul Renfro. Later he would explain that there are times for planning, times for implementing, times for considering, times for reconsidering, and times for drinking beer while looking at the sky.

We went downstairs into an apartment, in the living room a group of men were watching soccer and eating noodles out of Styrofoam bowls. Paul said they were illegals, Guatemalans, migrant workers. They were a constant source of inspiration to him. It is natural, Paul's words, that in this most bureaucratic age the last true improvisational thinkers should be called illegals. He said this loudly and with a tone of great public authority. The men did not seem to notice. Paul's room was filled with cardboard boxes, no wonder he slept on the roof. For several hours Paul and I filled the elevator with those boxes and brought them to the fifth floor and I carried them the rest of the way up. After emptying trash cans all day and cleaning up a second grease spill that was not my fault and being reminded not to talk to customers, it was a relief to work for a friend until the job was done instead of working for strangers until the clock ran out. Once we got everything onto the roof, Paul and I took another half hour to drink beer and look at the sky, I don't like to drink, but if you're just looking at the night sky and there's no one around trying to pick a fight it can be okay. Paul and I had profound conversations on many subjects such as science and the scientific method, in fact he recruited me as a fellow scientist, and then we opened the boxes and made a sort of assembly line, one box that was full of empty antioxidant cream tubes, and then several boxes full of two other kinds of cream, the kind you buy at the supermarket. One smelled like coconut and the other smelled like mint. Together they were the very odor of youth itself, Paul's words. My nose couldn't make that out. We poured both into a plastic tub, combined them, and then poured the mix into the antioxidant cream tubes using a little funnel, it was slow work, cream doesn't flow like water. When we were done Paul unrolled a large sheet of dark purple plastic and a hole-punching device and we punched out gels for what he called his proprietary penlights. Then he opened a box of plain white penlights, and we popped off the caps and slipped in the gels until all of them were done. Paul said that all was fair in love and war, and this was a war, the territory we were trying to capture was time to think. I never worried about having time to think until I moved to Panorama City, I had always just done my thinking, nobody had tried to keep me from thinking in Madera. Paul told me that in his research he had stumbled upon a simple combination none of the other lotion or cream companies had tried, and that by mixing these two commercially available creams and activating them with the UV penlight he could indeed make people look younger. Then he added unnecessarily that the creams we had blended had high SPF values, whoever applied them regularly would be protected from certain kinds of skin cancer, which was a side benefit, which was something we could also feel good about, while we were appealing to their vanity we were also looking after their health, it is the business of thinkers to be guardians, his words, to guard over the health and well-being of nonthinkers, someday we will need them around to park our cars and clean up our garbage.

Several nights that week I snuck out from Aunt Liz's, she never suspected anything, I snuck out and together Paul and I prepared cream tubes and penlights for sale, we labeled everything, Paul had custom labels printed, they looked medical. It all went smoothly, aside from my not getting enough rest, which was compounded by the fact that I was sleeping on the air mattress, sleeping with my hands and arms off the edges of the air mattress, careful not to roll off, though by dawn I usually found myself on the floor. It was an exhausting time, Juan-George, made pleasurable by real work, punctuated with long hours of being the floater and a session with Dr. Armando Rosenkleig, who continued to baffle me, I didn't know what we were supposed to be talking about and he was no help.

The day arrived, the day I was to leave behind my life as a floater and wage slave and start my career in sales, and instead of putting on my fast-food place uniform I put on your grandfather's suit jacket and hat and a crisp white shirt. I did my best to steer clear of Aunt Liz, I thought I could avoid notice and go straight to Paul Renfro's without her seeing me, but Aunt Liz was everywhere in the morning, Aunt Liz would not let me go without a solid breakfast, which to her meant eggs. I have always been partial to oatmeal but Aunt Liz was always pushing eggs. The beginning of life for the beginning of the day, her words. When Aunt Liz noted that I was wearing my traveling clothes, as she called them, instead of my uniform, I worried that I was finished before I'd even started. I thought she was going to ask questions about what I was up to. But she only said that she was relieved I'd finally stopped wearing my fast-food place uniform everywhere, if only she could do something about the binoculars around my neck. When breakfast was over I hopped on the bus and went to Paul's building. If I could go back and do it all over again, which I cannot do, which is impossible, I might have contacted Roger, or dropped by, to let him know that I wouldn't be coming in. I hadn't really considered that not showing up to work would be cause for alarm, I'm the type that once I've made up my mind I forget that the world hasn't been informed. So I didn't tell anyone what I was up to, and maybe I should have, although who knows what would have happened if I had, unintended consequences being what they are and operating like they do. Really what was going on was that in the middle of the night, while sleeping poorly, while not getting a good night's sleep, while debating whether I should pull myself off the floor and onto the inflatable mattress again, knowing that I would end up on the floor by morning, I couldn't help but think about rude commerce. Obviously, as Paul pointed out, the first step would be to secure time to think, the first step would be to use rude commerce as a tool to remove ourselves from the world of rude commerce, but then undoubtedly we would have additional money, we would have wealth to spare, and my mind reeled at the possibilities, which may have been one reason I was distracted from covering my tracks, so to speak, I was too busy looking forward, I didn't think I'd be coming back this way. Which was also why I missed the bus stop by Paul's place and had to get off at the next one and walk back.

He was waiting for me on the sidewalk with a large cardboard box full of antioxidant cream and ultraviolet penlights, he was wearing his valet parking uniform again, together we must have looked impressive, we must have looked like men of the world, we sure made an impact, a visual impact, I mean, when we got on the bus to Sherman Oaks people took notice. I had asked Paul where we were going and he'd told me he'd explain on the way, we didn't have time to waste, but once we were on the bus he didn't seem to be in the mood to explain, he seemed far more concerned with the safety and security of his box. Paul was blinking strangely, he was blinking as if by force of will, whatever automatic motor in the head that makes us blink without thinking was shut down or not operating correctly, and so he forced his eyes shut and open every twenty seconds, his mouth open, always open when he did this. I asked if he was okay, if he was feeling okay. The illegals had been up all night watching soccer matches, he explained, and construction machinery on the next street over prevented any sleep during the day, but otherwise he felt alive. Stepping off the bus had an emancipatory effect, Paul's words, he could feel it was going to be a good day, he said, and he let me carry the box from there onward. We walked several blocks through a business district in Sherman Oaks, language on everything, until we reached what Paul called ground zero.

* * *

You could see through the front windows, you could see machines, dozens of machines, people on treadmills and exercise bicycles and rowers and other machines I could not recognize or name, I had never seen anything like it, the only thing I knew from personal experience was the exercise bicycle, Wilfredo had a catalogue full of them. Everyone who was exercising was watching television, there were televisions everywhere, which I shouldn't have been surprised about, but I was, I couldn't help but be, and while everyone was exercising and watching television, everyone else, I mean people outside the so-called health club, everyone on the street, we all could see, or would be hard pressed not to see, the people inside the health club, exercising. Clearly, with the giant windows opening onto the sidewalk like that, those of us on the outside were meant to look in at those on the inside, but nobody on the inside seemed to care or notice anybody outside. They acted, strangely, as if the glass was one-way, as if they couldn't see us or anything going on outside, they moved and sweated and watched their televisions, it was like an aquarium without the water, it was like television.

Behind the front counter sat a woman in tight clothing, her ponytail tied up high, arms crossed tight across her chest. Paul walked up to her and said a few words, she picked up the phone, spoke into it, hung up, and recrossed her arms. When health club members came in, they swiped a card over a box, she nodded at them. I recognized her as a fellow wage slave and gave her a smile, she smiled back quickly with her mouth only, no other motion in her face. I sat on a bench, the box at my feet, I tried to place the smell in the air, laundry, sweat, and a third thing, an air freshener that must have been designed in a lab somewhere, there was no way to describe it. Paul sat next to me and explained that we were waiting for the head honcho, that he would liaison with the head honcho and then let me get to selling, he explained that he would love to stick around and help me, but that in order to keep up appearances he would have to return to the field office. I was about to ask him what he meant when the so-called head honcho came out. His name was Carter, he had a bumpy bald head and strange eyebrows, it looked like he had shaved off his eyebrows and then darkened the skin where they'd been, his skin looked like it'd been burned and then fixed by doctors, is the best way I can put it. He was large, I mean he was thick, I couldn't tell if he was in shape, or had been in shape but no longer was, there was no way to know whether he was built of fat or muscle without touching him. I realized immediately that he and Paul had talked before, which was a relief. Paul explained that as the West Coast regional sales representative for a pharmaceutical firm he couldn't name because of market research–related privacy concerns, all his words, he couldn't be more excited to roll out this new antioxidant cream through selected, by which he said he meant exclusive, outlets in Southern California, by which he meant Carter's health club. He then introduced me as a rising star on his sales team and told him I'd be handling the table today. I shook hands with Carter, his hand was warm like it had been resting on a radiator. Carter said that if there was anything he could do for me, and then he didn't finish the sentence. Paul and I set up a folding table near the entrance, just past where people swiped their cards, and together we arranged a few rows of antioxidant creams and penlights, and then he pulled out a little folding cardboard sign that listed the benefits of the product and so on. He said that there was one thing I shouldn't forget while I was working today, which was that we were in a temple, that we had entered a sacred space, that this was a temple to the body, and that the most important organ was not the brain, as some thought, or the heart, but the skin, without the skin the brain and heart would be useless. We had brought with us a product to honor that organ, we had brought with us the most advanced antioxidant skin cream available, and then he said surely I could riff on that for a while, surely I could elaborate on that pitch, he had many things to take care of, he was already late for the lunch shift, but soon there would be no more parking cars, he said, no more picking trash off dumpsters, he was putting his faith and trust in me, he had no doubt I would succeed.

* * *

I didn't have an opportunity to use Paul's sales pitch, exactly, I mean that by the time I'd asked someone what the most important organ was in the human body, they had already swiped their card and nodded at the girl behind the counter and were gone inside. Or, if they were on the way out, they pointed at their watches, or just smiled and apologized and kept moving. A few people paused long enough for me to say that the skin was the most important organ, but then they kept going, one said huh, and more than one said, as if asking, but not really asking, The skin is an organ? before going deeper into the health club or out the front door. Finally a guy approached my table, he was on his way out, he smelled like a fresh shower, his hair was still wet, he was wearing a suit and had a duffel bag over his shoulder, he asked me if this was the sort of shit his wife would like. I explained that the special qualities of the cream were such that when used in conjunction with the UV penlights it could make someone look younger after about two weeks of regular application. He grabbed a tube from the table, opened it, and held it to his face. His nose wrinkled up and then he said he wasn't about to step into the doghouse by giving his wife something that was supposed to make her look younger. He left without buying anything, but his presence at the table, his standing there for a moment or two, attracted a few more potential customers, which is related to Roger Macarona's ideas about the ideal number of cars in the drive-thru line, which I will cover later, if there is time. Anyhow, the next potential customer was a woman who had heard me talking about looking younger, she asked me whether the cream could help retard the effects of aging, were the words she used, on the backs of her hands. You might be picturing a very old woman, Juan-George, you might be wondering what kind of old woman goes to a health club and has maintained such keen hearing into old age, but this woman was not in the least old, I believe she was younger than I was, she couldn't have been much older than twenty-five, if that, and she was in excellent shape, with excellent skin, and the backs of her hands were no different than any other part of her. This is where the genius of Paul Renfro comes in, I mean if I had been trying to sell the antioxidant cream on my own I might have gone to a nursing home, or to the park where the wrinklies played cards, I mean I would have tried to sell the cream to those who could actually benefit from it. But as Paul explained later we were appealing to youth, to the vanity of youth, not the actual skin of old age.

While she was deciding whether to buy the cream, I mean she had put some on the back of her hand and was sniffing it, a man who had been standing behind her stepped up to the table, he said he had a few questions. He asked if the cream worked on men or was it just for women. I told him it was for everyone. Then he said he would be interested, but only if he could be sure it worked, he didn't want to throw away money on something that didn't work, he'd been snookered before. I said I understood, I said that we'd taken that into account with our money back guarantee. If he used the cream for two weeks and discovered it had no effect on him, which was unlikely, I said, it had been formulated by one of the greatest thinkers of the twentieth century, if it had no effect, or if he was unsatisfied in any way, he could return the unused portion for a complete refund, we stood behind our product that much, some of Paul's words and some of mine. The man nodded, he carefully read the cardboard sign that Paul had set up, he picked up a tube of cream to assess its weight, he flicked a penlight on and off. He was tempted, but he wasn't sure he was ready to pull the trigger, his words. What we needed, his opinion, was a trial period. Now the woman who was standing next to him chimed in, she thought that would be a good idea too. I suggested that a money back guarantee was as good as a trial period. The man said that with a money back guarantee it was up to the customer to return the unused portion, it was up to the customer to get his money back, it was up to the customer to wait to get his money back, and so on. With a trial, if the product is truly excellent, the customer pays, and if it's not, that's the end of that, there's no returning anything, no back and forth. If you stand behind your product a trial is the way to go. I considered what he said, I assessed it from all sides, and I thought about Paul and what he had said about the antioxidant cream, and I thought too about how long I had been there already without anyone stopping by the table, and here was an opportunity to actually move some product, as they say. I told the man I'd be willing to offer the product as a trial, I'd be willing to let him take a tube for two weeks, after which, if he was satisfied, we could meet back at the health club, two weeks from today, I said, we could meet right there and he could pay me. I asked him to write down his name. I gave him his tube and penlight and shook hands with him, I could see in his eyes, Juan-George, that he was an honest man, I could see that when the cream worked for him he would be back in two weeks to pay me, two weeks was not long in the scheme of things, I thought, what difference did it make if some of the money took a little longer to trickle in, people waited two weeks for their paychecks, didn't they? Once he had gotten his free trial, the woman who had walked up, the young woman who had been waiting to the side so patiently, she'd set her handbag on the table, ready to get her wallet out perhaps, and had now pulled it off the table, she asked whether I'd be willing to do the same thing for her. I couldn't see why not. And then, according to what I'll call Oppen Porter's corollary to Roger Macarona's ideas about the ideal number of cars in the drive-thru line, other people stepped up to the counter, other people interested in the properties of the antioxidant cream, other people who wondered whether I'd be willing to offer the same free trial deal to them, one after the other, in an unbroken stream of customers, or potential customers, I should say, until there was nothing left on the table but Paul's standing cardboard sign and my list of names.

If I knew then what I know now, I wouldn't have gone back to Paul's apartment building that day, and so I wouldn't have found myself standing on the sidewalk looking into a car windshield at a crumpled fast-food place bag with Paul's hand-drawn map on it. How strange, I thought, I remember thinking, that Paul's map should be staring at me from the dashboard of a car parked in front of Paul's building. How strange that that car should be the same kind as Aunt Liz's. How strange, and then it dawned on me, that Aunt Liz herself should be getting out of that car and walking toward me with an unhappy look on her face. What the heck did I think I was doing, she wanted to know, why the heck was I here instead of at the fast-food place, she wanted to know, Roger Macarona called her when I didn't show up to work and she had been looking for me ever since, she had almost called the police, she said that twice, the police. She'd had to cancel a whole slew of notary public appointments, which were her bread and butter, to wander the valley looking for me, first along the bus lines, then everywhere between her house and the fast-food place, and finally, luckily, she'd looked through my things, she looked around my room, and found, sitting on the dresser, this map, she held up Paul's map, finally here of all places. All of this was very serious, she said, she was very disappointed that I had somehow found time to see the one person she had expressly forbidden me to see, for my own good, that man Paul. I didn't deny it, I don't believe in lying, there's enough to keep track of already in this world, but I also didn't admit it, I didn't say anything, I just got into the car, I was shocked, I think, I was shocked and stunned and I kept quiet, to express how I was feeling I moved the seat back as far as it would go, I moved the seat back to what was a comfortable position for me but which would require Aunt Liz to turn around completely if she wanted to talk to my face. We rode in silence for a while, and then Aunt Liz cleared her throat. Here it comes, I thought. But the first thing she did was apologize, I hadn't expected that, she started by saying that she was sorry she hadn't thought of my feelings before, that she hadn't thought about how lonely I would be in Panorama City.

It was perfectly natural, her words, that I would try to make new friends, she couldn't blame me, but she wasn't going to apologize for keeping me away from that man Paul, her words, he was trouble, she knew it from the first time she laid eyes on him through the peephole in her front door. The whole thing was her fault, her words, because she had made the same mistake as her brother, my father, your grandfather, she had extended me too much freedom, how could she expect me to follow the righteous path without drawing me a map, I should have been following her map, not Paul's, it was a good thing she'd managed to find me, she'd been worried sick, she didn't want to imagine the alternative, all her words. It is difficult for me to remember how I responded to Aunt Liz, again it wasn't just her talking and me listening, though I didn't say much, I wasn't sure what she was getting at about freedom, about extending me too much, because between the fast-food place and Dr. Rosenkleig and our regular meals with the unlit candle I didn't feel free at all, I didn't feel like Aunt Liz had extended me any freedom whatsoever. But one thing about freedom is that you don't notice it until someone takes it away. Of course Aunt Liz had her own philosophy about freedom, which was that freedom isn't free. She said it repeatedly, I could not wrap my head around it. Even after she explained that she meant I would have to earn my freedom from her with responsible behavior, that when I proved myself worthy, meaning that I would make good use of so-called free time, meaning not getting involved in any unsavory business, even after that explanation I couldn't understand why freedom shouldn't be free. Free was right there in the word *freedom*. It was the most preposterous philosophy in Aunt Liz's arsenal of small ideas, Paul's later words. What Aunt Liz was offering, I came to understand, was the opposite of freedom, she would release me only once I began behaving like a prisoner. There are invisible lines, Juan-George, and then there are invisible fences.

# PART THREE

TAPE 4, SIDES A & B;
TAPE 5, SIDES A & B;
TAPE 6, SIDE A

# A NEW FRIEND

Aunt Liz found me under the covers, breathing my own air, she had been calling me to dinner and I had not responded. She was going to introduce me to someone new, she said, a surprise friend, so I would no longer be lonely in Panorama City. In fact I hadn't been lonely there at all, I met new people every day, I hadn't made friends with Paul because I was lonely, I had made friends with Paul because he was a fellow thinker. Aunt Liz wouldn't listen to my explanations, her ideas were fixed in her head. Which I talked to Dr. Rosenkleig about, Aunt Liz had made an emergency appointment, it was that day I finally had a conversation with Dr. Rosenkleig that was more than talking in circles. For the first time Dr. Rosenkleig sat straight up, he looked almost like he was leaning toward me, he didn't sway to the side, his eyelids didn't droop. His goal always seemed to be to make me say more, to liberate me from my words, to get me to use up all of my words, to let loose a flow of words until the source was dry. That day, though, he was responsive, he asked questions, he came up with an idea. He didn't look like a cat lazing in the sun anymore, he looked like a dog pointing into tall grass. I told him about Aunt Liz and her idea of freedom, and how she was trying to keep me from communicating with the one fellow thinker I knew, and how she was trying to quash any ambitions or dreams I had, and how in general she was steering me away from greatness at every turn, some of which were my words and some of which were Paul's. I told him about the lack of flexibility in her thinking, about the rigidity of her thoughts, and about her bodily proximity to the steering wheel. I told him that Paul had initiated me as a man of science, that he had taught me about the scientific method and about experiments, and about two principles he had developed in his youth, when he had been a promising young scientist, before his brain overheated, as he put it, which were, one, nature is always ironic and, two, there are no such things as constants, neither of which I really understood but, as Paul said, they were advanced ideas. Talk of science got Dr. Rosenkleig excited, he was a man of science, he believed himself a man of science, he wondered aloud if we could discuss my situation in those terms, from one scientist to another, which made sense to me. Clearly Aunt Liz and I were having trouble agreeing on what was best for me, we had different ideas about it, but rather than battling back and forth endlessly why not resolve the question with a scientific experiment? It was fortunate, Dr. Rosenkleig's words, that I had developed an interest in science, we could skip the preliminaries and get right to designing the experiment. There was no way to know whether Aunt Liz's plan for me was truly objectionable unless we subjected it to experimental technique. He stood and pushed the chair away behind him. He proposed something called a clinical trial. For one month, I would follow Aunt Liz's plan without questioning my feelings about it. Only then could I truly know whether she might have had access to some secret knowledge, some insight she couldn't fully articulate that was nevertheless informing her decision-making process. I objected that I couldn't just turn my back on Paul Renfro. Dr. Rosenkleig made the point that a month wasn't a long time, that for the sake of a scientific approach we should pursue this experiment, that it wouldn't win the war between thinkers and nonthinkers, of course, but that sometimes science had to pursue more modest goals, and that at the end of the month, having followed Aunt Liz's plan, if the results were less than favorable, we would know Aunt Liz's plan was baseless and I could escape, I would be justified in escaping, to work with Paul Renfro or do whatever it was I wanted to do for the rest of my life, but that in the meanwhile I should focus on putting Aunt Liz's plan to the test, empirically and wholeheartedly, like the scientist I had become. I considered Dr. Rosenkleig's suggestion quite seriously, turned it over in my head, ran through all of the possibilities, debated whether I was going to pursue it or not, and finally, in the end, after much serious deliberation, I made my decision. Despite his professionalism, despite his being a professional, I decided to give Dr. Rosenkleig the benefit of the doubt, I decided to focus on the positive aspects. Independent of the issues surrounding professionalism, it was a good idea to put Aunt Liz's plans to the scientific test, something that I felt confident I could do, something through which I could continue to pursue the sciences, through which I could advance thinking in general. All right, I said to Aunt Liz, all right, I said to her outside Dr. Rosenkleig's home office, after my session with him was over and I had considered his suggestion quite seriously, had turned it over in my head and looked at it thoroughly from all angles. All right, I said.

In the Tempo, I moved my seat forward, not all the way back anymore, because I was pursuing the clinical trial proposed to me by Dr. Armando Rosenkleig in earnest, and not half doing it while hoping for failure. Despite his professionalism, despite the mantle of professionalism, Dr. Armando Rosenkleig had acted like a human being at the end of our session, had spoken to me scientist to scientist, and I was impressed with that, with his wanting to test Aunt Liz's plan scientifically, and with his saying that if Aunt Liz's plan was baseless then I would be justified in escaping to do whatever I wanted. It was like watching a puppet come to life, for he was a puppet, I mean he had been a puppet in my eyes, a puppet of Aunt Liz, a professionally trained puppet of the educational system, and then suddenly he was alive, looking out for my best interests, helping me determine my best interests, in a scientific way, not just some trained puppet positioned in front of me to deprive me of all my words, to squeeze from me every last word on the subject, under the guise, under the disguise, of analysis.

C: Sleep, my Oppen, you need to sleep.
O: Just a few more things, I've got a few more things to talk about.
C: You need to heal, you need to come home and work on the house. [*Laughs.*]
O: I'll sleep when I'm finished, after I've finished telling Juan-George everything.
C: There's tomorrow, there's always tomorrow.
O: Yes, I'll sleep tomorrow.
C: That's not what I meant.
O: You sleep, Carmen, you sleep for the both of us, for the three of us, I'll be done soon.
C: *Ridículoso.*

We drove toward home and so I thought we were going home, but instead of turning down our street Aunt Liz drove to a single-story mini-mall, it seemed like there was one at every intersection, if you ever make it to Panorama City you'll see for yourself. This one consisted of a liquor store on one end, then two storefronts decorated with anchors and life preservers and a working miniature lighthouse up top, then around the L was a Laundromat, and at the other end was a dark window with a neon pyramid sign hanging in front, which your mother does not want me talking about. I didn't know it then but we were headed for the Lighthouse Fellowship, Aunt Liz was introducing me to the Lighthouse Fellowship, she was introducing me to a surprise friend from that youth-oriented Christian organization, she was trying to wholesomely ease the loneliness she imagined I was feeling. We parked and I followed her through a door that had a porthole in it, I followed her into the Lighthouse Christian Fellowship coffee shop, the theme of cargo netting and life preservers continued inside, but the furniture reminded me more of the Madera St. Vincent de Paul on South B Street than anything you'd see on a ship, although I must admit I've never been on a ship. Later, I would learn that the furnishings themselves were supposed to look poor, they were supposed to reflect a sense of humility, they were supposed to display a Christlike indifference toward material things. But it was a mixed message, as they say, because the tables were all particleboard with fake wood veneer, the furniture itself was a lie, pretending to be what it wasn't, an indicator, I didn't notice it at the time, but it was an indicator that whatever was being achieved at the Lighthouse Fellowship might not be what it seemed. Not to mention that Jesus wouldn't have settled for particleboard and wood veneer, being a carpenter, being the son of a carpenter.

Aunt Liz scanned the room systematically, looking for the person we had come to meet, and when that person, whose name was Jean-Baptiste, who was bald and black and about my age, when he sprang up from the chair he was sitting on I knew he was going to be the surprise friend. I had just stepped into a dense nexus of invisible lines, and yet I had no idea, I couldn't see it, I could see only the spirit of industry and exuberance, I could see only young people sitting in groups and discussing issues, or filling out forms, or sticking labels onto envelopes, or playing music, or making coffee. The Lighthouse Fellowship, on first glance, and without any knowledge of the invisible lines involved, seemed, in contrast to the world outside, more energetic and more transparent, a first impression probably colored by JB, by his springing up from the chair and greeting me as warmly and sincerely as anyone in Panorama City had greeted me so far. He shook my hand, then he put his palms together like he was going to clap, but at the moment his hands came together he held them in place, clasped them tight enough that you could see the tips of his fingers change color. He pursed his lips. I would come to recognize this as JB's let's get started gesture, he used it to establish himself as the facilitator of whatever group or situation he was in, to declare himself at the center but not in the center, which was how he put it. He liked dividing things with language, he was constantly clarifying his words in ways that made sense to me while he was talking but became more obscure with each passing second. As opposed to the words and ideas of Paul Renfro, which bloomed and grew and expanded in the mind, JB's hair-splitting, which got more and more precise as it came out of his mouth, dissolved completely once he and his clasped hands and pursed lips had disappeared.

The three of us sat at a low table. JB asked Aunt Liz if it was okay if he gave me a little introduction to what he was about, then he went into an extended speech, some of which came out so quickly I do not remember it, he declared that he was not there for the hard sell, that he wasn't trying to convert anyone, that he wasn't trying to sell any product. He explained that he had the easiest job in the world, he had a product that sold itself, his job wasn't even a job, he was just a conduit, he was just a facilitator, all his words. Being bald and black gave him a double whammy of wise man, his words, good thing God made him a talker. JB talked about God's will and being reborn in Christ, the meaning of which I came to understand later, but which without any background sounded strange, every plain word he used had a secret second meaning unknown to me at the time. Then we turned to more concrete matters, as they say, we discussed my leaving Madera and coming to live with Aunt Liz. JB had lots of questions. He asked why I hadn't decided to stay in Madera. Aunt Liz frowned at that. I explained that I had come to Panorama City to become a man of the world. JB said he too had wanted to be a man of the world, but after many years of pursuing that false goal he had discovered something better, something everlasting, something not subject to fortune's shifting winds. You can imagine how appealing that was to me, you can imagine how appealing that would be to anyone whose whole life had been a concatenation, a Paul Renfro word meaning chain, whose whole life had been a concatenation of unintended consequences, you can imagine how JB's words entered my head and bounced around in there, pinging and ponging against all the other words, knocking into the idea of being a man of the world, which was still a half-formed idea, knocking it off its pedestal, replacing it with the idea of a life free from circumstance. Once Aunt Liz could see that JB and I were getting along, she got up and said, You know where the house is. I said that of course I did, and as I was saying it I saw JB nod at her, she had been addressing him.

JB thought we should have some fun before heading back to Aunt Liz's, he thought we should be able to come up with something better than sitting around the Lighthouse Fellowship listening to guitar music and Bible talk. He suggested mini-golf, and then a shooting range, he seemed dead set on going somewhere together. I didn't have an idea, I've always believed that fun can happen anywhere, anytime. All I could think of was how I'd like to share the details of my clinical trial with Paul Renfro, just to get his take on it, not as an interested party but as a fellow thinker and man of science. The problem, of course, was that one of the experimental conditions was that I wasn't supposed to see Paul Renfro, but since I was the principal investigator I figured it wouldn't matter if the experiment didn't start exactly on time. It didn't seem fair that I should abandon Paul without filling him in on what was happening, he was my friend, after all. In hindsight, which people say is twenty-twenty but which I think is not quite that clear, in hindsight I would have done a clinical trial of Paul's ideas first, rather than Aunt Liz's, but as Paul explained much later, Aunt Liz was the one paying Dr. Rosenkleig and in the so-called professional world research typically follows the sponsor. I told JB I had an errand to run, if he wouldn't mind driving to North Hollywood, I told him I had left something behind on Paul's rooftop patio, though I didn't mention Paul's name. JB said that he was game for whatever, his words, and we went to the parking lot to his fantastic car, a metallic gold car, which JB informed me was a classic, a Datsun, a 280Z. It was difficult for me to get into, physically, but once I got the seat reclined properly I was comfortable, my head was almost at the same level as my feet. Riding in it was like coming down a waterslide, except I was dry and the view was of the road ahead. I told JB that I was partial to bicycles, but that if I ever had a car I would want it to be this car. He smiled and said, his words, False goals, false goals.

I don't want to worry your mother any more than she's already worried, I don't want to worry you in there, but she's asleep right now, she's completely asleep, her breathing is deep and relaxed, and so I can tell you now what I know, what I know that she does not. Your mother, your sweet mother, she believes I'm being dramatic, she believes I'm worrying over nothing, or not nothing, exactly, but she believes I'm going to be coming out of this hospital someday soon, whereas I know that I'm destined to meet the terminus here. What happened was that yesterday, while your mother was in the cafeteria, she's been by my side this whole time, but she has needs, you have needs, you stimulate her appetite, while your mother was out I heard the nurses talking. The curtain hung between us, I was out of their sight and so out of their minds, they spoke plainly in the hall, thinking nobody was listening, one of them said I wasn't going to make it through the night, meaning tonight, meaning I will never see another sunrise. To tell you the truth, Juan-George, I never did spend much time thinking about death, I never really considered the fact that I was going to die, I always assumed that the terminus would be a far-off thing, and to hear that it was less than twenty-four hours away, to hear that I wasn't going to make it through the night was a shock, it still is a shock. Yet I knew immediately what had to be done, I knew what had to happen to ensure that you would benefit from my experience. If you had asked me two weeks ago what would I do if I had only one night to live, I don't know what I would have said, but when I heard those nurses talking there was no time for dreaming up an answer, I knew right away. The other nurse, when the first one said I wasn't going to make it through the night, the other nurse said, Let nature run its course, at which point I knew I was being cared for by at least one fellow thinker. Bless that curtain! They never would have said these things to my face, Juan-George, they never would have told me these things directly, and yet, thanks to that curtain, they spoke freely, and in so doing they gave us a gift, they drew back another curtain.

On the way to Paul Renfro's building JB said he wanted to get everything out in the open, to clear the air, his words, he wanted to illustrate what he meant by false goals, what his life was like before he discovered the Lighthouse Fellowship, he always spoke in terms of discovering the Lighthouse Fellowship, as if it hadn't existed until he got there. Before he discovered the Lighthouse Fellowship, he said, he'd hit rock bottom in his pursuit of false goals, he had become the lowest of the low, he had hit physical and spiritual rock bottom, which was one of the things that he had to do before he could seek recovery, he had to get to the point where he was living only for himself before he could give himself over to a life focused on others. He'd had false starts before, he'd always put too much emphasis on good deeds, he'd tried to hoard good deeds as a ticket to heaven, which wasn't how it worked, you could do all of the good deeds in the world and if your heart was just adding them up, if your heart was just a calculator, it didn't mean a thing, you couldn't enter the kingdom. Before he was lucky enough to hit rock bottom without killing himself, his words, he drank too much and committed petty crimes, he hated himself and he self-medicated, because he had never come across a mechanism for effecting change in his life path. Little did he know that the mechanism was right there in front of him, the mechanism was let go, let God. One day he was flying in a small plane with some buddies, from L.A. to Las Vegas, and they were carrying a decent amount of cash and an indecent amount of cocaine, his words. Out over the desert something went wrong with the plane. Everything went silent, all they could hear was the wind, and his friend the pilot said they were going to have to make an emergency landing in the desert, he was going to have to glide it in with no power and land on the desert floor. Which was what happened, he radioed that they were going down, he guided the plane toward a flat spot on the desert floor, the silence of it was eerie, JB's words, he knew something bad was coming, and he prayed, he hadn't prayed since he was a kid, he promised to lead a righteous Christian life if God would spare him. The something bad came in the form of a large rock, a rock his friend did not see, a rock no one saw until they were right up on it, until it tore off the right side of the landing gear and the next thing JB knew he felt like he'd been punched in the face by the biggest fist you could imagine. When he awoke he was the only one alive, wreckage everywhere, no emergency vehicles in sight. He grabbed his buddy's backpack, filled it with food, water, cash, and cocaine, and hiked out. What followed were two more years just like before, no praying, no righteousness, no gratitude for having been spared. But he was tested again. JB was always talking about tests, about ways in which the Lord was testing him, which is probably where I got the idea that I was being tested, I got this idea later, it has to do with Maria the Psychic, who your mother doesn't want me talking about, I entered the whole Lighthouse situation thinking I was doing the testing, and somehow, I think it was JB, somehow I got the idea that I was being tested, too, I was being tested and tempted, more on that later. JB's test came in the form of a stab wound, he was stabbed, someone stabbed him in the middle of a fight he should not have been in. In any case the knife punctured the sac around his heart and he nearly died. He woke up in the hospital and, standing at the foot of his bed, he saw. He stopped his story, I looked over at him, I was lying practically on my back in the Datsun, he stopped his story and stared straight ahead at the road, the sun was setting, the day was coming to an end. He told me that he saw the dead pilot, he saw all of his dead buddies standing at the end of his bed. They didn't say anything, they only stood there, this was for the whole time he was in the ICU. The minute he got out of the hospital, which was just a year before I met him, he went straight to the Lighthouse Fellowship and started living a righteous Christian life, with humility, he was just a conduit, all he had to do was stay out of the way and let the Lord do his work through him.

His story made an impression on me, Juan-George, I had never heard of ghosts appearing at the end of hospital beds,

I thought the Lord must have had something special in store for JB. I wondered, too, what it would be like to be a conduit myself, what it would be like to have that experience, it was more of an idle curiosity in that moment than a deep feeling, but then again the ground was stable under my feet, I hadn't yet been buffeted by what JB had called fortune's shifting winds. I was concerned about Paul, we had pulled up to his building, I wasn't sure how I was going to explain to JB that I needed to talk to Paul about the clinical trial, JB hadn't given me a chance to explain while we were in the car, he had talked the whole time. And so I told him I'd left something on the roof, on the penthouse patio, which was true, I don't like to lie. We took the elevator to the top floor and went out the door I'd used before, the one with the alarm bell on it, but this time a bell rang. JB didn't seem fazed, he pulled a card from his wallet and wedged it into the door jamb and the bell went silent. Old habits, he said. The patio looked so different I wondered if I'd accidentally come into the wrong building. Everything was gone. Everything was cleared away. Later Paul would explain to me that zoning issues had resulted in a total impasse between him and the building's owner, which was the reason he had been arrested, which was the reason the charges had been trumped up, but at that moment I couldn't comprehend why someone had taken all of Paul's things and disposed of them like this, especially the massive supply of valuable antioxidant cream and ultraviolet penlights, we had amassed an arsenal of rude commerce in the war for time to think and now it was gone. JB asked whether I was okay, he asked me if I needed to sit down. Before I could answer, a man appeared on the roof, holding an aluminum baseball bat, he asked if we were with the asshole who'd made a mess of his building. I couldn't speak, my tongue swelled in my mouth, I couldn't make words. The man informed us that if we were looking for all that shit it was gone and that we should get gone too. We could take the stairs or he would send us down the quick way, his words. JB and I walked to the door, we walked past the man with the baseball bat, he smelled like coconut and mint.

I couldn't believe that Paul's entire penthouse patio was gone. It was as if I'd found out that there never had been a Paul Renfro, that I'd made up everything, that those late night conversations about the scientific method with a fellow thinker had been figments of my imagination. I came to my senses, Juan-George, I mean it was ridiculous to imagine that I'd made him up, but the feeling stuck with me, the feeling of showing up on that roof and seeing nothing left, everything swept away. JB started the car and we drove away and while I was feeling shattered, completely shattered, JB laughed, not at my being shattered but at what had just happened. He told me that I knew how to have fun, that he'd never had so much sober fun in his life. He told me that back in his heyday he would have thrown that guy off his own roof, no questions asked. I told him I couldn't believe there was nothing left, I couldn't tell him about Paul Renfro, I told him I couldn't believe the roof had been swept clean of everything. He didn't ask me to explain, he only said that I should stick with the Lighthouse, that I needed the Lighthouse. I had the feeling he was right, that feeling stayed with me for a while. Later, Dr. Rosenkleig told me that on the roof I had experienced the loss of the father all over again, a so-called variation on a theme. He suggested that discussing my father's death through the lens of Paul's disappearance might help us dig deeper, which made no sense to me, I couldn't see what one had to do with the other, but then again Dr. Rosenkleig lacked insight into the workings of the human mind, which was why he had become a professional in the first place.

Later that week I found JB and his gold Datsun waiting for me after work. I asked him if Aunt Liz had sent him to monitor my activities. He told me he hadn't seen Aunt Liz since we had all sat down at the table together, he told me he'd come to pick me up and take me to the Lighthouse, he was a soul tender, his words, and my soul needed tending. All I had to do, his words, was come with him and keep my eyes and ears open. That sounded easy enough. We arrived just in time to hear the speaker, Scott Valdez, founder of the Lighthouse. Everyone had arranged the chairs facing the front, toward a simple podium, though some people stood along the walls or sat on the floor or on tables, I don't quite know how to say it, they made a show of being informal. We took two seats in the back and I kept my eyes and ears open. Scott Valdez began by saying that he was going to talk about grace, he spread out his arms, which were alarmingly short, and repeated the word *grace*. Or maybe his arms were normal length, it's impossible to know, maybe they were normal length but his body had swallowed them at the shoulders. He was built like those football players, linebackers I think, I don't know much about football, I was only on the team at Madera High for one day, it wasn't my talent. He had a massive round head, with spiky hair on top, his head looked like a pineapple. And I didn't see this then, I was looking at the front of Scott Valdez, I didn't see it until later, but when he sat down a bulge appeared at the back of his head, above his neck, or at the top of his neck, a bulge of flesh appeared there, like a pillow, flesh that had nowhere else to go. He was a man of strength, his physical strength reflected his spiritual strength, JB's words later, which made me wonder what the bulge of flesh represented, spiritually. Scott Valdez's face cramped up and he said to everyone that Jesus is Lord and whosoever believes in him shall have eternal life. Which didn't mean much to me, but in pursuing Aunt Liz's plan one hundred percent, without any reservations, I set my feelings aside, feelings being mutable unlike God's immutable love, JB's words. Scott Valdez said that

Jesus' father loved the world so much that he gave his only begotten son, so that whosoever believed in him should have eternal life, this was straight from the Bible. The father in question here was not Jesus' actual father, but God the father, the first of the three Gods. The Old Testament of the Bible was about him and the New Testament was about Jesus. The Holy Spirit didn't have his own testament. This was because there was a rule somewhere that the only thing that couldn't be forgiven was talking against the Holy Spirit, and so to avoid talking against him by accident, nobody talked about him at all. I listened with an open mind, I have to admit I was confused, so many new ideas were flying into my head with nothing to connect them to. But the main subject of Scott Valdez's talk was grace, this is the important part, Juan-George, not because you need to know what grace is, I don't think you do, if you want to know more you are free to find out, but because Scott's words echoed in my head in a particular way. He talked about how God's grace was strong enough to forgive all of our sins, and then he said that while being a good person was important, it wasn't enough, good deeds weren't enough to earn entrance into the kingdom of heaven. All the good deeds in the world without accepting Jesus as your lord and savior would land you in hell with the rapists and murderers, Scott's words. Which didn't sound right to me. At the pearly gates, Saint Peter, I don't know why God himself couldn't let people in, at the pearly gates Saint Peter wasn't going to pull out a calculator and add up our good deeds. When Scott said that, when he mentioned the calculator, I realized that I had heard it before, I had heard it and much of what Scott was saying from JB's mouth. This was a revelation, Scott could talk all day about grace and it wouldn't have had the impact that the word *calculator* did. Because grace had nothing to attach itself to in my head, while the calculator was already in there. It dawned on me that JB was a repeater. He collected things that Scott said and spread bits and pieces to people Scott hadn't met. When JB talked about being a conduit, he talked about being a conduit for God, but he was in fact a conduit for Scott Valdez.

I have talked before about how the head gets filled with other people's words, how in sleep we transform those words and make them our own. The measure of a man's thinking is in how those words are transformed, the measure of a man's thinking is what he does with other people's words, they must penetrate him deeply, they must penetrate him to the core, they must filter through his piled-up experiences and opinions, and they must return transformed. I didn't have this philosophy straight while at the Lighthouse Fellowship, it came later, I knew only that JB had repeated Scott Valdez's phrases without transforming them at all. What came out was what had gone in. Which meant that the phrases hadn't even grazed JB's core, they'd only bounced off a series of mirrors inside JB.

After Scott Valdez was done talking JB introduced me to him, he displayed me to Scott as if I was a fish he had caught. Scott extended his short arm and welcomed me warmly but in his eyes I didn't see the instant friendliness I had seen in JB's eyes, in Scott's eyes I saw something else, he was a fellow thinker.

# FRENCH FRY MAN

At work the next day, Francis and I were sitting at the table behind the fast-food place, watching the drive-thru. Roger always said this about the drive-thru, you wanted three cars in it at all times. If there was just one car, you should drag ass to let a line build up, if there were four cars you'd better pick up the pace. It was the one thing of fucking value, his words, he'd ever learned from working in nightclubs. Francis was smoking, he always smoked during break. He was smoking and blinking behind his large glasses. There was one car in the drive-thru. Francis took a drag and told me that this was the end of the line for him. He wasn't coming back the next day, he was done with the fast-food place. He hadn't told Roger yet, he wasn't going to tell Roger, he wanted to shaft Roger. He made me promise not to tell Roger. He was telling me now, he said, because he wanted me to know that he'd enjoyed working with me, that in my own way I'd helped him stay on his path toward film school. I didn't understand how I had helped him. I wasn't going to question it, though, and so I thanked him. Also half the things that came out of his mouth made no sense to me, he was always quoting movies I hadn't seen. For example, he said to me, his words, It's a strange world, isn't it? And I said that yes it seemed strange, but that it was the only world we knew, so who could say? Of course he wasn't really asking me, it turned out to be a line from a film, it was the last line from his favorite film. Then he asked me what my vision of an ideal world was. Once I was clear that this was not another line from a film, I answered, I hadn't ever really thought about it, or at least I didn't think I had, but when I opened my mouth the words came out. In my ideal world everyone knows everyone else, bicycles and binoculars get the respect they deserve, there is no such thing as money, thinkers have time to think, everyone is as lucky as I am, and people are buried where they want. I could see that Francis wasn't really listening, he was only waiting for me to finish talking, he had only asked the question as a prelude to his own answer, which he had been thinking about for a long time, he said. In his ideal world, everyone knew all the films he knew, and they communicated only by using lines from films. With each line came implications and shades of mood and meaning, all perfectly communicated from one person to another. In his ideal world, he would hardly have to talk, he would only have to quote. He took a drag off his cigarette and said that I was all right, but that talking with me was the opposite of all that. He flicked the butt toward the dumpster, I would pick it up later, and pointed at the drive-thru line, which was now six cars.

* * *

People incorrectly use the idea of a ladder when they talk about getting promoted, it would make more sense to use the idea of caulk, because promotions don't come from hard work or honest effort but because a crack has opened up and must be filled. If Francis had not walked off the job I would not have become a french fry man no matter how hard I worked. In fact, if I had worked hard enough to make myself indispensable, I never would have received a promotion. I was unaware of all of this, I did not know any of this yet when I came home from the fast-food place after my next shift, when I came home from the fast-food place no longer a floater but a french fry man. I told Aunt Liz the good news, I let her know I had been promoted. She was floored, her words, that I'd made such quick progress. Aunt Liz set the dining table in the dining room, she lit the candles, I hadn't expected that. I thought it was reserved only for guests and for when I got a place of my own, but Aunt Liz said she was so proud of me, she was willing to make an exception. She set the table and lit candles and put back into the fridge the casserole she was about to reheat. She opened the freezer and pulled out some frozen packages I had not seen before, something she said she had been saving for a special occasion, surf and turf, her words, which were lobster and steak. Your grandfather had never been very good at celebrating, Juan-George. There was always something else coming, even when something good happened, there was always something else around the corner, something that either took away what you'd achieved or surpassed it so much that your earlier celebrating seemed hasty, your grandfather's philosophy. Aunt Liz made a point of celebrating, she had taught herself, her words, she had decided years ago that if something good happened she was going to stop and acknowledge it, damn the torpedoes, her words. This was while she was preparing dinner, the steaks were in the broiler and the lobster was in a pot, she had opened a bottle of bubbly wine, I drank ice water. She raised a glass to my success. I was pleased that she was pleased. We ate our surf and turf in the dining room, on opposite sides of lit candles, over a fancy tablecloth. She looked softer in that light, her reddish brown hair and reddish brown lipstick didn't scream at you that they matched, her hair didn't look as no-nonsense as usual, her leopard print pants were below the table. Aunt Liz said that if we had eaten like this every night, if we had lit candles every night, we wouldn't appreciate the specialness of the occasion. I wondered aloud, I still wonder this, how did people celebrate before electricity, when candles were part of the normal routine? Aunt Liz said that I was well on my way to becoming a contributing member of society in Panorama City, and, what was more, a respectable citizen, with a sense of personal responsibility, people could look at me from across the street while I was waiting for the bus to come and could see that I was not some foreign substance mucking up the gears but an essential cog in the smooth functioning of the city itself. I liked the sound of that, essential cog. That night I celebrated wholeheartedly with Aunt Liz, without reservation, without questioning the nature of promotions, and without second-guessing. I had the feeling, I don't know how to describe it, the feeling of everything coming together in harmony. It's difficult to imagine now how I could have felt like that. We were celebrating a fluke. And yet what remained with me was not the unsound reason for our celebration but the warm feeling of sharing a happy moment with Aunt Liz, however brief.

Brief because Aunt Liz had a dark magnet inside her. When she'd finished half of her food and a second glass of bubbly she turned the subject to my father, her brother, your grandfather. She smiled, she was still smiling over my promotion, she smiled and asked me to imagine if only my father had gotten me started earlier with something like the fast-food place, imagine where I'd be today, considering how quickly I'd gotten my first promotion, imagine where I'd be if my father, her brother, your grandfather, hadn't been so laissez-faire, her words, in raising me, or failing to raise me. The smile was still on her face only now she was working to hold it up, she was trying with her face to hide the fact that she'd talked herself into the same corner she was always talking herself into. Your father, she said to me, your father was a good man. She told me about how he'd been in his youth, how energetic he'd been, how nobody could ever seem to keep up with his zest for life, how when he was an infant in his stroller he would whistle like an adult, how he always wanted everyone to stay up late and wake up early with him, how he had always taken life by the horns, if life was a bull he took it by the horns and flipped it onto its back, her words. But by the time I came along he had already been destroyed by that woman, my mother. Aunt Liz told me that my mother had been trying to destroy herself her entire life, and for some reason my father thought he could prevent her from doing it. Then she succeeded in destroying herself, which destroyed him. She sacrificed herself to ruin him, Aunt Liz's words. Which was why I grew up in Madera, doing nothing but riding my bicycle around, comporting myself like a village idiot, it was because my father, who had been a fount of energy in his youth, had been drawn into the spider's web and lay stuck there unmoving for the rest of his life, rendered passive, passive and impassive, by that woman who left us when we needed her most. At this point Aunt Liz wasn't trying to hold back, she wasn't trying to find her way out of the corner she'd talked herself into, she said instead that she was afraid, frankly, her word, frankly, she was afraid that I was in turn going to destroy her, that half of my nature came from my mother, that her destructive disposition was in me somewhere, and that my promotion had raised such hopes in her she couldn't help but fear she was being drawn into some kind of trap, like my father, your grandfather, her brother had been when his hopes were raised about turning that remote piece of land into a vineyard. Your father never should have died, she said, I'm the old one, I'm the older one, she said, I should have died, not him, but your mother killed him, she said, she killed him and she kept killing him long after she was gone.

My promotion had raised hopes in me, too, Juan-George. As I mentioned, I had not yet learned the nature of promotions, Paul Renfro had not yet illuminated for me how these things happened in the so-called real world, what these things really meant. And so in those sweet first hours at my new post I immersed myself completely in the thrill of the promotion, the sizzle of frozen fries sinking into hot oil, the fact that I'd become an active participant in food preparation. Not to mention that from the catbird seat location of the french fry hopper, I could watch Ho and others working the front counter, and I could see all the way past Roger's tiny office to the freezers containing the giant bags of french fries and all the frozen dirt and grime that came off the trucks every week, and beyond that to the giant dishwasher where Harold, the new floater, who arrived at work in a special van, who was brought to work every morning by some kind of counselor, was standing with a finger in his nose or ear, or mouth, as if the tip of his finger would come off if it was exposed to open air. It seemed, for the first day, ideal. But on the second day, the second time I came into work and set myself up at the fryer, I felt something else creeping in, it was the feeling of opening your lunch to find the same thing that was there yesterday. I couldn't quite understand it, I had moved up in the world, as they say, I should have been grateful, and instead I found myself watching Harold, watching the new floater, roaming the restaurant, doing all his variety of jobs, doing none of them very well, and I realized that I missed, already, being the floater, I missed not knowing what my job was going to be, from day to day. I felt chained to the fryer. I tried passing the time by making up tunes, I made up tunes and whistled them, or I didn't really get a chance to make up tunes, I was still feeling my way around the notes when Roger told me to shut the fuck up, he couldn't concentrate on whatever he was concentrating on in his office with me making that spooky racket, his words. With great freedom comes great responsibility, someone said once, well, it doesn't work the other way around.

It was a low moment. But low moments are more valuable than high moments, because when you reach a high moment you just want it to go on forever, which is impossible, whereas when you reach a low moment you look everywhere for a way out, and so things present themselves that you might not have noticed otherwise. I had just lifted the fry basket out of the hot oil and secured it to the rack so that the grease could drain before the fries got dumped into the trough under the heat lamp, I had just done that, and I saw, lying atop all the other fries, a single fry, normal in color and texture and width but exceptionally long. I had possibly seen one before, they occurred every hundred fries or so, but not before having been in a low moment had I recognized, not until Roger Macarona told me to shut the fuck up, had I recognized its potential. I set aside the abnormally long fry, and from that moment on I made a point of setting aside every abnormally long fry, I pushed them to the edge of the trough until I had enough to fill one of our cardboard fry cartons, at which point I shifted my attention to the counter, to determine the recipient. I could pick whatever customer I wanted, it was liberating, I was no longer bound by my job description, which is an example of the thinking man's way to empowerment, Paul Renfro's words. First I picked the most interesting person of the day, he had no hair, he had shaved his head, and instead of regular clothes he wore an orange sheet, like a toga, he had running shoes on and a big white plastic digital watch. I wanted to reward him for being interesting, by giving him what were in my opinion the most interesting fries, but for some reason he didn't notice his interesting fries, maybe he had so many interesting things going on in his life already that interesting fries didn't make much of an impact.

After some deliberation I decided to bestow the fries on the meekest customer of the day. When I first heard that the meek shall inherit the earth, I felt bad for the meek, because after the Rapture they would be left behind with the sinners, but JB said I had my stories mixed up and that in this particular speech inheriting the earth was a good thing. I don't know if Panorama City is bolder than other places, but it took some time until a meek person stepped up to the counter. He was a skinny and pale man, bald except above his ears, and when he ordered he couldn't seem to bring his eyes to meet Ho's. I had to leave my station, I had to leave the french fry hopper to get close enough to hear him speak, he nearly whispered his order, which, fortunately, included french fries. I returned to my station in time to position the carton of abnormally long fries where Ho was sure to grab it, and everything went according to plan, as they say. In that moment, the moment of him walking away with the abnormally long fries on his tray but not having noticed them yet, I felt quite good about myself, I had given the meekest customer a preview of his future inheritance, french fries coming from the earth, I mean, via potatoes. I had not only solved the problem of my lack of freedom but also changed someone's life in the process. I had not yet realized, or rather Paul Renfro had not yet enlightened me, that most people despise change, that most people, when faced with a change in their lives, will ignore it for as long as possible, until they are forced to face it. Most people are not thinkers like you and me, Paul's words. The meek man went to his table with a preview of his earthly inheritance right there on his tray and, because he was so meek, there was no telling what his reaction was, or whether he even noticed.

That disappointing attempt got me thinking that all of the energy I had put into selecting the right customer had been misplaced and that instead I should focus on putting together a carton of fries with more obvious impact, with what Francis would have called mainstream appeal. Which got me started collecting some shorter fries along with the longest fries. I had realized that an entire carton of long fries might look, to someone without a set of reference fries, unremarkable. I began to arrange for a customer, for a random customer, interesting or plain, meek or proud, a carton of fries expressly designed to highlight the single abnormally long fry, a carton that might replicate the joy of discovery I had felt upon finding that first abnormally long fry among the rest. When the carton was ready I turned to the counter. The customer standing there had what some people call a mousy face, people who have never looked closely at a real mouse. I listened to make sure she ordered fries, which she did, and then I personally delivered the special carton directly to her tray, which disturbed Ho, who was working the register, he scowled at me, he looked like he wanted to kill me. Ho did not respond well to having his space invaded, as he put it, he did not respond well to a lot of things, and sometimes he would be overcome by some kind of spell, and he would mumble nonsense words, his eyes staring at something in the distance, all of which was explained by the fact, Roger Macarona's words, the fact that Ho was a refugee, or had been a refugee, from someplace in bumfuck Asia. In general, though, if you did not invade his space or catch him during one of his spells, Ho was a nice fellow, you could always talk to him about cards, he was a poker fanatic, and his shirts were always perfectly ironed, he did them himself.

The woman didn't notice the fries on her tray, and I almost lost hope that I could bring anyone to pay attention to their fries, and indeed she would later claim that she had not noticed them until she got to her table and sat down to enjoy a nice peaceful meal alone and without any disturbances, her words. From a corner of the dining room I heard a squeaking sound that I would accurately describe as mousy, and then she was at the counter again and Roger was asking her whether there was anything he could do. I heard her say that she had received a carton containing an obscenely long french fry, that she had looked at that fry alongside the others in the carton, and that she couldn't imagine how a fry this long had come from a real potato. It was disgusting, she said. Her mind, she said, flashed immediately to an image from her childhood, which had been an unhappy childhood, though that didn't come out until later, to an image from the *Guinness Book of World Records*, of the man with the world's longest fingernails, and this image, which had come to her by involuntary recall, her term for it, this was not a laughing matter, her words, the image had so disgusted her, prompted by the obscenely long fry, that she had lost her appetite completely. She made a gagging sound that convinced me but that Roger later said was fake. She demanded from Roger Macarona that something be done, starting with holding accountable whoever was responsible. Together they looked at me, the tallest employee, six and a half feet tall, standing at the fry hopper, the evidence was my body itself, my height, I was making fries in my own image, as they say, and, her words now, I had picked her, I had singled her out for harassment, when all she wanted was to eat anonymously and in peace. Roger walked to where I was, it was only a few steps, really, he walked over and silently loaded a cardboard container with a bunch of average-length fries, with the freshest fries in the hopper I might add, though I wouldn't expect her to know it, he loaded it up, not a word to me. Of course I thought I had ruined everything, I thought I was about to lose my job, I was trying to do the math, as they say, in my head and figure out where and when I had gone wrong, maybe I had not deserved the promotion after all, I thought, but I didn't yet understand the nature of promotions, I couldn't bear to face Aunt Liz, I thought, after she had so courteously arranged a real job for me and I had ruined it, especially while I was doing my best to apply myself to Aunt Liz's plan for me, all of these thoughts were going through my head, and then I saw, I couldn't bear to look directly at Roger, I saw out of the corner of my eye Roger, his back to the woman, wink at me before turning to deliver the new carton of fries. Then the new carton of fries lay on her tray next to the carton with the obscenely long fry sticking out of it. You could see now that the seemingly average bunch of fries in the offending carton were in general shorter than those in the replacement, further evidence against me. She stood there like she was waiting for an elevator, looking at nobody. Roger took the offending carton from her tray and threw it away. She said, I heard her say, her voice wasn't so mousy, she said that Roger didn't understand, she didn't want new fries, her appetite had been ruined by the old fries, she couldn't get the image of a horrifying spiraling fingernail out of her head, it was disgusting, she wanted Roger to do more than replace her fries, her problem wasn't solved by new fries, what he was doing, her words, was trying to replace the heater in a building that had already burned down because of the original heater. Roger said that he thought they were talking about french fries, what did heaters have to do with it? This was a ruse, he admitted later, he had gotten her point completely. He declared himself responsible for the food only, he had no control or influence over what mental images popped into her head, and while he was sorry for, he used her words, her flash of involuntary recall, he couldn't exactly go back in time to her childhood and prevent her from opening the *Guinness Book of World Records.* Kids are naturally curious, he said, what can I do about that? As a paying customer she declared herself entitled to compensation for her negative experience, she described the whole incident over again now, as if Roger hadn't witnessed it and hadn't heard her describe it already, and he listened patiently without interrupting her, nodding the whole time, which was when we heard about her unhappy childhood. After she re-detailed everything that had been said and done, Roger said that he was very sorry for what had happened to her, and if there was anything he could do to make up for the unpleasantness of her dining experience at the fast-food place, anything at all, she shouldn't hesitate to ask.

I didn't realize it then, I didn't even realize it when he did it a second time for a customer whose chicken bites weren't cooked as well as they should have been, I mean they'd been precooked, they weren't uncooked, that would have been dangerous, they just hadn't completely unfrozen in the center, and Roger had done the same thing, he had offered to do anything at all to make it better. Even then I hadn't understood, Roger had to explain it to me, he asked whether I'd noticed that nobody ever took him up on his offer to do anything at all for them. If he had offered coupons or vouchers or a refund, his words, they would have snatched them up, that's what customers did, they wanted to hold on to their money, it was their nature. But by asking them whether there was anything at all he could do for them, he was in fact offering them nothing. He was telling them that if they wanted something, they would have to ask for it, and if they had to ask for it, Roger's thinking, they would have to give up what Roger called the moral high ground, which customers cherished even more than money. If they managed to ask in a roundabout way, Roger explained, using words like compensation or recourse, he waited for them to ask directly for money or coupons, but they never did. The woman never got past the word *compensation*, she huffed and puffed and left without even taking her food to go, vowing never to return to the fast-food place in as loud a voice as she could muster, to which Roger replied in a calm and soothing near whisper, so that everyone in the restaurant had to quiet down to hear him, which they did, that she could make whatever dining choices she liked, that this was America, that she was free to go, and that he was sorry she was having a bad day.

Once she was gone, he shrugged his shoulders and apologized to the other customers for the commotion, as if to say that she was unbalanced and overreacting and we were all better off without her, or at least that's what it looked like to me, I had seen that look before, I didn't like it. Roger had been cruel to the woman, I thought, and I said so. He explained that he had been nothing but accommodating with her, but that she was clinging to an unrealistic expectation of customer satisfaction, that the problem lay in her mind, not in his actions, he explained that individual customer satisfaction was not important, it had never been important, that the emphasis on individual customer satisfaction was only a strategy, a business strategy, a means to an end, and that it had become shopworn, customers had begun taking advantage of it, which was damaging the business ecosystem, like picnickers feeding the bears. I told Roger that I had only wanted to brighten the woman's day with the same wonderful feeling of discovery I had experienced upon recognizing a very long french fry sitting atop a pile of otherwise normal fries, I had only wanted to provide a unique and exceptional dining experience, I hadn't meant to cause any trouble or hurt any feelings. Roger shook his head at that, he said I hadn't caused any trouble at all, what I had done was root out someone who was trying to take advantage of the fast-food place, I had eradicated vermin, his words, I had done a very good thing. But from now on I should maintain a consistent variety of fries in each carton, because people had certain expectations when they dined at the fast-food place, expectations that should be met, not exceeded or fucked with in any way, and consistency was the hallmark of the fast-food place, Roger's words, it trumped quality every time. Even though Roger said I had done a good thing, I couldn't help, I can't help but be haunted by the image of the spiraling fingernail.

## GRACE

A few nights later, I told Aunt Liz I was going to take a walk around the block to settle my stomach, to aid my digestion, not that her cooking hadn't been delicious, it had been, I'd just eaten it too quickly. Which was entirely true until I started down the block and noticed a glow behind the sheets hanging in the window of the milky blue house. I had tried knocking on the door several times already, after work, to speak with the inhabitants about their lawn, or about their patch of wilderness, which took up the space where others would have kept a lawn, I wanted to introduce myself as a new neighbor, and let them know how much I appreciated their not cutting the grass to within a literal inch of its life, as Aunt Liz had done and kept doing, or as her gardener kept doing, I should say, on her orders. But nobody had ever answered. This time when I knocked a fellow who looked like a young Indian chief answered the door, his name was Chuy. I complimented him on the wilderness that was his lawn, but he said the place wasn't his, he was just visiting. He asked me where the pizza was, what had happened to the pizza. I told him I was not the pizza guy. He asked me if I was the police, I said I wasn't. A car pulled into the driveway then, which turned out to be the pizza guy. Chuy disappeared with the pizza and someone named Nick came to the door to pay. He invited me in, it was his house, or his grandmother's house, or it had been, before she went into a home, she had memory and balance problems. Nick's hair was slicked back and he had a goatee, or part of a goatee, on the point of his chin, and a tiny mouth compared to the rest of his face, it was fascinating to watch him eat pizza with it. Chuy lit what he called some Buddha and smoked and passed it on to the other guy on the couch, who passed it on to Nick, who put his pizza down to have a puff, who passed it on to me. When in Rome, wear a toga, your grandfather used to say. I took a puff, I inhaled and then let it out quickly. I am not a smoker, I have never been a smoker, but I could see immediately that one of the appeals of smoking is that when you let the smoke out of your mouth you feel like a dragon. A few moments later, or a few hundred, who can say, I couldn't remember what I'd just thought, or what I'd said, or what someone else had said, and so I spent much of my thinking trying to chase down what I'd forgotten. I became uncertain about what these people really looked like. The harder I stared the less concrete their features became, like when you try to look at a dim star dead on and it disappears on you. The rolled cigarette came around again and I was offered some more, and I pinched it between my fingers as I had seen the others do and I held it up to my eyes and looked at it closely. I wanted to penetrate, with my eyes, whatever this thing was, whatever was burning in there, but it was impossible. I could feel, I mean I could sense, how this thing was connected to maintaining one's yard in a wild state, I understood how these guys, or how Nick, specifically, might, were this something he smoked routinely, ignore many practical aspects of life, of which gardening, or landscaping as they called it down there, was only one. I asked Nick about his lawn, I asked him what his philosophy was. Chuy said, his words, Again with the lawn? Nick shook his head at Chuy. Plain and simple, he said, his grandmother's gardener was an asshole, he had problems with some of Nick's plants, strictly hobby plants, and so Nick had to fire him, which was why the lawn looked fucked, because also Nick had been too busy to mow it. Then he asked me to shit or get off the pot, his words, meaning pass the cigarette. As you can imagine, I was disappointed, as you can imagine, I was sad to discover that a respect for and fascination with nature in a natural state, or close to a natural state, was not the only reason someone might have a patch of wilderness around their house. I kept deciding to leave but my body felt like it had melted into the chair. I kept thinking I had come up with profound realizations but then found I couldn't put them into words. I felt hungry despite my full stomach and ate a slice of pizza and watched them play a golfing game on their television. After a while, or a hundred whiles, I became concerned that if I didn't leave soon I would never get up. On my way back to Aunt Liz's house my mind spiraled in a million different directions as to how I would explain my extended absence, how I would explain that I had gone on an hours-long walk, how I had stayed up long past our bedtimes. Except Aunt Liz was sitting at the kitchen table doing her crossword puzzle, and she looked up and welcomed me back and asked me if I'd had a nice walk, without any concern in her voice whatsoever.

I spent an eternity brushing my teeth. I stared at the picture with footsteps on the beach, trying to unlock its secrets. I kept having realizations, and then when I tried to remember them, or recall them, in words, I mean, I couldn't seem to put them back together. Every new piece of philosophy in my brain revealed itself to be a mirage, and yet I kept feeling I'd discovered something profound. I couldn't lie on the inflatable mattress, it was too wobbly, I lay down on the floor instead, I liked the way it felt against my ankles and calves and shoulder blades and the back of my head. My flesh felt like it was becoming part of the floor. I thought of your grandfather, I wondered what it had felt like to lie there while his body gave out, or whether his body had given out so completely that he'd never experienced lying there at all. I wondered what he would have said about me being down in Panorama City, I think he would have supported it one hundred percent, he had always wanted me to know something of the world. And yet I wished he had been there the other night at dinner with Aunt Liz, to confirm or deny what she'd had to say about my mother, your grandmother, and her destructive nature, which was supposedly half my nature, though I'd never felt destructive, I'd never been interested in destruction.

That night I dreamed, Juan-George, that I could read as well as any scholar, everything clicked, like those dreams where suddenly you can fly, and you sort of think, oh, that's right, now I remember how to fly. I had that feeling in the dream when I remembered, so to speak, how to read, and everything seemed clear to me, the world opened up like a book. Only to dissolve upon waking, as they say.

On those days when I didn't have to see Dr. Rosenkleig, I got into the habit of going to the Lighthouse Fellowship after work. Someone was always there, there was always a friend to make, and as part of my clinical trial of Aunt Liz's plan I did my best to stop thinking, in the name of science I did my best to accept the Lord Jesus Christ as my personal savior. I didn't reserve any part of myself from pursuing Aunt Liz's plan, I didn't go through the motions while my heart was somewhere else, I was genuine in my intention. And yet what I felt in my heart wasn't faith so much as effort. When you feel only effort in your heart, Juan-George, you know you are on the wrong track, my philosophy. I met effort with more effort, I wanted to absorb as much as possible, Scott and JB had given me my own Bible, it was black and the pages had gold edges on them, you could see the gold when you had a bunch of pages pressed together, it was symbolic of the flock, JB had said, I wasn't sure how. It also had a built-in fabric bookmark, no symbolic function, and in the New Testament some lines were written in red ink, which meant that Jesus said them. I would go to the Lighthouse after work, I would go to the Lighthouse and sit at one of the tables with a tall glass of ice water and open my Bible and listen to people talk. These were not always biblical discussions, in fact I was surprised by how few of the conversations were biblical discussions, to some extent it was a relief, I didn't feel like people were going to pop-quiz me in front of everyone, but on the other hand I enjoyed hearing people talk about the Bible, if only because I became more and more curious with each passing day what lay between the pages of that book. Sometimes I sat alone, staring at the words, picking out a few here and there, trying to teach myself to be a stronger reader, and someone would see me concentrating very hard on my Bible and look pleased. I couldn't get too far and I didn't want to sit there always staring at the first page, so I turned to pages farther in and stared at the words there. Your grandfather used to say that my gift was gab, by the time I figured out a couple of words in a row, I would forget the words I'd just read, I couldn't quite decode words and hold a sentence together in my head at the same time, I still can't, it's like the machinery is missing,

I hope you won't have the same problem, people tend to make judgments. Not Paul, of course, Paul helped me see the value in what I thought had been a handicap. Reading and writing are mankind's greatest tools, Paul's words, but we've abused them, we've managed to turn our own tools against ourselves, we've managed to bury ourselves with our own shovels, bury ourselves under piles of nonsense left behind by people from the past, nonsense that muddles our vision, that makes it impossible to see things as they are. Not reading and writing means not being muddled, and an unmuddled vision is invaluable, which means valuable.

I was staring at the words when Scott Valdez walked up, I hadn't spoken to him since I had first met him, I had spent more time with JB and others. Scott stood in front of me with his pineapple of a head and said that he had noticed my studiousness, my seriousness of purpose, his words, and my interest in the Old Testament. And then he said the name of the chapter I was reading, which I realized as he said it was pronounced like Joe with a B at the end, and not like a job you would work at. Which is the thing about reading, just when you think you've solved a word, it turns out to be wrong. He asked me what I thought. I told him I was doing my best to understand. He said that God tests us each in our own way. I agreed with that, everyone was different. It wasn't until later that I was able to absorb the words of Job, right then I had no idea what Scott was talking about, really, and I don't lie, I don't like to have to keep track of an alternate universe that doesn't exist, but in that moment I didn't feel like telling Scott I wasn't getting anywhere with the Bible, I didn't want to disappoint Scott, I wanted to understand the Bible. But as I said before, Scott was a thinker.

Scott waited until I was about to leave, I hadn't made it much farther in the Bible than where I'd started. He asked me to come into his office, which in some ways reminded me of Roger the manager's office at the fast-food place, I mean it was about the same size, except that instead of being cluttered and full of piled-up things it was neat and organized. Scott sat in his chair, which looked adjustable but was locked in an upright position. His short arms moved a computer monitor to the side so we could see each other. I was terrified that he wanted to talk about Job, I felt like I had been caught in a lie, a lie I hadn't really told, but a lie that had settled on me, like a pigeon. He told me how much he appreciated my help around the Lighthouse Fellowship, how much my enthusiasm meant to him, how despite my short time at the Fellowship so far I'd become a part of the family, thanks in large part to my friendliness and can-do attitude. He thanked me for all of the lightbulbs I'd changed and apologized for taking advantage of my height, of my being the tallest person in the Fellowship. Getting down to brass tacks, his words, he wanted to give me a token of appreciation. I let him know that I enjoyed being helpful, that I didn't need anything. He handed me a tape recorder. I thanked him, I didn't know what to say. He told me the gift would make sense in a moment. He pulled open a file cabinet, grabbed a thick zippered binder, something a businessman might carry around, and set it down in front of me. I unzipped the binder and looked inside. A dozen plastic pages with four cassettes on each page. I didn't know what they were for, I spent a minute counting them up, waiting for Scott to talk. He told me that it was the King James Bible, old and new testaments, with music and atmospheric sounds. He didn't say anything about me not being a strong reader, he didn't say anything about how I would be able to get through the Bible on tape but not on paper, he never said anything about my reading skills or lack of reading skills. It would have been the easiest thing in the world for him to say that since I obviously struggled with reading, I should listen to the Bible on tape, it would have been completely natural to say that, but Scott didn't say that. Juan-George, I did not yet know that the Lighthouse Fellowship was a hotbed of philosophical and spiritual perversity, I did not yet know that while I was trying to be faithful, while I was trying to understand, I could not be, and I would never understand. But I want you to know that regardless of his beliefs, independent of his beliefs, Scott Valdez was not only kind to me, but kind to me in a way that involved thinking and use of the imagination, he had taken a moment to picture the world through my eyes, and he had seen that my gift was gab rather than the printed word, he had come to that insight, he had acted on it, and yet there was no sense of victory. He wasn't interested in gloating over his powers of perception, he wasn't interested in stepping into my shoes and then stepping right back out, it was more important to him to help me achieve what I was trying to achieve, which at the time was to read the Bible.

So began my religious education. It wasn't your grandfather's wish that I should have a religious education, he had always felt that religion had done him no good and that he had been lucky enough to have the mental fortitude to escape it, he didn't want to trap his son in the same situation, which Aunt Liz thought was a shame, which Aunt Liz thought was throwing the baby out with the bathwater, all of which I learned after your grandfather died, all of which I learned from Aunt Liz over the dinner table on those rare occasions when she felt like sharing a piece of family history, which usually had to do with being exasperated with her brother, my father, your grandfather, and the life he had led and the way he had brought me up, triggered by her concerns that through situation and weak will and lack of religion your grandfather had single-handedly brought the family line, the Porter family line, to an unnecessarily premature end, to a collapse, what Paul Renfro would scientifically call submitting to entropy, to a collapse she would realize, as she was saying all of this, was embodied by me, embodied by her nephew, a realization that would be followed by a series of apologies for the implication, her word, that I represented some kind of Porter family dead end, an implication physically refuted, I can now say, by you, Juan-George.

That night I listened to the first tape, where God spends a week creating everything and Adam and Eve get kicked out of the garden. Some later sections sounded like a telephone directory without the numbers, just name after name, I wondered why God had left them all in. It is a confusing book, Juan-George, it contradicts itself, I don't know why anyone would found a religion based on it. But I can't really say, I wasn't there. It took a while before I got to Job, before I understood what Scott meant about God testing each of us in our own way. Job was a rich, happy person and a great believer in God. Satan, who is the villain in the book, seemed to think that the only reason Job was so faithful was that he was lucky and rich. What if, Satan wondered, what if you made Job's life miserable? Would he still believe? It was a sort of experiment, a clinical trial he wanted to run. Now, I'm not God, I'm not working with all of the information God had, but if I was God I would have stopped everything right there. For some reason, though, God tells Satan he can do whatever he wants. So Satan takes Job's riches away and kills his children, which is a terrible thing to do. And Job remains faithful to God. He passes the test. But his children stay dead. The Bible doesn't get into what kind of test they were undergoing, they just die, that's it for them. People are always being tested in so-called biblical times, God and Satan can't seem to leave them alone. Another time God tells a guy named Abraham to kill his own son, and then just when Abraham is about to do it, God tells him not to. Another loyalty test. And again, the guy's son has no say in the matter, his job is just to lie there and be killed.

## TEMPTATION

O: Are you asleep, *mi amor*?

[*No response.*]

O: There is a spider on your face.

[*No response. Breathing.*]

O: That's a little trick, Juan-George, to make sure someone's really asleep. There's no spider.

When Maria the Psychic walked into the Lighthouse Fellowship coffee shop she didn't walk in like a member of the church, but she also didn't walk in like a coffee shop customer would, she walked in as if she was walking into a stranger's house, she tiptoed across the threshold, one hand on the doorjamb, and said hello like it was a question. I had never seen her before. It had been what people liked to call a slow day for God, nobody had come in for coffee or flyers or guidance. I'd been peeling address labels and applying them to envelopes, Jan and Mark were doing the stuffing and sealing. They were longtime Lighthouse members, always together, pale, they looked like they never went outside. Jan had Band-Aids on her fingers from all the paper cuts, Mark had strange, wiglike hair, I mean it was big and dark and curly, but more than that, there was a strip of stubble at his hairline, it looked like he'd shaved his head and plopped a wig on over it and the wig had fallen back on his head exactly one quarter inch. I waited for him to say something, typically Mark did all the talking when he and Jan were together, I don't know why, Jan's voice was more commanding, Mark's words always sounded like they were going into his mouth rather than coming out. I waited, Mark said nothing. He and Jan pretended that Maria did not exist, which surprised me. I walked over, I left the labels and envelopes, I introduced myself and asked her if there was anything I could do. She told me her car wouldn't start, she asked if we had any jumper cables. I turned to Jan and Mark, I assumed they had heard the question, she hadn't whispered it, neither of them looked up, I asked them if they had jumper cables and Mark mumbled that they did not. I couldn't understand why he was being unfriendly. The coffee shop existed for situations like this, to draw in strangers, to attract with the promise of familiar things people who might listen to a word or two about Jesus and the church. I walked back to Scott Valdez's office and asked him if he had jumper cables. He did. He made sure that I knew how to use them, which I did, I'm not a driver, I don't drive, but I have always been handy with cars, there was always some repair work for me to do around Madera. Scott threw me his keys and went back to doing whatever he was doing, reading the Bible, probably. When I emerged from Scott's office back into the coffee shop area, Maria had retreated to just outside the doorway of the coffee shop, she was barely visible. Jan and Mark kept their eyes down, they reminded me of the people at the bus stop the time I brought fries and a Coke for the skateboard kid who hadn't showed up. They were paying intense attention to nothing in particular, you could see it a mile away.

Once I got outside, once I stood in front of this small Latina woman with dark hair, once I saw her in the light of day, I realized she was making my heart pound, which took me by surprise but also made me more inclined to help her and more confused about Jan and Mark. I suppose you will have heard by now of the expression *inner beauty*, people like to talk about inner beauty to make sure that everyone doesn't fall for outer beauty, which can be deceiving, which often isn't an indicator, really, of what someone's going to be like. But you know, there are certain women, when you see them, when they enter a room, it doesn't matter what their personalities might be like, it doesn't matter if they are thinkers of depth and sophistication, it doesn't matter if they are just plain mean, you still have to, you're compelled to, pay attention to them. Whether you like it or not you know where they are in the room at all times. Maria was one of those women, and once I stopped worrying about Jan and Mark, it was difficult for me to think of anything or anyone else. This is known as love-at-first-sight, which Paul Renfro later called romantic love, which he said many poems and songs had been written from, and which was in fact a tactic of future generations reaching back through time to assert their right to exist, his words.

You can expect to suffer from it at least once in your life. Your mother and I, as I've already mentioned, didn't exactly begin our relationship with love at first sight, in fact we did not experience that at all, which does not mean we are not in love, which does not mean we didn't find true love, lasting love, love which had I not ended up in this hospital bed would have gone on into old age. But when Maria looked at me, looked at the keys in my hands, and smiled, well, that was something different. In some ways Maria reminded me of your mother, an imaginary younger version of your mother, your mother as she might have been had she not had to work so hard her whole life, she was about the same height as your mother, though thinner, and her hair was the same color, though more evenly so, and she was Mexican, though from, I would discover later, a prominent family, and she was beautiful, as your mother had been once, as I could still see in your mother, or, I don't know how to say it, Maria's outer beauty reminded me of your mother's inner beauty and in some ways her outer beauty too.

* * *

Her blue Camry was at the other end of the parking lot, I had the keys to Scott Valdez's white Mustang. I opened the trunk and pulled the jumper cables out, prepared to hand them over. Maria shifted her shoulders and said that she would need the jump, from the Mustang, not just the cables but the actual boost to get her car started. I wondered aloud how we might bring the Camry close enough for us to jump-start it. She suggested that I could drive Scott's Mustang across the lot, to bring it alongside the Camry, I mentioned that I didn't drive, and so she suggested she could do it. I was sure Scott wouldn't mind, after all, Jesus would have moved the car, if he knew how to drive, which he wouldn't historically, but divinely he could figure it out. Maria got behind the wheel and started the car and put it in gear, I think, I was standing next to it, holding the cables in my hand. Suddenly Scott appeared, throwing his short arms across the hood, red-faced and yelling at her to get the hell away from his car. I explained that she was the woman who needed the jump-start, but Scott didn't seem to hear me, he was entirely focused on her. She told Scott that this had nothing to do with him, she just wanted to get the Camry started. He demanded his keys, he put out his hand, he demanded them. Then he told her he was happy her car wouldn't start, it served her right, his words. Maria looked at me, I was frozen where I stood, she looked at me and said at least someone around here knows how to behave like a Christian, then she turned to Scott and said that he had just bought himself a karmic ticket to a living hell, her words. I explained to Scott that I was just trying to help. He told me that I had no idea what I was dealing with, that Maria did the devil's work, that it always starts with a little help here, and a little help there, and next thing you know you're out in the desert being tempted, did I remember the part where Jesus is out in the desert being tempted? I hadn't gotten there yet. He told Maria to stay at her end of the parking lot, to leave his flock alone, he told her to call the auto club. She walked away, toward her car, then into the storefront at the other end of the mini-mall, the one with the neon pyramid in the window. She disappeared behind rustling doorway beads, like a fish jumping back into water. Scott asked for his keys. He pulled me into his office and explained that while naturally it wouldn't be obvious to me, Maria had refused to accept the Lord Jesus Christ into her heart and had instead pursued a path of necromancy and devil worship. She had followed a black path, his words, and I should avoid her at all times. The battle between good and evil played itself out everywhere, he said, and our mini-mall was no exception.

I could not comprehend how someone so naturally beautiful and seemingly kind could be aligned against all of the values that Scott Valdez held in high esteem but I didn't say anything. I went back to Jan and Mark and the labels, and when I heard the tow truck in the parking lot, the auto club tow truck coming to give Maria's dead Camry a jump-start, I felt a pang in my heart. At the Lighthouse Fellowship I had come to understand what was proper and what was improper, what was holy and what was unholy, what was good and what was bad, and yet my heart was going in the exact wrong direction. I wanted more than anything to ride a bicycle around the block. Riding a bicycle is the way my head figures things out, the pedals go around in circles, like thinking, but the bicycle moves forward, like an idea.

The next day after work I headed to the Lighthouse again, but when I got to the mini-mall some mysterious force drew my eyes to the other end of the parking lot. Some mysterious force told me that I shouldn't enter the Lighthouse but instead go talk to Maria. Some mysterious force needed to know what was going on behind the bead curtain and neon pyramid in the window. At the time, in the moment, I felt like I was experiencing temptation, I felt like something ungodly was tempting me over to the other side, if anyone had asked me what I was doing as I walked over to Maria's storefront I would have said that I was succumbing to temptation. I would have used the word *temptation* rather than the words *some mysterious force*, in part because I had begun to see life as a test, I had begun to get the feeling that I was being tested by God, that rather than testing things myself, rather than being the lead investigator in my own clinical trial, God was running a clinical trial, in which I was the lead subject, which is no way to live, Juan-George, anyone with half a thought in their head could have told me that God wasn't organizing a whole universe simply for the purpose of testing me. And yet there was the Bible, in the Bible God was always testing everyone, over and over again God took time out of his busy schedule of earthquakes and athletic conquests and glorious sunsets to put individual faithfulness to the test. Such thinking seems absurd to me now, Juan-George, it seems preposterous in about five different ways, but at that moment it was very real. You will no doubt go through a period in life when you believe that you are at the center of everything, it is an interesting period to go through, it is good for the development of one's thinking, but it is also one of the most important periods to come out of. The moment I walked into Maria's place of business, the moment I passed through the bead curtain, I believed, or I felt, or I thought it possible, as I once had felt or believed or thought possible in the early parts of my childhood, that I, Oppen Porter, was at the center of the universe, that I was being tested by God, that I was up there next to the judge, so to speak, being put on trial, and I was terrified, I knew that by walking into Maria's place of business I was betraying Aunt Liz, and God, and Dr. Rosenkleig, and JB, and Scott Valdez.

The waiting room was tiny, with a couch and some magazines, a poster of a dolphin. A voice in back asked me to come further. I passed through a second bead curtain into a dark room of complicated rugs and overstuffed chairs, mirrors, velvet, and the smell of incense. It was as if Maria had visited the Lighthouse Fellowship and decided to make her place the exact opposite of it, nothing was plain or humble, everything glistened, even in the dimness. She stood on the other side of a small round table with a beaded chandelier hanging over it. It made a strange pattern of light on her face. She said that she knew I would come. I apologized on behalf of everyone at the Lighthouse Fellowship for the bad treatment she'd received at our end of the parking lot. She called me a sweetheart, she thanked me, she asked me to sit down, I couldn't refuse. She wore a tight tank top and a long flowing skirt, her skirt was as modest as the tank top was not modest, and when she sat down it was difficult not to notice the tank top, or the areas of her body it didn't cover. As a sign of gratitude she offered me a reading, she explained that she could look at my hands and tell me things about myself, she asked me to lay my hands on the table, faceup. Then she said a number of things I didn't understand about the lines on my hands, she pointed out the life line, the fate line, the love line, and bumps. As Maria's hands moved over mine I experienced the presence of a strong spiritual force, unlike anything I'd ever experienced at the Lighthouse Fellowship. I experienced it without any effort on my part. Maria followed the lines on my palm with her fingertip, her eyes were on mine. She told me that I was the kind of person who didn't take things at face value, she told me that I was the kind of person who had to know everything for himself. She told me that I had considerable unused capacity that I had not yet turned to my advantage. She said I had experienced a tragedy recently, which of course was the loss of your grandfather. The next statement she made, while tracing what she called the fate line on my hand with her fingertip, her eyes closed now, was that I was going through a strong period of questioning, that I was having my doubts about the Lighthouse Fellowship. Those were her exact words, that was the degree of specificity she could achieve without knowing me at all. So as you can imagine I had many questions for her. I have since realized that the best thing about the future is that it remains in the future, but back then I wanted to know how everything was going to turn out for me, you can imagine how many questions I had, they bunched up inside my mouth, all of them trying to get through at the same time. What came out was gobbledygook, even to Maria. I took a deep breath, on her advice, and I considered what might be the most important question, I considered what might be the number one question I could pose to someone who had access to the so-called other side, who could tap into, her words, the spirit realm. This kind of thinking took a great deal of energy, I expended all my strength trying to focus on one thing. With her hands resting on mine I could have taken forever. I wanted never to be separated from her, from this force, I wanted never to go back to the Lighthouse Fellowship, that was for sure, or at least while her hands rested on mine.

## BINDER

My thinking was interrupted by screeching tires, honking, and a crash. Maria jumped up, the spell was broken. I followed her through the waiting room to the edge of the outer bead curtain. Everyone who had been inside the Lighthouse Fellowship was now in the parking lot, and people were coming out of the Laundromat, too, and the liquor store. JB's gold Datsun was on the other side of the street, facing the wrong way, smashed on the side, a box truck was up on the sidewalk. I hid, I stayed behind the curtain, no one could know that I'd gone to Maria's. Scott Valdez, I could see him across the parking lot, Scott Valdez was not looking at the accident but across the parking lot toward me, no, directly at me, his gaze penetrating the bead curtain, a look of blame, I thought. I heard sirens approaching. Then I realized Scott wasn't looking at me, he couldn't see me, he was staring at Maria.

At first I thought JB's accident came *ex nihilo*. Whenever you have the opportunity to say *out of nowhere*, say *ex nihilo* instead, Paul's words. Then I remembered a scene from a few days before. I'd been sitting with JB at the Lighthouse Fellowship, talking about something or other, when Scott had walked up to our table. It was morning, Scott's hair was wet and spiky, his head really did look like a pineapple, I wondered if it would look less like a pineapple if his hair wasn't so spiky, I remember wishing I could take a picture. Of course, Scott was a thinker, that's the thing about thinkers, Juan-George, you never know what they're going to look like. Or what we're going to look like, I should say. Don't forget how Aunt Liz turned away Paul Renfro for looking shabby. I wondered how many people had missed being exposed to the kindness and sensitive thinking of Scott Valdez because his head looked like tropical fruit. In any case, Scott asked JB how he was doing, they nodded at each other. And then he asked me how my Bible studies were coming, he quizzed me about my reading, he wanted to know what I thought, this was before I skipped to the New Testament, in fact this was when I decided to skip, I was deep into Jeremiah, and so I talked about Jeremiah, I talked about how God made Jeremiah hide a linen girdle down by the Euphrates just to make a point about the people of Judah, it seemed like an awful lot of work just to make what the teachers in Madera used to call a visual aid. Scott pointed out that in the Old Testament God made the prophets do all kinds of things, things God could have done with a snap of his holy fingers. He thought it had something to do with letting everyone know who was in charge. JB shifted in his seat, he said that Scott should know all about that. Scott didn't say anything to JB, he said only that he was looking forward to discussing Jesus with me, he was interested in my fresh perspective on the material, his words. After Scott walked away JB, who had after all facilitated my arrival at the Lighthouse, said I should be proud that Scott had become interested in my thoughts, that Scott was an incredible leader, for whom it was an honor to facilitate, and that no one, not even himself, had ever gained Scott's ear quite the way I had in such a short period of time. JB said that he himself might have become a leader of Scott's caliber, if he hadn't taken the Lord's word to heart. He could have led an amazing church of his own, but that wasn't what the Lord wanted from him, the Lord wanted him to be a facilitator, a humble facilitator, someone who operated behind the scenes to bring people together, which was what he'd done by bringing Scott and I together, by facilitating my gaining Scott's ear. JB said he'd come to understand that humility was far more important than power, to him at least, and that Scott could have all the power he wanted. His power would do him no good whatsoever in the next life, JB's words. I didn't notice, I should have noticed, that everything out of JB's mouth had a flip side.

An alarm is going off. Your mother is awake. She'd been sleeping so peacefully. Are you all right, *mi amor*? The beeping is coming from the other room. I wish you could see what is happening here, Juan-George. The hall has been quiet all night, just someone's television in the distance, and me talking into this tape recorder, your mother's trips to the toilet, medication beeps, the hum of the air or the freeway or both. Now the hall is full of light and nurses, I don't know where they've come from. A sleepy doctor, the night doctor, I recognize him, he was a year older than me in high school, his hair is sticking up in the back, he's walking quickly, his arms swinging like an ape. The alarm is still going. What's happening? Your mother is going to check. I can't turn my head far enough to see where she's gone. [*Pause. Carmen's voice, soft and unintelligible in the background. Distant commotion. Someone shouting:* Clear! *Buzzing on the tape.*]

I visited JB after his accident, I took the bus, sat in front as usual, and I brought my tape player with me. I listened to the Bible in one ear and the world in the other. JB had gotten out of emergency surgery and was in the ICU, I told him I would pray for him, for a speedy recovery, but he didn't seem to see me. He mumbled toward the end of the bed, where nobody was standing.

Later I asked Scott whether he'd gone to see JB and he looked at me seriously and said he'd visited JB one time too many. I asked how that was possible if JB had been in the hospital only one day. Scott explained that he'd always stepped in to rescue JB from whatever problem he'd gotten himself into, but JB always found his way back to trouble. I didn't understand why this would happen, how this could happen. The next time I saw Dr. Rosenkleig I didn't want to talk about what was inside my head, namely thoughts that didn't fit the boundaries of the clinical trial I was trying to run, so I asked him about it. Dr. Rosenkleig said that the Lighthouse Fellowship was a little Band-Aid, and JB's wounds, his emotional wounds, required stitches, required round-the-clock care. JB's time at the Lighthouse Fellowship was bound to end badly, again and again, because he needed a different kind of help from the kind the Lighthouse Fellowship could provide. It was a fine place for me, Dr. Rosenkleig couldn't blame Aunt Liz for introducing me to it, it was a fine place for me to develop a sense of community, but it was not a complete system for dealing with the traumas of the past. JB had too much pride in himself to admit defeat, and so he continued moving forward, patching up one tiny defeat after another with one tiny untruth after another, after which these little defeats and little untruths began to accumulate, which led to what Dr. Rosenkleig called a total breakdown. JB had too much pride to deal with the little defeats as they came, he could not acknowledge them, he was too busy being born again, and so he collapsed, which is what they call a cautionary tale, Dr. Rosenkleig's words. He took a long sip of tea and looked at me as if staring could hammer home his message. I had the strange feeling again, for the second time, that is, that the puppet had cut his own strings and come to life, he had cut himself off from the professional strings and expressed something real. Then he went on and on about how JB was in need of therapy, about how only through therapy would JB have any hope of progressing, instead of repeatedly regressing, and it was as if the strings were getting tied right back on again, as if I had seen the bare walls behind all of those plaques and degrees just long enough to wonder whether deep inside that feline head of Dr. Rosenkleig's, behind that professionally inexpressive face, under those wavy mounds of salt-and-pepper hair, there was a tiny thinker, shouting to be heard.

And then one night over a casserole, an Italian casserole, with pasta and vegetables and ground beef, Aunt Liz pulled out a three-ring binder. We were at the kitchen table as usual, with the single candle unlit. I had never seen the binder before, I had no idea it existed. It had been thirty days, she said, since I'd arrived. I had been in Panorama City for one month, and she wanted to do what she called a check in, she wanted to talk about how I was adapting to life there. Her no-nonsense hair shimmered under the kitchen lights. I hadn't realized she'd been tracking my progress, I told her I felt like I had just begun my journey. She frowned, put on her reading glasses, her eating glasses, and licked her finger and flipped the page. First of all, her words, I had made significant progress with Dr. Rosenkleig. The so-called professional talker and listener thought I was adjusting well, he thought I was putting in a good effort, he wished only that I would talk more about my father, your grandfather, he thought that in due time I would open up to my feelings and begin the mourning process in earnest, his words, as reported by Aunt Liz. I should mention that I'd decided, it was during my second session, not to talk to Dr. Rosenkleig about your grandfather, I kept those feelings and thoughts to myself, he had not proven himself capable, my thinking, he hadn't proven himself able to handle those kinds of ideas and feelings, he had buried his thinker too deep. Then Aunt Liz flipped the page and said that Scott Valdez had given me high marks as well. To discover that Scott was reporting my progress, my quote-unquote religious progress, was baffling, the whole message of the Lighthouse Fellowship was that only God knew what was in one's heart, only God could be the judge. And yet here was Scott, telling Aunt Liz how impressed he'd been with my level of participation, their words. Aunt Liz smiled at me, her eyes proud and perky above those reading glasses, and I felt like I was back in one of those parent-teacher meetings your grandfather had taken me to, those meetings we'd attended when he was still leaving the house, on the way back from which he would pick apart everything the teacher had said, he would wonder aloud what kind of morons were running the educational system, he would pledge to write a letter the next day. True learning, your grandfather's words, cannot be evaluated by morons, school was an accountability cult. Aunt Liz moved on to the fast-food place, apparently she had been speaking regularly with Roger, it was the first I'd heard of it. Turned out he hadn't expected me to move beyond floater, he hadn't expected me to succeed as a french fry cook. She said, she read, this was a quote from Roger, she said that I had become an integral part of the fast-food place machine, that I was a trusted fan belt in the fast-food place engine, and that he looked forward to my service well into the future. In fact, Aunt Liz said, she had a secret for me, a private message from Roger, something I wouldn't be allowed to share with my fellow employees until it was announced a few days from then. Roger had informed her, this was the secret, he told her that I was going to be named the next Employee of the Month. He had singled me out, specifically, because of my top-notch handling of an unhappy customer and her irregular french fries. Aunt Liz shivered with excitement. There was going to be a photo shoot and everything, her words, they were going to put my picture on the wall. I had seen the plaque before, of course, the plaque hung to the side of the counter, everyone could see it, customers and employees. I had seen it and wondered whether I could ever become Employee of the Month, I had pictured it as a jewel in the crown, so to speak, befitting a man of the world, but the longer I worked at the fast-food place, the smaller the jewel got, until I finally had it in my hands, or on my head, so to speak, at which point it became so small it disappeared, and the crown along with it. The closer you get to any goal, the more it looks like a false goal, my philosophy.

And then Aunt Liz closed her notebook and told me how happy she was that I'd come into her life, despite the challenges, despite the awful event that had led me to come to Panorama City, meaning her brother's, my father's, your grandfather's death, not his double burial, she clarified. She opened up to me, as they say, and she talked about how she had always felt like she was growing up in my father's shadow, how he was the one everyone thought would succeed. It was a different time, of course, women didn't have the options they did today, her words, but nevertheless it was clear to Aunt Liz that she was not the pride of the family. And so she stumbled from one job to another, she married Alan, I did not know she had been married, she married Alan and he left her after six years, at least she got a house out of it, she didn't seem to be able to succeed at anything, but she was a good Christian, she remained humble, she knew that if she stayed the course her life would one day open up, she would one day be called upon to do something great, something greater than verifying and certifying people's signatures on bank loans and real estate documents and living trusts. Already, Aunt Liz told me, already, only one short month after I'd arrived, already I seemed like a different person, already we had made headway against her brother's, my father's, your grandfather's failure to guide me in any meaningful way, already my life was taking the shape of the life of a respectable citizen, of a responsible member of society. She had been called, her words, and she had answered, I was her answer. I'm not sure how it came to be, the reason is probably attached to the great chain of unintended consequences, but Aunt Liz's calling in life turned out to be preventing me from pursuing mine.

I lay on my inflatable mattress that night, breathing my own air, all manner of thoughts spinning around my otherwise empty head, and I found myself picturing a certain person who ran a certain business near the Lighthouse Fellowship. You see, a substantial part of my paycheck had been going toward frequent secret discussions of past, present, and future events, and that the person with whom I discussed these events was providing far more insight into the workings of the human mind than the so-called professional Dr. Armando Rosenkleig, and the discussions themselves, the acts of discussion, resulted in a much more intense spiritual experience than anything I'd felt at the Lighthouse Fellowship. It was her hands, Juan-George, it was her hands on my hands, her eyes on my eyes, it almost didn't matter what we talked about as long as her eyes were locked on mine and she was feeling her way around the lines and bumps of my palms. And so you can understand, Juan-George, why I found myself making an appeal to this person, why I found myself trying to broadcast my thoughts to her, why I hoped that she of all people might give me some advice. It was a form of prayer, I realize that now, not all prayers are addressed to God. I wanted, I don't dare say her name, your mother will wake up instantly at the mention of that name, I wanted her, the one who had led me into temptation, as they say, I wanted her to take me away, to liberate me from the nexus of invisible lines and invisible fences, I wanted to be with her, and even more, I wanted to be, I didn't know how to express it then but now I would say I wanted to be, I needed to be, outside Aunt Liz's dominion, outside the confines of her three-ring binder.

I was awakened by a tapping at my window. It was one of those nights where the wind picks up only after the sun is down, one of those nights when you awaken in the dark to the sound of the world being torn to pieces, and so at first I thought it must have been a branch tapping the window, which happened in Madera all the time, and so in my half-awake state I thought I was back in Madera, a Madera branch tapping at my Madera window. Of course once I had climbed what I like to call the ladder of awareness, I realized, first from the squishy feeling of the air mattress, then from the odor in the air, the odor of freshness, of Aunt Liz's air fresheners, I realized I could be in only one place. But there couldn't be a branch tapping against my window, none of Aunt Liz's trees came anywhere near touching the house, she'd planted them all well away from the house and kept them neatly pruned. The one time she had visited us in Madera, you can imagine how she felt about our patch of wilderness, the one thing that irked her most, her words, were the trees right up against the house, which in her opinion was like a billboard of ignorance, only the ignorant let trees rub up against their houses, that was how rats and squirrels came in and nested, that was how moisture and rot took hold, and, what should be obvious to everyone, it was a fire hazard. It finally came to me, someone, some person, was tapping at the window. I remembered my prayers. I don't dare utter even the beginning of her name. I rolled off the air mattress and onto the floor, my legs tangled in the sheets. I raced across the room to the light switch and flicked it on, but then I couldn't see out the window, I could only see my own reflection. I turned off the light and went to the window again. It took a moment for my eyes to adjust, I had been blinded by the light. Then I saw that the person standing outside was not who I had been praying to but Paul Renfro.

# PART FOUR

TAPE 6, SIDE B;
TAPE 7, SIDES A & B

# GOFER

My friend, he said, I need your help. He stood outside the window, briefcase in hand, giving me that newly hatched alligator look, that tiny smile at the corners of his mouth, as if nothing was out of the ordinary, as if we had just seen each other the day before, as if this was the typical way someone came to visit, knocking on your bedroom window in the middle of the night. I asked him where he'd been. He shook his hand in the air and explained that he'd had to untangle himself from his real estate problems, meaning his penthouse patio and the zoning board, and jump through what he described as a series of hoops before he could again pursue what it was he had been called upon to pursue. Hoops, his words, specifically arranged to prevent any kind of original thought or action on the part of the individual. He was lucky to have the practical knowledge, he called it, to be able to navigate all of the hoops, else he wouldn't be standing outside my window but rather rotting away in a cell somewhere while the human race expired from its own stupidity. Look at Galileo, his words. He started to come in through the window, but I sent him around to the front door. Aunt Liz was catatonic with her sleeping pills, night mask, and white noise–nature sound generator. He wore a dark blue suit with a crisp white shirt and a striped tie, in the light of my room he looked like a businessman, or he would have if his clothes had fit, the pants had been rolled up and the jacket sleeves extended well past his wrists. His briefcase was still made of cardboard but had been cleaned or replaced with a new one. He sat on my desk chair and explained that the period in his life ending with the antioxidant cream was over, that he was changing his stripes, going the straight-and-narrow route. Anything less than the straight-and-narrow route would be unfair to those who stood to gain most from his thinking, meaning mankind. I must set aside the personal, he said, this is not about me, none of this is about me, I am but a humble representative of my species on this planet, I have no more right to assert myself individually, he said, than an aphid. I feel no need, he said, to stand outside the race of man, I am a humble servant, a humble servant of the future of mankind, and I have resolved now, in this period of clarity, in this period of utter and complete clarity, in this period so clear I have experienced the ability, twice in the past week, to see through solid objects, I have resolved to use my powers for good, and good alone, which I was doing before, more or less, which I have been doing all my life, but which I have hampered with a modicum of selfishness, an infinitesimal modicum I have since erased, he said. Then he asked me how I had been adjusting to life in Panorama City.

I told him everything. I'm not going to repeat it all, I told him everything I've told you. Afterward he explained that no matter how I entertained myself, making french fries for short-tempered people was a waste of my time, and that Dr. Rosenkleig was not interested in my scientific analysis of anything but was only trying to modify my behavior using a series of techniques first developed by Watson, Pavlov, Skinner, and others. Paul said that Dr. Rosenkleig would strip, using the language of science, using the techniques of science, hiding behind the mask of professionalism, would strip away every interesting part of myself and replace those parts with a prefabricated system, a program, a computer program but for the brain, a series of thoughts and behaviors I would run through from the moment I awoke to the moment I went to sleep, so that I would be left with only the vague feeling that I was not living my own life, that I was a shadow of myself, sleepwalking through my days, until my death. As for the Lighthouse Fellowship, from what I'd told him it sounded like the ultimate hotbed of spiritual and philosophical perversity. The revelation of an eternal soul should occasion drinking of beer and looking at the sky, Paul's words, because the word *eternal* means, above all, that we have time. But at the Lighthouse Fellowship the revelation of an eternal soul seemed to have resulted in the opposite reaction, resulted not in a sense of expanding time but collapsing time, resulted in an overwhelming sense of urgency. Which was baffling, utterly baffling, he couldn't think of a single thing more baffling in the whole wide world. And furthermore, Paul said, the lighthouse itself, as a symbol, made no sense. Someone had declared it a Christian beacon of some sort, but a lighthouse wasn't something that led you to a safe harbor, a lighthouse was something that you avoided at all costs, a lighthouse was something you stayed away from lest you and your ship be dashed on the rocks. The most perverse message a lighthouse could ever deliver, Paul's words, is come here and be saved.

I told Paul that I'd learned enough already about the life they were trying to squeeze me into. I wanted to quit my job at the fast-food place, I wanted to quit seeing Dr. Rosenkleig, I wanted never to go back to the Lighthouse Fellowship, I wanted to go wherever I wanted and do whatever I wanted, whatever it took, whatever it would take, to become a man of the world. Paul put up his hands. All aspects of Aunt Liz's plan were in direct conflict with the fundamental rights of man, he said, nobody could possibly argue with that. But he reminded me that there were times for planning, times for implementing, times for considering, times for reconsidering, and times for drinking beer while looking at the sky, and this was a time for planning and considering, not yet a time for implementing.

We were seeking homeostasis, his word. I did not know what homeostasis was and said so. For starters, he said, I need lodgings. The government had taken all his money, so he couldn't rent a room anywhere, and living on the streets was out of the question. Aunt Liz certainly wasn't going to let him stay. We discussed him possibly sleeping in the garden shed, but the gardener, being a professional, would rat him out, no question. We discussed him sleeping on the roof of the house but police helicopters were always in the neighborhood and would surely spot him. Then I remembered the access panel in the closet. I had poked my head up there when I first arrived from Madera, I had stood under the panel and pushed it out of the way and jumped up so my head poked through the opening. I'd caught a glimpse of the space above my room. It wasn't an attic, there wasn't room for an attic, it was a low crawl space of lumber with a peaked roof, lined with insulation and crowded with heating ducts and wires, but it was, as they say, our only option. I made a stirrup of my hands and lifted Paul so he could get a good view. He hauled himself up completely, which I did not expect him to do, which I did not expect him to be able to do, he was stronger than he looked. He asked for his briefcase and a flashlight. Aunt Liz had a tool drawer in the kitchen, not that she ever fixed anything herself, depending as she did on professionals for everything. I fetched a flashlight and pulled my desk chair into the closet. You never know when something useless might come in useful. I couldn't ever sit on the chair and also get my legs under the desk, the chair was too high, or the desk was too low, neither was adjustable. I had a plan for raising the legs of the desk, but after Aunt Liz's reaction to my wanting to modify the bed I had put it on the so-called back burner. But for these purposes the height of the chair was ideal. I stood on it and poked my head up through the access. I handed Paul the flashlight. I don't need to see, he said, I don't need my eyes, I need only to breathe the air to know that this atmosphere is conducive to advanced thinking, ideal for the kind of powerful thoughts I expect to assemble in the coming weeks.

Paul had not had a decent meal in a long time, he'd been subsisting on too little too long, he'd been subjected to, his words, cruel and unusual cuisine. I couldn't raid Aunt Liz's pantry without arousing suspicion, so I suggested that Paul and I step out to the fast-food place to find something to eat, the drive thru was open twenty-four hours, I was sure we could walk up and get something to eat, if the right people were working I could even get us a table inside, after all, I was about to be named Employee of the Month. But Paul seemed reluctant to leave the ceiling. He declared himself setting up for a long stretch of advanced thinking. Perhaps it would be better if he didn't show his face to the world at this moment. I understood. Some burgers, Paul said, and some fries, please. I'll be up here working and waiting for your return. Do not forget, he said, that you are advancing thought right now, and that if the great thinkers hadn't eaten, if the great thinkers hadn't been provided with nutritious victuals, we would still be dwelling in caves, instead of beautiful homes like this one.

I snuck out the front door and made my way to the bus stop. The wind gusted and howled, the air was full of dust and debris, I wiped the fiberglass bench with the edge of my hand and I sat and waited for the bus to come, I lifted my binoculars to my eyes and scanned up and down the road. But it was too late, or too early, I should say, it was well past midnight, and the buses weren't running yet. Paul had said before, he had said that the history of mankind is full of bad ideas perpetuated by hungry thinkers, by thinkers who if their blood sugar levels had been higher would have seen the error of their thinking. Look at the Bible, he said, it is one extended chronicle of malnourishment in barren lands leading to cockamamie visions swallowed whole by a famished population. I didn't have time to wait, the quality of Paul's thinking was at stake. I knew the way, I knew how to get there, I had seen the landscape from the front seat of the bus, it would not be complicated to walk. When I had first driven into Panorama City with Aunt Liz, there had been no difference between Panorama City and whatever it was we had been in before Panorama City, but now I had come to recognize intersections and businesses, I had come to understand the landmarks that made one block different from another. All intersections had at least one mini-mall, unless they had a gas station or a fast-food place already, and most mini-malls had liquor stores, but only one had a butcher shop. The way to the fast-food place would take me past that butcher shop, then three liquor stores, two check-cashing places, a house where someone had parked a tractor-trailer in the yard, a boulevard with palm trees running down it, and a big chain drugstore. The streets were deserted. I could have walked down the middle of the road the whole way.

When I was a boy I would sometimes pretend that a catastrophe had wiped all other people from the earth. I pictured not having to go to school, and instead going into town and picking out any bicycle from the shop and riding it up and down the aisles of the grocery store and eating whatever I wanted to eat. The pretending stopped, usually, when your grandfather's voice reminded me I was not alone, your grandfather's voice calling me to breakfast. But somewhere along the line he stopped calling me to breakfast, he started staying in bed through breakfast, and so I could keep the pretending going past the door of my room, past the porch, even keep pretending as I rode my bicycle to school, until I saw the first car cruise past in the distance or someone in their driveway fetching the newspaper. For a while it was thrilling to imagine having the world to myself. If there's nobody, there's nobody to tell you what to do. But the thrill wore off, Juan-George, the thrill turned into something else, which was that I needed to feel the presence of other human beings, even if it meant I couldn't do whatever I wanted anymore.

There were no cars in the drive-thru, I walked up to the window. Ho sat with the headset on the countertop, he'd set up his computer game, he was playing video poker, waiting for customers. Ho worked more hours than anyone, it was a matter of pride with him, he used to joke that he didn't like to sleep, bad dreams. I tapped on the glass, which didn't sound like glass, which looked like glass but sounded like plastic. The wind whistled through the drive-thru. I must have been quite a sight, standing at the window in the middle of the night, my clothes flapping in the wind, but if Ho was surprised at all he didn't show it. He nodded at me before I even said a word, left his chair and computer, and walked around to the side door to let me in. When I got inside, he simply said hello and asked me to help myself to whatever I'd like, someone named Carlos was working the kitchen, he could help. That was Ho. Stand too close to him with some french fries at the counter and he wanted to kill you, but appear out of nowhere on a windy night, looking like a maniac, and he became a gracious host. I went to grab burgers and fries from under the heaters, but Carlos insisted on making them fresh, Carlos said he wouldn't have me eating the garbage that had been sitting there all night, it was destined for the dumpster, the late-night *borrachos* had had their fill hours ago. Carlos made the burgers fresh, and the fries, too, while I waited. The smell of cooking made me hungry, I hadn't realized how hungry I was, my body needed fuel, I needed to feed myself before the long walk home, and so I ate a couple of the burgers and some of the fries. Then Carlos made more for me to bring home. Throughout all this Ho remained focused on his video poker, he didn't budge an inch. Which contributed to the feeling that time had stopped.

Outside, though, the wind had calmed and changed direction. People had started to appear on the streets, and cars. Sunrise wasn't far off. I walked as quickly as I could, I extended my stride to get the burgers and fries to Paul in the ceiling as soon as possible. I didn't run, Juan-George, I don't run, because when you run people chase you. People and animals. Always better to extend your stride. Unfortunately, when I arrived at the house, having taken so much time to walk to and from the fast-food place, and having been delayed by Carlos's insistence on making the food fresh, and perhaps also by my needing to feed myself, Aunt Liz had already established herself at the kitchen table, where she was sipping coffee and flipping through the newspaper, one page at a time, reading each page completely and then flipping to the next. She lived according to the philosophy early to bed, early to rise, which was not her philosophy alone but had come from somewhere else. She could see the front door from where she was sitting, she could see me walking through the front door, trying to be as quiet as I could, and the look on her face was pure horror. She shouted that she thought I was a burglar. I said that burglars don't typically use the front door. She demanded to know where I'd been, she thought I'd been in my room, she thought she'd heard me in there, stirring in my sleep, she was going to wake me when she'd finished her newspaper. What if she'd gone in there, she asked, and found me missing? I didn't know what to say or do so I kept my mouth shut and stayed put. Then she saw the bag, she needed to know what was in the bag, she asked me if it was from the fast-food place, she asked me how I had gotten there. I told Aunt Liz that I had been unable to sleep because of the wind, and that Panorama City was oddly peaceful without anyone on the streets, and that while walking I'd gotten hungry and gone to the fast-food place to eat, at which point Aunt Liz, whose face had turned red, cried out, Enough! I had not lied, I had told the truth, I was on my way to telling the whole truth, but Aunt Liz stopped me before I could. Later, Paul Renfro would say that I'd obfuscated perfectly, he had heard the whole thing from up in the ceiling, despite his nearly being catatonic with hunger, he had heard me and said that I had done a perfect job of obfuscating, his word. Sometimes all it takes, Paul said later, is telling the whole truth until people can't bear it anymore. Aunt Liz glared at me, she removed her reading glasses, she glared at me with utmost seriousness, a seriousness underscored by the fact that she had not yet put on her face, as she liked to say. She said that the reason it was so peaceful was that nobody in their right mind would go wandering around Panorama City in the middle of the night, it was too dangerous, which didn't quite make sense to me, there had been nobody around to make it dangerous, but she didn't give me a chance to speak. She held her hand up like a stop sign and said that I was not permitted to go out at night. As a matter of fact, she said, I wasn't to go out at all without telling her where I would be, she wanted to know where to find me at all times. I nodded, her glare softened. It's not safe out there, she said. You don't understand, she said, you've never understood, the world is full of people dying to take advantage of someone like you.

# DOUBLE AGENT

There are worse things in the world than being taken advantage of, was what I came up with after I had made my way back to my room. I pulled the chair into my closet again and poked my head up into the ceiling and passed Paul Renfro the bag of burgers and fries. I apologized for the fact that they weren't warm but he didn't seem to mind. He poured whole ketchup packets in his mouth and then filled his mouth with fries and chewed until he was able to swallow. Aunt Liz knocked on my door and said she was going to drive me to work this morning, she was going to deliver me herself, we were leaving in a half hour, she didn't want me getting into trouble on the streets of Panorama City. Paul asked if I could bring him some water as soon as possible. And some pushpins or thumbtacks. I knew Aunt Liz would take a while to get dressed and made up, she would not be caught out in public without painting her face, which I took for granted at the time but which gets stranger the more I think about it. I provided Paul with pushpins recovered from Aunt Liz's corkboard, she kept a corkboard by the phone, with pictures and cards and old invitations on it. All of the pushpins were in use, but I was able to remove some without disturbing the alignment of the pictures by causing some pins to do double duty, holding up more than one picture or invitation by taking advantage of where they overlapped, which was a perfectly reasonable way to arrange a corkboard. I provided Paul with water from the laundry room, where Aunt Liz kept a water dispenser. I lifted a still-sealed jug into the ceiling for Paul to drink from. It was quite heavy, he could hardly move it, he said it must have been five gallons at least. I wanted to make sure he had enough water for the whole time I would be gone, it could get hot up there, I wanted to keep him hydrated so that his thinking could be clear and productive instead of delusional and incorrect.

After I had gotten him everything he needed, I announced that I couldn't possibly go to work. I had carefully considered Aunt Liz's plan for me, I had run a clinical trial testing her plan, or most of one, and I had found it lacking, I had found all aspects of it wanting, I needed as soon as possible to return to my original plans and goals, which were to come to Panorama City, and become a man of the world, and return to Madera, and find Carmen again. Paul reminded me that this was a time for planning and considering, not implementing. Paul said that without these lodgings, without this hermitage, his word, he would have no chance to advance his thinking. He couldn't risk expending his energies on legal struggles. If I truly wanted to help him, he told me, I would have to do so while arousing as little suspicion as possible, which meant, he was sorry to tell me, acting as though Aunt Liz's plan for me was working just fine, as if the Lighthouse Fellowship was fulfilling my spiritual needs, as if Dr. Rosenkleig was making some kind of progress, however he liked to measure it, as if I'd rather do nothing more than make french fries for people who barely seemed aware they were eating. Aunt Liz knocked again. Paul said, Make it through today and tonight we'll fix everything, tonight we'll work on your plan to become a man of the world. I did not have time to shower, I prefer to shower every day, but I did not have time, I pulled on my fast-food place uniform and went out. Aunt Liz drove me to work, where I found a balding photographer with a walrus mustache sitting on bags of equipment, waiting to shoot my Employee of the Month photo.

Which is why, when you pick through my old things, which you will, which I won't blame you for doing, feel free to explore the bits and pieces I've left behind, most of them once belonged to your grandfather, I've never been a collector, other than bicycles, but which is why when you find my Employee of the Month photograph, they gave me an extra copy, unframed, you'll look at me, at your father, and you'll think there is something missing. It is me, I am missing, I mean my body is there, my face, my uniform, all of that, but I am not there inside. I mentioned before that your grandfather used to say that he was only a passenger in his body. I never fully understood what he was talking about until I saw that picture of myself as Employee of the Month, shot the day after Paul Renfro moved into Aunt Liz's ceiling. I'm sure others could have done a better job, I'm sure others could have put on a more convincing smile, I'm sure there are those who go about their daily business in service of something else completely unrelated, who turn off their thinking for the promise of some other later thinking, but I have no idea how they do it. There is such a thing as pretending to live, Juan-George, I'm not good at it.

I spent that day terrified they would see through me and know I was only pantomiming, and suspect me of hiding something, and search the house, and discover Paul Renfro in the ceiling. But Roger Macarona did not notice. Melissa did not notice. Wexler did not notice. Harold, who couldn't be expected to notice anything other than his fingertip, did not notice. The Employee of the Month photographer did not notice. The customers certainly did not notice. Aunt Liz, who not only dropped me off at work but also picked me up afterward to take me to Dr. Rosenkleig's, did not notice. She only asked me whether the fast-food place bag I was holding was the same one from that morning, I told her of course it wasn't, she said it stank, I moved my seat all the way back. But surely, of all people, Dr. Rosenkleig would notice. This was his stock in trade, as they say. I am not a liar, I tell the truth, but when Dr.

Rosenkleig asked me that day how my clinical trial was going, I knew what he wanted to hear, and I delivered the words like fries on a tray. I told him that the clinical trial was going surprisingly well, I told him that Aunt Liz had chosen correctly for me. I told him how proud I was to have been named Employee of the Month, I used some of Roger Macarona's previous words to express my disbelief, I told him how much it meant to me to have a job and duties I could call my own. I told him how someday I hoped to be a manager myself. I told him how much it meant to me to be a part of the larger fast-food place family. I had believed that once, I'm not sure for how long, or when I stopped believing it, but I didn't believe it anymore and I told Dr. Rosenkleig that I did. I told him that the Lighthouse Fellowship had put me in touch with a spiritual side of myself I hadn't known was there, and that I felt bonded with so many members of that vibrant spiritual community I didn't feel the need to make new friends anymore. I told him, in short, the opposite of everything I felt, I expressed myself using the exact opposite words, including, because I knew it would get back to Aunt Liz, and because I knew Aunt Liz would be pleased to hear it, including telling Dr. Rosenkleig what a relief it was to be somewhere where nobody treated me like the village idiot.

That afternoon, after Aunt Liz drove me home, I went up into the ceiling for the first time. The access panel was barely large enough for me to fit through, but I managed somehow to rein in my elbows and pull myself up. Once there, I couldn't believe my eyes. Paul had transformed the space completely. It was as if his briefcase, which had always contained more inside than seemed possible from the outside, had exploded. Papers everywhere, tacked to the beams, wedged between the studs, tucked into the insulation, piled in the corners. The dozen or so pushpins I had requisitioned from Aunt Liz's corkboard were engaged in astonishing feats of redundancy, each one pressed through the corners of countless pages, diagrams, charts, and notes. A settled smell of fast-food place food thickened the air. The water bottle sat in the corner, open, a sheet of paper over the top. Paul had found a string of Christmas lights somewhere and connected them to the spare electrical outlet for the air-conditioning blower. I asked him whether he wouldn't rather have a regular lamp, I could probably find him one, and he said that he preferred the Christmas lights. At first they had bothered him as too festive for sober thought, his words, but then he realized that all the colors added up to white, and that the separation of colors was conducive to splitting the brilliant white glow of revelation into individually colored bands of thought. The space had turned out to be a boon to advanced thinking, as he had always suspected it would be, the attic being the cranium of the house. The only problem was gaining access to the toilet, he needed a way to get down to the bathroom and back again without leaving any traces, which was to say without leaving the desk chair sitting in the middle of the closet. He had been urinating in the overflow pan below the air-conditioning coil, he'd had to urinate slowly to prevent the pan from filling up, but otherwise it had been draining completely. As long as I could provide a daily trip down to earth for his more solid business it would suffice. I helped him down for that essential purpose, and once his feet hit the ground he seemed deeply uncomfortable, like a raccoon out in the middle of the day. He didn't breathe normally until he was finished and safe again up in the confines of his thinking space.

He showed me that he could make his way, via my ceiling, to the ceiling over the living room, from which he could see through a vent the front entrance. If someone came looking for him, he said, he'd be the first to know. This was crucial, he explained, because since we'd worked together last, meaning on the antioxidant cream, no more of that, he added, he was on the straight and narrow, since we'd worked together last, he had suffered a series of persecutions of unimaginable variety, his words. Not once during the course of them had he encountered a fellow thinker, he added, which resulted in the double indignity of not only suffering but also having nobody understand the context of his suffering. I had no idea, I would have tried to find him had I known, had I not been pursuing my clinical trial of Aunt Liz's plan for me. That was when he explained to me about clinical trials typically being tilted in favor of whoever sponsors them, and about my failure to define my terms. He blamed me for none of it, he could never blame a fellow thinker for any attempt to advance knowledge. Even missteps count when you're moving toward this kind of goal, his words.

I had forgotten, I think, or not realized, or I had gotten entangled in the wrong part of my head, I had forgotten that despite the avalanche of difficulties I'd faced, and the eruptions of unintended consequences arising from my every action, I'd forgotten that I had been in fact advancing knowledge, in my own way, a bit at a time. I reminded Paul that I was still seeking the path toward becoming a man of the world, not having found it as Employee of the Month, or at the Lighthouse Fellowship, or in Dr. Rosenkleig's chamber of framed diplomas, or anywhere else for that matter. Paul blew out his cheeks and exhaled. The time had come for him, he said, to talk to me about provincial types.

He asked me to picture a man of the world in my head. He asked me if I saw in my mind's eye a watch on a chain, or a three-piece suit, or alligator shoes. Sure, I said, sure I did. He informed me that I was actually picturing a provincial type, not a man of the world. You can always tell a provincial type by the way he makes a show of reading the newspaper, a provincial type will always hold the newspaper high, and it will never be the local paper, and he will read it as if nothing else matters, but when the provincial type is finished, Paul's words, he leaves his newspaper all over the place, he never folds it properly, he treats it as something to be disposed of sloppily, to be cast aside, with none of the importance it had held for him only moments before. In this way, he demonstrates that he is above the so-called fray. He has used the newspaper to confirm himself, to confirm what is not true, that he is a man of the world, and now he must discard it, he must cast it aside, or be drawn down to its level. But in fact he operates at exactly its level, Paul's words. A newspaper puts the whole world onto a few pages, and provincial types put the whole world into their wine cellars, or well-stamped passports, or art collections. They collect, and they congregate, in packs and clubs, fraternities and cooperatives, civic groups and associations, behind labels and pins, on plaques and lists, in registers and yearbooks. They announce at every turn, in every manner imaginable, their worldliness, but in actuality their response to the human condition is to winnow and huddle, Paul's words, they turn their backs on the world and call it living. This is why provincial types love to say that great minds think alike, it is one of their favorite phrases. But in actuality, and in biological fact, Paul's words, small minds think alike.

He squinted at me like he was trying to look through a dirty window, and then he said that the true path was not wide or straight, that he could take me only as far as the trailhead, that above all things a man of the world stood alone, that to deny our fundamental solitude was to persist under a most dangerous illusion. He put his hand on my shoulder and said that sincere friendship, the kind of friendship we shared, was a great balm, but it was only a balm, it did not change the so-called ground rules. There was knocking at my door below. Aunt Liz asked what I was doing, she thought she'd heard voices. I stuck my head down through the ceiling panel and told her I'd been listening to my Bible, she'd been hearing my Bible on tape. Dinner was ready, she said, could I come to dinner?

I don't have time here, Juan-George, to tell you about every meal I ate, or every face Aunt Liz made, or every moment of my life, I wish I did, I wish I could take you back in time with me, so that you could stand on my shoulders, so that you could know your father firsthand, but I cannot, there isn't time, there isn't enough tape in the world. But though the terminus approaches, though the dawn I won't see is coming, I want to take a moment to tell you about that night's dinner with Aunt Liz. It wasn't what was said, I was not a great conversationalist that night, I was mainly trying to keep from arousing any suspicion. Aunt Liz talked, she'd spoken with Dr. Rosenkleig, she expressed pleasure and surprise at my turning over a new leaf, her words. I didn't know what to say, I couldn't prop up the illusion, but I didn't dare topple it either. I watched Aunt Liz's hand gripping the spaghetti spoon and putting noodles on my plate, I saw the spots, I saw the muscles and tendons, I saw the strength and the weakness all at once. She went back into the bowl with the spaghetti spoon, this time specifically to grab me an extra meatball. She looked at me, her no-nonsense eyes peering over her reading/eating glasses, and asked whether there were enough meatballs on my plate or would I like another. And I had the feeling, the overwhelming feeling that Aunt Liz knew well the solitude that Paul had talked about. She was always reaching across the divide.

After dinner I returned to the ceiling, I was ready to begin, I was ready to hear what Paul had been working on, and I was ready to assist him however I could, whatever I could do to counteract the pantomime of my life. I was ready to be a double agent, I was ready to fake my way through daily life in order to sustain the illusion that I was on board with Aunt Liz's plan for me. I found Paul lying on a mattress of insulation he'd stripped from between joists, silver with pink fiber guts spilling out the sides. He wore new clothes, and I wondered where he'd gotten them, until I noticed the odd stitching and realized he'd turned his suit inside out. I cleared my throat, but he remained on his back, arms out to the sides, not moving, not speaking, staring at the papers he'd tacked above his head. After what I would now call a protracted silence, he explained that he was reading his old notes, refilling his mind with the basic questions he was trying to solve, he hadn't even reached the point at which progress could be made, he was still catching up with himself, with his former self, he was making himself into a duplicate of who he'd been, this was a fragile phase. He had faced so many obstacles, obstacles upon obstacles, in his journey, that along the way he'd become someone who faces obstacles, rather than someone who advances thinking, and the only way back was to become his former self, a duplicate of his former self. What he was doing was reabsorbing all of his old ideas, was catching up, so to speak, was starting again from where he'd last been interrupted, which was something mankind itself couldn't do, would never do, there was too much history. So-called scholars tried to absorb the research in their fields, but it was mostly paperwork, the contrails of careerism, Paul's words, and as a result those scholars stood on the shoulders of ants. I asked Paul what some of the basic questions were, maybe I could help him think them through from my inflatable mattress, maybe we could engage in some parallel processing, I didn't use that term, I hadn't yet learned that term from Paul, I used some other words I can't remember. Paul told me he appreciated the offer but he himself didn't really know what the basic questions were, he hadn't gotten that far.

You see, Juan-George, people tend to be impressed with complex ideas, but the basic questions are the hardest part, the basic questions are the most difficult challenge to any serious thinker. Answers get all of the glamour and attention, answers are what everyone seems to be after, but the real value is in basic questions. This is because once you have an answer you stop, you're done, but life doesn't stop, you become a plaster statue, life begins to pass you by, only by asking questions can you keep moving, and only by asking the right questions can you keep moving in the right direction. Or to put it simply, to put it in clear and concise terms, you have a choice, you can either feel smart or be smart.

The next day I sleepwalked through work, nobody noticed. Then Aunt Liz dropped me at the Lighthouse Fellowship for a scheduled Bible group. The discussion topic was Letting Go, Letting God, and it was about how God has a plan for every one of us, and how we can try to fight it but in the end we must all submit to his will. I hadn't expected to engage in the conversation, I had planned to sit in the circle of uncomfortable chairs and nod from time to time while my mind wandered elsewhere. I was only counting down the hours before I could get back up in the ceiling again and help Paul advance thinking for the sake of mankind. But some of the talking made its way into my ears, and all the references to God's plan reminded me of a boy I knew in Madera when I was younger. He and I had been friends, I mean I was friends with everyone, this was before I became a shield, this was when we were very young, our lives were just getting started. He had a baby sister, they were playing at a winery with some other kids, and I don't know exactly what happened but the baby sister stepped into a puddle, which turned out to be deeper than anyone thought, and she drowned, she was two years old, it was terrible. I don't need to tell you every tragedy I've heard of, turn on the news, they keep coming, I don't mean to add to your burden, I mention Natalie's death only because if God indeed has a plan for everyone, then what kind of plan is living for two years before drowning in a muddy puddle? Since it was already in my head, I mentioned this story to the Bible group. Jan's face turned red and she started to pick at her Band-Aids. Mark, who was leading the group, who was what JB would have called the facilitator, responded to the story of Natalie's death in the strangest way, everyone else looked sad, nobody likes to hear about that sort of thing, everybody looked sad and made faces of sympathy, they made faces that told me it would be okay if I got emotional, they made faces of support, but Mark's face was something different altogether. Mark's wiglike hair migrated farther back on his head, his eyebrows raised, and he looked like I'd just offered him a cookie or a hundred dollars. I had brought up, he said, something he had been wanting to talk about, I had brought to the table the exact question he wanted to address, and I had done it better than he ever could have, he had been planning to talk about an earthquake in Portugal, I had made it personal. If indeed we are living according to God's plan for us, Mark said, then why is there suffering in the world? A seeming paradox, Mark said, he had a thing for paradoxes, and yet the answer was simple, Mark said, so simple many people missed it completely, the answer was best phrased in the form of a question, Mark said, or two questions, which were, Who are you to question God's plan? Is your wisdom infinite like God's wisdom? Everyone around the table agreed that Mark had made a good point, that there must be some reason for suffering, known only to God, something we couldn't see from where we were standing, so to speak. Now I don't claim to know everything, Juan-George, in fact, I claim to know very little, my areas of expertise are limited and very small, but it seems to me much more reasonable to say that there is no plan, that the reason Natalie drowned had nothing to do with God's will, it was an accident, it happened because she didn't know how deep the puddle was and didn't know how to swim and her big brother was distracted pulling apart a pomegranate. Why am I here in this hospital bed, dying of my injuries, shortly before you are scheduled to arrive? Is it so important to God that we do not meet? I am interested, I have always been interested in trying to make sense of the world, your grandfather was always interested in it, too, and even more so in trying to make the world fair, to make it a fair place, but life is unfair, usually, and sometimes an accident is just an accident. Mark talked about Natalie, who he had never met, and about earthquakes, I can't count how many times he used the phrase *needless suffering*. He smiled when anyone in their right mind would have kept their face serious, he talked about things that were horrible, he talked about things that anyone with any room in their head would recoil from, amputation, combat, poisoning, starvation, and he said that these too were gifts from God, the significance of which would not be revealed until after death. He mentioned Job, everyone perked up, he had ventured into the Old Testament, he seemed pleased with himself, he mentioned Job and misquoted a passage, I did not correct him. There's an expression, seeing something in a new light, it was like that. I could see the cracks, and I could see the dust in the cracks. The Lighthouse Fellowship was a beehive of perversity, the lighthouse was a perverse symbol, all of these things were in my head. They overlay everything I saw and heard. I don't blame the people at the Lighthouse Fellowship, Juan-George, I don't begrudge them their beliefs, everyone is different. I just want you to keep in mind that what we see, what we think we see, I should say, is always changed by the words in our heads, which means that even when we're all looking at the same thing we each see something different.

A moment ago I asked why I was here dying in this hospital bed, only a month before you are scheduled to arrive, and when I said it I realized I haven't told you the story. I'm going to interrupt my walking out of the Bible group, I'll get right back to it, because first I want to tell you, because it's more important, I want to tell you how I ended up in this hospital. I haven't told you yet about leaving Panorama City and returning to Madera, about finding your mother again, about setting up housekeeping, as they say, in the old house, I hope I have time, but if the terminus takes me first, your mother was there, she can tell you all about it. What happened was that a few days ago I was riding my blue-flake three-speed Schwinn, as I used to do before your grandfather died, I was riding into Madera. Your mother was home napping, you make her tired sometimes, and so I was riding into town for some groceries. It had been a long time, Juan-George, since I'd been able to enjoy that simplest of pleasures, listening to the burring sound of tires on asphalt, feeling the breeze on my face. And then, as if summoned somehow by my presence, a familiar vehicle appeared on the horizon. The Alvarez brothers' pickup truck, coming my way, drifting across the yellow line toward me. Then there is a blank spot in my memory, I don't know what happened next, my next memory is of waking up here in the Madera Community Hospital.

I excused myself from the Bible group as if I was going to the restroom, which was at the back of the Lighthouse Fellowship coffee shop. I thought I would have to sneak past Scott Valdez's door, it was open, but he wasn't at his desk, his office was empty. I went out the back door, the sunlight was blinding white, everything was bleached. I followed the alley to the end of the mini-mall and came back around to the front. I wasn't planning to see Maria, I was just trying to get away from the perversities, to get fresh air, but as soon as I saw the neon pyramid in the window I knew I was going in. Your mother is snoring at the moment, I can say Maria's name, I don't dare utter it when your mother is in that shifting-around half sleep. I am a jealous god, she likes to say, which is from the Bible, she'll tell you she doesn't remember any of it from school, but that's a direct quotation. I've mentioned before that while I was down in Panorama City your mother had many suitors, I am not jealous of any of them, I am not the jealous type. Your mother says it's because her suitors never so much as nicked her heart. Maria, on the other hand, says your mother, stole my heart, Maria threatens our bond, no matter how far away she is, in distance and time, no matter how I might claim to have no feelings about her now. Your mother says that what's written on the heart stays on the heart, true feelings can never be erased, only written over, they lurk beneath, circling like sharks. That is her philosophy, I'll let her share it with you, later. For my part I can only say that my feelings for Maria and my feelings for your mother reside in two different parts of my heart, and that except for putting my life down on tape, except for telling you my experiences, I haven't done much visiting of the part with my feelings for Maria in it, I haven't seen any reason to, she is gone, long gone, I wouldn't even know where to find her, and besides, I am happy in the part that belongs to your mother.

I went into Maria's storefront, I went into her psychic adviser shop, I pushed through the bead curtain into the waiting room. Empty and quiet. Usually she was there right away, or I could hear her talking with another client and I would wait my turn. I listened for her voice, I heard nothing. I sat on the couch and waited, there was a magazine about boats. I flipped through it and looked at pictures of yachts. I wondered, when I was finished with the magazine and still had not seen Maria, I wondered whether she had heard my psychic appeal to her several nights before, whether she had heard it but had not responded, whether she was avoiding me. But then I heard something, it sounded like someone had knocked over a glass, an empty glass. It clanged but did not break, then rolled across the floor. I walked through a second bead curtain into the room where Maria did her readings, with the round table, and the crystal ball, and the chandelier that had cast strange patterns of light on her face. Empty. Then more sounds, something else knocked over, furniture, from farther back, there was a solid door, I had never been through it. Something told me to go in, whatever was going on didn't sound right. I thought Maria might be in trouble, I was in the part of my heart that belonged to her, I acted without thinking. I nudged open the door, I must admit I thought of myself as coming to her rescue, I thought about how grateful she would be that I'd interceded.

If there's one thing I can't recommend, it's thinking of yourself in an outside way when the situation requires you only to be yourself. I poked my head into the room, ready to save the day, and I found an empty business office, or a business office I thought was empty. I looked down and saw, on the floor, Maria, blocked partially, or mainly I should say, by broad shoulders, short arms, a fleshy neck, and a head that even from behind looked like a pineapple. Maria's eyes were closed, and her mind must have been somewhere else, because, being psychic, she should have known I was standing there, even nonpsychics know when someone is looking at them, but she was distracted, her mind was elsewhere, I lingered there only long enough to verify, only long enough to understand what was happening, which was obvious at first glance, which was that they were doing what men and women do, only long enough to verify and certify that what was happening was happening mutually, I mean, that it wasn't a violation, that she wasn't being attacked. I lingered only to make sure, to be sure she didn't need to be rescued. I might have lingered there a moment longer than necessary, I wanted Maria to open her eyes, I wanted her to see me standing there and stop everything, but she did not, she was lost in pleasure.

* * *

I did not go back to the Bible group. I went to the Laundromat. I watched clothes tumble around inside a dryer. Words echoed in my head, something Scott Valdez had said, the first time I met Maria, when Maria had asked me for a jump start, Scott had said, his words, The battle between good and evil played itself out everywhere, and our mini-mall was no exception. I watched a skinny man pull out items from a rolling wire laundry basket and fold them on a high counter. Maria and Scott, Scott and Maria, it made no sense, they hated each other, I had seen it, I had heard it, seething hatred. Maria had heaped scorn on the Lighthouse Fellowship, which was Scott's organization, which was Scott's mission in life, his calling, and Scott had even more viciously and publicly attacked everything that went on behind Maria's bead curtains. Yet my eyes had not deceived me, as they say. I couldn't watch the skinny man calmly folding his clothes anymore, I turned my eyes to the dryer again, it better suited my thinking, which was tumbling in circles, or which tumbled a half circle before free-falling through space.

Eventually, Aunt Liz pulled up at the Lighthouse Fellowship and went inside to look for me. I stepped out of the Laundromat and sat on the hood of her car. She emerged from the Lighthouse looking panicked, she thought I'd run off again. I told her I'd been waiting outside and that she must have missed me. Scott Valdez came out then, he came out of the Lighthouse, he had come through the back, he came out and told Aunt Liz that he knew I hadn't wandered off, he told her that I was a real asset to the Lighthouse, he told her I always kept the Bible group on their toes. I looked into his eyes, his too-close-together eyes, and I saw only sincerity, and I knew then that Scott, too, was a double agent of sorts, a better double agent than I could ever be. Scott gave me a big grin, his cheeks looked flushed, he patted my upper arm. There was no fear in his eyes, not the slightest trace, I knew that he had not seen me, that he and Maria had had no idea I'd seen them. I knew, too, because I've always studied people, since elementary school I've studied people, I knew that this wasn't the first time for Scott and Maria, this had been going on a long while, what I had witnessed in the office was not the exception but the rule. Which meant that the jumper-cable incident had had nothing to do with a battle between good and evil. It had been a lovers' quarrel.

# PART FIVE

TAPE 8, SIDES A & B;
TAPE 9, SIDE A

# FALLOUT

As these things usually are, Paul Renfro's words. Look at the Trojan War. I wasn't interested in the Trojan War, I wanted to know why and how Scott and Maria had ended up together. On that point, Paul had no answer other than to say love is blind, truly blind, not blindfolded, when you're dealing with love you don't get a choice, even when you think you do, there's no blindfold to remove, you just have to accept it. Scott and Maria could seethe all they wanted, they could talk about good and evil until they lost their voices, but they were in the grip of future generations asserting a right to exist, Paul's words. We were in the ceiling, I had gotten in the habit of climbing up there after Aunt Liz had taken her sleeping pills and gone to sleep professionally, to let the balm of sincere friendship do its work. Night after night, Paul and I discussed every subject imaginable. If I had been wiser I would have recorded our discussions, they would have proven more valuable to you than this thin slice of my experience. Every other thing out of Paul's mouth was something I did not understand, my head filled with his words. The only thing we didn't talk about was what he'd scrawled on the notes hanging from the walls and joists, he would say only that he'd finally had the time and space to successfully reabsorb all of the thoughts and ideas he'd written on all of those scraps and sheets of paper, he'd for the first time in years managed to turn himself into a duplicate of his former self, so that he could push forward, through the development of several basic questions, push forward his thinking. He described his thinking as a large rock, the size of a small mountain, that had to be kept rolling, that if it came to a stop might never roll again, due to the differences between the coefficients of static friction and kinetic friction, Paul's words, which I remember but still do not fully understand, as opposed to most other people's thinking, presuming they thought at all, presuming they hadn't given over their thinking responsibilities to so-called common sense, which was, other people's thinking was, more like a tumbleweed, meaning it was not as dense as his thinking, and therefore not as difficult to move forward, but also much more sensitive to the whimsy of shifting winds.

He said to me, this was a few days into his stay in the ceiling, he said that the one thing he needed that the ceiling hadn't given him, the one last obstacle to his thinking, was freedom of movement, everything else was ideal, but his blood wasn't circulating freely, it might have been exacerbated, Paul's word, by the fast-food place food, which thickened his blood, or the warm air, the warm dry air of

Panorama City, but freedom of movement, or the lack thereof, had become an obstacle, the last in a long line of obstacles. I asked him if he needed to come down, if he needed to walk around the block, I had taken walks around Aunt Liz's block many times, it had been most salutary, though I probably didn't use that word, Paul probably taught me that word while I was telling him about the walks, I offered to help Paul down from the ceiling to let him roam the streets of Panorama City at night. I explained to him that at certain hours the streets were completely empty, we could imagine we had Panorama City all to ourselves, thinkers only. But for Paul coming down from the ceiling was out of the question, even in the middle of the night he couldn't risk interacting with the terrestrial-minded masses. His thinking, his cloud, had become like a soap bubble, contact with coarser elements would destroy it. How, then, to achieve movement? We devised the solution together, I can't deny that I was part of the thinking process that lay behind the ingenious but ultimately doomed solution, doomed but also not doomed, resulting as it would in your eventual arrival, I can't trace all of the unintended consequences here, it's not my job to do so, I can only tell you what we did and what came after. There was a network of crawl spaces and openings up there, Paul had explored them on his first day, I mentioned that he'd found a way to observe the front door. Near my room, not far from my room, above the area we would later realize was the kitchen, the roof above peaked in a continuous line toward the living room. The living room had high ceilings but the kitchen did not, meaning that there was an area above the kitchen where the roof was peaked but the ceiling was low, it wasn't a big area, it covered maybe half the floor plan of the kitchen, but providing he stayed on the beams it was big enough to allow Paul Renfro to pace back and forth while developing his thinking, it was big enough to allow the kind of unfettered movement Paul was in desperate need of. The space was unlit, but some light crept in from three separate sources, which were a dim glow from Paul's Christmas lights, shafts of daylight coming through a ventilation grate, and, occasionally, if I left them on, overspill from the ceiling-mounted kitchen lights. The only problem, which was a problem we solved together, was figuring out how Paul could do his pacing without making too much noise. What happened, what ended up happening, was that I went down into my dresser and pulled out four pairs of socks, these socks were too big for Paul's feet, we had to stuff them with newspaper so they would fit, we stuffed the socks and put Paul's feet into them, and then put three more pairs of socks over that, and it was like, his words, it was like walking on air, he didn't make a sound.

I was often in a half-waking state when Aunt Liz banged on my door to ask me to breakfast, I was often existing with one ear in the real world and one in the dream world, which was what led me to picture, or hallucinate, or dream one morning that your grandfather George was typing again, which meant alive, he was alive again, I thought. I heard the sounds of typing, I heard your grandfather typing his Letter to the Editor, it was the sound of home. Then I remembered that he'd died, I remembered what an indignity it was that he'd been buried next to someone called Kutchinski and someone called Brown, miles from his hunting dogs Ajax and Atlas. I climbed the ladder of awareness, I mean I awoke completely, and I recognized the dream for what it was. But the typing continued. I thought first of Paul, I thought at first that Paul had found a typewriter, I thought that he'd found a typewriter and had followed an idea so deeply that he'd forgotten to fear exposure. Then the sound changed, it didn't sound so exactly like typing, and I realized it was coming from outside, from the walnut tree outside, a tree situated well away from the house. I opened my window to see what the source was, and I saw what I'd never seen before, or never noticed before, at the top of several branches, a group of tiny birds making typewriter noises at each other. Hummingbirds, chirping. I ran to get my binoculars but by the time I'd returned to the window they were gone.

By the time you're able to see me, Juan-George, I'll be gone. It's unthinkable, but it's so.

When I walked into work that morning I saw for the first time my Employee of the Month photograph on the wall.

It was shocking to see my face up there, on display. I've already talked about what it looked like, I've already told you how I wasn't present in the image, despite the image being an image of me, I've covered that, but at that moment, at the moment of me first seeing that picture up on the wall I experienced shock at the evidence before my eyes, at the evidence that I'd been turned into, as Paul had warned I'd be, that I'd been turned into a shadow of myself. When Roger brought my own copy to me, in a manila envelope, the copy that you'll find among my things, I told him I wasn't feeling well, I told him I was going to have to go home, I told him I was going to have to take a sick day. He looked me up and down, he winked, he pointed at the Employee of the Month photograph up on the wall, and he said that I'd earned it, what the fuck, just this once.

I didn't go home. I ended up at the Lighthouse Fellowship, or at Maria's, I should say, I didn't want to enter the Lighthouse Fellowship. I walked through the first bead curtain and sat down to wait for Maria, I didn't know what I was going to say, I didn't know what was going to come next. She pushed her way through the second bead curtain a moment later, I could see immediately what I had seen in Scott Valdez's eyes, she had no idea I'd seen what I'd seen. As far as Maria was concerned nothing had changed. She flashed the same smile she'd always flashed, she touched my arm the way she always touched it when she led me to the table where she did her readings. We sat across the table from each other and she held my hands the way she always held them at the start of a session. You see, Juan-George, for her these gestures had not changed, their meaning had not changed. Yet for me each one was a blow. She did not love me back. It's nature's way, the exception is being loved back, if everyone who loved was loved back, nature would move sideways for a while, then collapse, Paul's words. Maria asked me if there was anything specific I wanted to ask her about, did I have any pressing issues, she sensed that I was troubled, the details were hazy, her words, there was a lot of interference between the earthly plane and the higher planes, she said, because of sunspots, it had been on television. She looked to the envelope on the table, I had set it there when I came in. There is something, she said, of great importance in that envelope. She asked me if I had opened it already, I said that I had. She asked me to tell her how I felt about what was in there. I told her I didn't know how I felt, I knew only that I was supposed to feel proud but didn't. She asked me to open the envelope for her and show her what was inside. She said that she knew what was inside, of course, but she needed more specifics, the sunspots and solar flares had been interfering with her abilities. I handed her the picture. She looked at it for a moment and then held it to her forehead. She described how helpful the image was in cutting through the celestial activity and accessing the higher planes. She said that my father was proud of me, but not for what was in the picture, he was proud of me for something that hadn't yet happened, for something I hadn't yet done but would do soon, they know no time in the higher planes, her words.

She put the photo back into the envelope and I asked her if there was anything else, if there were any general readings, if she might gather any more insight about the future. I did not care about the future, Juan-George, or I should say I don't care about the future, perhaps it is best to say that I don't concern myself with the future, if you spend all of your time living in the future, you tend to miss out on what's happening right now. Which is something I knew a long time ago, forgot for a while, learned again, forgot, and learned again while talking to you, while talking into these tapes. But I asked Maria for another reading so that she would again lay her hands on mine, I wanted to recapture that feeling, that spiritual feeling I had never felt at the Lighthouse and had always felt at Maria's. She lay her hands on mine, she closed her eyes, she asked me to close mine, too, but I did not, I could not, it was dawning on me that the feeling was gone, that the feeling would be gone forever, that there was no way to recapture an old feeling by going through old motions. I looked at her face, at her beautiful face, the light from the chandelier casting a pattern on it, and I sent her a message, from my mind, I aligned my thoughts like a magnet aligns metal filings, I sent her a message with every part of my mind. Open your eyes. She did.

* * *

I crossed the parking lot, the envelope in my hand, someone yelled hello from the Lighthouse Fellowship but I didn't even look to see who it was. I rode the bus back to the fast-food place, where my shift was ending, I bought a bag of burgers and fries from a puzzled Roger, and I waited outside for Aunt Liz to pick me up. When she arrived I pushed my seat all the way back and handed her the envelope. She pulled out the picture, smiled, and shook her head at the same time. Don't you look handsome, was what she said. All through dinner she kept remarking that I looked handsome and respectable in my Employee of the Month photograph, I didn't know what to say, as you know I thought the picture was terrifying, as you know I thought the photograph looked like my body without me in it, I wondered how Aunt Liz could not see this. After dinner I went straight to the crawl space with the bag of food, my evening talks with Paul were my lifeline, everything else was falling apart. He had been pacing, he said, or practicing a form of pacing, on the beams over the kitchen and trying to push forward the mountain rock of his thinking, and despite the limited headroom he'd been able to experience the freedom of movement he'd been looking for. I was pleased to hear this, I was pleased to hear that Paul would be moving his thinking forward, and I said so. He shook his head, he shook it slowly and said that unfortunately lack of movement was not what had been impeding him, or was not the bedrock source of what had been impeding him. He was thankful for the elegant solution we'd come up with, meaning the socks and the beam, but being able to pace, or practice a form of pacing, had only opened up to him another series of obstacles.

## THIEF

Aunt Liz sat me down for breakfast, she sat down with her coffee and her newspaper, she had finished the crossword puzzle already, she had put on her face and was ready to drive me to work. She sat me down in front of a pile of waffles and said that we had to have a serious talk about something she didn't want to address but needed to. She asked, her exact words, she started by asking, Am I correct in saying that we are the only two people living in this house? My heart stopped, my throat swelled, I couldn't speak or see. How had Aunt Liz detected Paul Renfro? He was silent, or he was near silent, he was quieter than the squirrels on the roof, they landed on the roof with a thump, it was a long jump from the trees. If I hadn't known he was there I never would have heard him walking back and forth on the beams. I couldn't answer, I was incapable of speaking, I stared at her, which was for the best, which Paul Renfro would later explain to me was the foundation for the legal concept of the Fifth Amendment, the founders had had more than one moment just like this, Paul said, between their wives and their slaves, chopping down cherry trees was the least of their indiscretions. I didn't answer Aunt Liz's question, I thought she'd discovered that Paul was living over the ceiling in my so-called quarters, I was paralyzed and waiting for her to speak, which was good, in situations like these it is best to be quiet and wait. Don't try to eat anything to cover up the fact that you're not talking, which was my mistake, I took a big bite of waffle to cover up the fact that I wasn't answering Aunt Liz's question, but my mouth was dry, my body had responded to her question by drying out my mouth. This could have been, this would have been a bigger problem, but then Aunt Liz spoke again, and amazingly enough the subject was not Paul Renfro, the subject was not a third person living in the house, the subject was pushpins. There were only two of us living in the house, she said, and she knew she hadn't gotten rid of a bunch of pushpins, which meant that I must have taken, without asking, and in a dishonest way, I must have stolen, she hated to use that word but she had to call a spade a spade, I must have stolen a dozen pushpins from her corkboard, there was no other reasonable explanation for the fact that they were missing, that the remaining pushpins were doing double, and in one case triple, duty holding up her invitations, photos, and keepsakes. I chewed my waffle, I nodded, I drank some orange juice to wash it down, I do not like the flavor of orange juice and maple syrup combined, I don't know how both together became part of a traditional breakfast. I admitted that I'd taken the pushpins. I can't remember the last time I felt so relieved. My feelings were not synchronized with Aunt Liz's face. She hoped I could explain myself to her satisfaction, she knew that there must have been some kind of misunderstanding, she expected me to take this seriously. I apologized for taking the pushpins, I told her the truth, which was that they appeared to be employed redundantly, that I didn't think it made much of a difference that I'd taken some for my own purposes, I didn't mention Paul Renfro, of course. Aunt Liz then said I was treading on a slippery slope, and though I might try to minimize, her word, what I'd done, I'd in fact stolen something from her, I'd taken her property and not returned it. I argued, not forcefully, but enough to make my point, that as long as the pushpins were still in the house, which they were, I hadn't really stolen them, it was more along the lines of not returning a screwdriver to the tool drawer. She said that I'd made a good point there, which surprised me. But to her mind I had come very close to stealing, and any kind of theft, no matter how seemingly inconsequential, put me on a slippery slope, meaning who was to say I wouldn't begin stealing bigger things, and from other people, who was to say I wouldn't find myself in more serious trouble if she didn't nip this behavior in the bud?

Now Juan-George, I must pause this scene to highlight two pieces of language Aunt Liz used, two pieces of language that seemed transparent to me, I mean I hadn't noticed them, I hadn't thought about them until Paul Renfro illuminated them for me later. The two pieces of language are *slippery slope* and *nip in the bud*. Paul, who had been listening to the whole conversation from above, who had been pacing on the beam when he heard the conversation, Paul explained that nonthinkers, those who weren't going to move history forward in any way, those who preferred to let others do their thinking for them, loved the term *slippery slope*, he explained that *slippery slope* was a favorite term among those who wanted to erase distinctions between discrete things in order to better control those around them, which I did not understand and so remember. It is an insult, Paul's words, to compare a person's behavior to a slope, it is degrading to one's sense of agency. And talk of nipping something in the bud turns people into trees and bushes to be pruned, anyone who talks about nipping something in the bud is playing the role of gardener, anyone who talks about nipping your behavior in the bud wants you to become a plant. These are dangerous phrases, Paul's words, and people use them every day.

Aunt Liz said that if in fact what had occurred was a failure to return the pushpins after borrowing them, then I could return them to her right away and we could consider the whole issue resolved. If, however, I could not return the pushpins, she would have to consider this an act of theft, and we would have to figure out what to do from there. I told her I'd be happy to return her pushpins, I'd be happy to bring them back, I apologized for inconveniencing her, I apologized for borrowing them without asking. I rose from the table and walked to my door, which I'd been keeping shut, I walked to my room and Aunt Liz followed me, I wasn't sure how I was going to get the pushpins out of the crawl space above the ceiling without causing Aunt Liz to ask more questions about what was going on, but sometimes all you can do is move forward and stay nimble, sometimes you don't know what's around the bend, but you can't afford to slow down and think about it, you just have to find out when you get there, you have to trust that you'll know what to do. Aunt Liz was right behind me when I opened the door to my quarters, I told her I'd be right out, but she followed me inside. There really was no way to climb into the crawl space without ruining everything, and Aunt Liz did not look like she was about to leave my room, and so I prepared myself, in my head, I prepared myself to deal with the consequences of admitting, untruthfully, admitting that I'd stolen them and didn't know where they had gone, or could not return them, or something like that. I realized that I would have to make up a story, that I would have to come up with something credible to explain how I'd not only stolen the pushpins but also lost them, and as I have mentioned earlier I'm not a liar, I don't lie, and so I didn't have any practice at that sort of thing, I didn't know where to begin. I looked around the room, I thought maybe something in the room could help me get started, something could prompt a story I could then embellish, Paul's word, but I wasn't getting anywhere, the ivy wallpaper was not helping. Then I saw, sitting on the little writing desk that I had never used, because the desk chair was too high and the desk was too low, you'd have to be a skeleton to fit in there, a skeleton with a very short torso if you wanted to actually write something there, I saw, just in front of the chair, on the middle of the desk surface, lined up like toy soldiers, points sticking up, Aunt Liz's missing pushpins. I did my best to pretend I knew they would be there, I picked them up with my right hand, one by one, and squeezed them between the first two fingers of my left hand, in a line, and then between the next two fingers, which is the safest way to carry pushpins if you don't have a box handy. I went back into the kitchen, Aunt Liz still following, and replaced the pins where they'd been. I told her I wouldn't touch them again, and that I needed a quick shower before work, I would be a few minutes. I could have gone to work without showering, I had showered after work the day before, I didn't actually need a shower, I needed to go back to my room to figure out how the pushpins had ended up on my desk.

The first thing I did when I got into my room, after shutting the door behind me, was to pull the desk chair into the closet and stick my head through the hatch to ask Paul what had happened. He was not there. I pulled myself up and looked around. He wasn't anywhere. I came down and scanned the room. Nothing. I went into the bathroom and found Paul sitting in the bathtub, concealed behind the shower curtain, hands wrapped around his right ankle. He explained that he'd heard our conversation, he'd known where it was going, it had been obvious, and so he'd torn down all of his papers, he'd pulled out all the pushpins, and he'd jumped down from the crawl space to deliver the pushpins to my desk. Unfortunately, in doing so, he'd twisted his ankle, he didn't know how badly, it had made a snapping sound, he was pretty sure he could walk on it, really he was just waiting for me to help him get back upstairs, he didn't like being down here at all, despite the shower curtain being closed he felt exposed, he was anxious to get above the ceiling and start thinking again.

# RETURNS

Two days later Aunt Liz reinstated, on a probationary basis, her words, my bus privileges, in part because she had an early notary appointment in Woodland Hills, which was not on the way to the fast-food place. I was delighted to find Clarence behind the wheel, Clarence who stayed to the right, who preferred living in Panorama City to being a black man in Minneapolis, I felt immediately at home in the front seat with Clarence driving, of all the drivers Clarence was my closest friend, Shaniece was second, she was friendly enough but limited in her ability to pay attention to a long story. We drove the old route toward the fast-food place, as usual, past the mini-mall with the butcher shop, past the big rig parked in someone's driveway, but when we got to the fast-food place, or the stop for the fast-food place, I should say, I didn't stand. I could only picture in my so-called mind's eye the way Aunt Liz beamed when she saw my Employee of the Month picture, the way she seemed so proud of it, it was the last thing she should have been proud of, I had become Employee of the Month because I had, without intention, tortured some poor woman with irregular french fries, I had, without intention, entertained, in a manner sordid and abject, both Paul Renfro words, I had entertained Roger Macarona, and he had decided to reward me for it, and anyone could look at that picture and see that it wasn't me in there, that I'd gone absent. I couldn't continue the charade, I needed something else, I needed to do something different, something that I could be proud of if I saw a picture of me doing it. Which I don't recommend as a technique, I don't recommend ever imagining how what you're doing would look as a picture, you tend to lose awareness of your immediate surroundings. Clarence turned in his seat, he turned to look at me, and he said, Your stop, Oppen. My stop. I had created a groove in Panorama City, so that someone like Clarence would remember where I got on and where I got off, it reminded me of the way everyone in Madera knew me by my bicycle, the way they all knew I'd be coming into town to look for something to do, or riding out of town, maybe with groceries, to head home. I told Clarence that I wasn't going into work, I couldn't do it. I told him I was looking for my own path, I told him I'd rather ride the bus a little while. Clarence nodded, he said, his words, I been there. Nothing, he said, nothing better for sorting out your head than a nice relaxing bus ride, leave the driving to me, you let your mind do its work. Which was how I came upon something that had always been there but I had just not noticed, which was that riding the bus was a way of thinking, which was that all modes of transport had been for me ways of thinking. I have mentioned already how riding a bicycle stimulates both thought and ideas, the rotation of the pedals and the forward motion of the bike, and everyone knows that walking, walking with a proper gait, can stimulate all kinds of regular thought, which was Paul Renfro's preferred technique, and I'd discovered already how motor coaches, I mean big buses, can stimulate sleep if you're synchronized with the rising and falling of power lines, but this was new, I'd stumbled upon a new way of thinking. Which was advanced in its own way, the key was to make the mind like the bus, the key was to let thinking proceed, let the thinking happen with its regular rumble and turns, speeding and slowing, let the thinking do its thing, but then at regular intervals stop the thinking motion completely, sort of crystallize everything, it's difficult to describe, I've never tried to actually describe it, the stopping and the starting. Stopping to let ideas on and off, then rolling along with some thinking to the next stop. Not unlike what's going on with this tape recorder.

The bus is a parade of noses and lips and eyes, and different colors and styles of hair, and different clothes, of course, all kinds of people wearing all kinds of clothes, shoes, boots, sneakers, sandals, and you can see in the way people carry themselves, you can see whether someone is having a good day, or whether they're in a hurry or just puttering along, you can even see those who would be in a hurry if their bodies would let them move more quickly, but their bodies won't, you can see it on their faces, they haven't quite resigned themselves to moving through the world at the speed of their bodies. You see fat people and skinny people, and fat people who want to be skinny, and fat people who are happy how they are, people of all different colors, speaking all different languages, all of them dreaming all different dreams, Juan-George, it's an amazing thing to ride the bus for a few hours. Clarence used to say that the world was always unfolding in front of him, no two days were ever the same, he was always on the move. I tell you, if driving had been my talent, you know where I would have ended up, of course then there would have been no you, but I don't want to trace the consequences, after all that's not how things turned out. It does make you wonder about someone like Phil, when Phil was driving you knew not to talk to the driver, you knew not to try to make friends with him. He never waited for someone to move their car out of the way, he always drove out into the left lane, people were always honking at him, it was no wonder he crashed the bus eventually, but that was later, and he argued successfully that it wasn't his fault, and for all I know he's still driving that bus around Panorama City, if you ever go down there and end up getting on a bus being driven by someone called Phil, he has a square head and red cheeks, just get off and wait for the next one. Phil only wanted to plow forward, plow through the streets and through the day. I suppose we need those kind of people, too, but still, what a shame.

* * *

It was while riding that bus, it was while watching people get on and off the bus, that I noticed a shopping cart pushed up against a bench, abandoned there, a regular old-style metal shopping cart with a supermarket logo on it, wheels in the grass, in the patch of hard yellow grass, looking lonely and lost, I don't quite know how to put it. I had been riding the bus for a while, we had looped back to come the other way, I had ridden to the end of the route and back, and so I wasn't far from places familiar to me, I knew where the cart had come from, a supermarket several blocks away, Aunt Liz shopped there sometimes. And so I decided, after saying goodbye to Clarence, after thanking him for the ride, I decided to get off the bus and walk that cart back to where it belonged. I don't know what possessed me, Juan-George, but when you're looking for your own path, you've got to trust your gut, and my gut was telling me that this stray shopping cart needed to go home, needed to be with its own kind, not bumped up against some bus bench blocks from the market it belonged to. I pushed it along the sidewalk, it made a terrible rattle, those wheels were designed for smoother surfaces than the sidewalks of Panorama City, I pushed it along and I whistled a tune, or I was still getting warmed up, I felt my way around the notes for a while, and nobody stopped me, nobody told me to shut the fuck up, as Roger had done, it was altogether a beautiful moment. My mind wandered in a most pleasant way, it felt like it had been ages since my mind had been able to wander the way I liked. When I reached the grocery store parking lot, I returned the cart to an area about halfway in, where carts are supposed to be returned, I pushed the cart into the back of a long line of carts, the cart in front obliged by lifting its hinged back panel, one fit into the other, and the lonely cart I'd found became one with the others, returned to where it could fulfill its purpose. Having returned the cart I'd found, I wandered the lot, bringing other shopping carts back to the designated area, until an employee came out of the grocery store and made it clear that I was doing his job for him, which would have been cool, he said, except it was really the only time he could get out of the store all day, and the more carts were spread around the lot, the longer he got to stay outside, and the longer he got to stay outside, the happier he was, and not just because he could sneak a smoke but more importantly because it sucked to be inside, his words, his manager was always crawling up his ass about something. At which point I wished him good luck and went on my way, there would be other carts elsewhere.

I spent the rest of the day collecting shopping carts from around the neighborhood and returning them to their respective stores. Sometimes I had to ask people where the stores were, I didn't recognize the logos on the carts, in general people were helpful and decent, as they always were in Panorama City. Only once, when I tried to retrieve a cart that was upside down in an alleyway, upside down so it wouldn't roll away, I later realized, only that one time did I encounter any resistance, when an old woman came out of her apartment onto her balcony, it was only one story above the alley, she must have heard me out there, she came out and yelled down that it was her cart, that she kept it there, that I had no business taking her cart away, that it was the only way she could carry the things she had to carry, that I should keep my hands off her cart. I obliged, I upturned it and apologized. And then, two carts later, I was walking down a street not unlike Aunt Liz's, I was close to Aunt Liz's, I was in her general neighborhood, and I saw a cart tipped on its side on the grassy parkway and I went to pick it up, I knew where to return it, in fact it was the grocery store I'd returned the first cart to. I became aware of a rumbling behind me, a vehicle coming down the street very slowly. I looked over my shoulder, I tried to do so casually, as I did it I felt anything but casual, I half expected to see Aunt Liz or a police car, but it was a pickup truck with a panel truck back end, full of shopping carts. The driver asked me if the cart was mine, I said it wasn't, I told him I'd found it, I was returning it to the market, someone had abandoned it. He looked at me strangely, he looked up and down the street and asked where my truck was. I told him I was walking it back, and he said I must have a lot of time on my hands. No more than anyone else, I said. He told me his name, which was Roland, and that it was his occupation, it was his vocation to drive around collecting abandoned shopping carts in various neighborhoods, stores gave him a small reward for each cart returned. I told him it sounded like a nice job and he said it had been, until he'd jacked his back, and so right now he was having trouble and could use a hand, was I interested? It was the end of his workday, he said, he was heading to drop off carts now, he didn't need my help just yet, but if I was available tomorrow, we could meet up in the morning. We arranged the time and location and he drove away. I pushed that last cart all the way back to the grocery store, whistling the tune I'd composed and thinking I'd finally discovered the perfect job.

As a result of all this, I missed a session with Dr. Rosenkleig. I mean I missed it deliberately, I was aware I was supposed to be at his office, and instead I continued returning shopping carts. In our previous session, he'd declared, from under that mass of salt-and-pepper hair, he'd declared that the key to the future lay in the past. And so he'd wanted to talk with me about your grandfather, he'd wanted to open the subject of your grandfather's death and how it had affected me. Despite his string-cutting moments, Dr. Rosenkleig was a puppet, and a professional, and I wasn't going to talk to him about your grandfather. My reluctance made him, Dr. Rosenkleig, all the more suspicious that I was covering something up, some emotional wound, his words, it made him all the more concerned that I wasn't willing to wrestle with issues from my past, it made him all the more concerned that I wasn't facing my demons. I searched high and low, as they say, for those demons, Juan-George, but I couldn't find them. And so my plan, my own plan, involved me missing all future appointments with Dr. Rosenkleig. Later, much later, I received a piece of information that was shocking and illuminating and yet to be expected, which was that even if I did not show up for a session Dr. Rosenkleig got paid, which meant that the best strategy for him, financially, I mean, in a business sense, beyond speaking and thinking as slowly as possible, was to hope nobody ever showed up.

I knew that Aunt Liz wouldn't be pleased with the plan I'd made up, with the plan I'd discovered on my own for myself in Panorama City, I knew she would object, because it was not her plan for me, I knew she would not be happy that I'd missed work and Dr. Rosenkleig, I knew I was in for a long discussion, that I was, as used to happen sometimes when I was a boy, that I was in so-called trouble or hot water with Aunt Liz, but frankly I wasn't worried, I could take whatever Aunt Liz wanted to throw at me, I could handle any of it. Because I'd become, as I had become in Madera in my youth, I had become a shield again, but where in Madera I had been shielding the weak, the targets of bullies, in Panorama City I was shielding Paul Renfro. I was protecting and shielding a thinker, I was providing him with a place to think, uninterrupted by quotidian concerns, his words, I was a shield and a protector of the most valuable thing I had come across in Panorama City, the delicate iridescent soap bubble of Paul Renfro's advanced thinking.

Aunt Liz was not yet home when I arrived. I climbed into the crawl space, or I stuck my head up there, to see how Paul was doing. He'd been working on his obstacles, he'd been outlining the nature of the obstacles to his thinking so that he could begin to ask the essential questions about the obstacles that would permit him to advance his thinking, his mind was a thicket, he said, but he was hopeful, he was going to pace his way there, the movement remained an essential component of his thinking, or his preparations for thinking, his ankle ached, he'd come down on it hard, but the swelling had gone down, and he'd found an old board upstairs that he was using as a sort of crutch, to keep the weight off his bad ankle while he paced on the beams, it was ideal, the whole situation was ideal, his words.

## MYLAR

Something is happening. The mylar balloon in the corner of my room, the balloon on which I have been watching the reflection of cars and trucks and their lights flowing on the freeway, the balloon bobbing and swaying in the air-conditioned breeze, is reddening, it is glowing. I am afraid, Juan-George, I am afraid, and I am not afraid. The terminus is approaching, I can feel it.

I am going to be asked, by no one, by some mysterious force, I am going to be asked to let go of all this, and I am not going to have a choice, and I am going to let go. The traffic is fading, the glow is lightening, the redness is glowing, my vision is narrowing.

I see a bright light. This is just as I have heard it described. I don't want to go, Juan-George, but I don't have a choice. Tell your mother every day that she was the love of my life.

It looks like I am not going just yet.

* * *

I have a few moments left, perhaps. I must tell you, I forgot to mention it, I did go back to the health club, I went back exactly two weeks later, to collect money from the sale of Paul's antioxidant cream, even though Paul was gone, even though I was supposed to be in the middle of my clinical trial, I went, I snuck down there by myself, I sat on the bench in the entrance for a few hours, nobody came, but someone had left an envelope, one person had left an envelope with my name on it, and a check for twenty dollars, with a happy face on the memo line, I never got a chance to cash it, I don't know what became of it.

Oh, Juan-George, the red glow is piercing my eyes, I can feel the terminus approaching. There's no manual to life, there's no arrow pointing at what's important and what isn't, you have to feel your way there, and of course if you had a thousand years you could do it on your own, but nobody gets a thousand years, most don't get even a hundred, life is short even when it is long, and so we have to listen to other people, we have to listen to others and then decide for ourselves, based on what we've heard, what's important and what isn't, which seems simple enough but is in fact treacherous because if everyone believes something it's probably not true.

Your mother is stirring now, I was hoping she would sleep through my passing, I didn't want to subject her to this, I am closing my eyes, I am going quietly.

* * *

I am here, I am still here, it is dawn and I am here. The sunrise, it was the sunrise, what I thought was death was the sunrise reflected on the balloon. Your mother has gone downstairs, she's at the cafeteria getting herself some tea. It is tomorrow, I have made it through the night, I have lived through the night, a miracle, the doctors said I wouldn't. It's a miracle I owe to you, Juan-George. You, your future ears, listening to this, you have helped me, you have reached back through time and kept me alive just a bit longer.

# UNINTENDED CONSEQUENCES

Aunt Liz, when she got home, she looked like she hadn't slept in days, her reddish hair had flopped down, her zebra print shirt was wrinkled, she opened the door and stared at me for at least ten seconds before saying anything. And then she said that she didn't know what to do with me. She said that she couldn't believe this had happened again. She had heard from Roger the manager, she had heard from Dr. Rosenkleig, she had driven all around town, she had checked the Lighthouse Fellowship, she had even gone back to that man Paul Renfro's building, she had found only an angry landlord. She didn't know what to do with me, she repeated that again and again. She was at the so-called end of her rope. How could she be expected to look after me if I continued to behave like this, if I continued to relapse, was the word she used. I had been doing so well, my one-month evaluation had been so positive, what had happened, why the backsliding? Had the positive reinforcement gone to my head? She decided it had started with the pushpins, and though she'd agreed

I'd only borrowed them they had caused her a great deal of undue concern, and she should have come down harder, she should have practiced some tough love at that point. She wouldn't, she couldn't be a party to my delinquency, she had taken me in with the hopes of undoing some of the damage my father, her brother, had done, or the damage that had occurred as a result of him doing nothing, she understood that I was still adjusting, Dr. Rosenkleig had told her that the process inevitably involved taking one step forward and two steps back, as he put it, or two steps forward and one step back, she couldn't recall, but in any case the time had come to step forward again, the time had come for me to shape up, another day like today, she said, and I don't know, her words, all she could say was, I don't know. As she spoke, I didn't respond or argue, I didn't tell her about my new job returning stray carts, I didn't tell her about how riding the buses had led to a new way of thinking, I didn't tell her anything about my own plan for my own life. It was all one long piece of uninterrupted speech from her mouth, and as she spoke I listened to something else, something only I could hear, because only I was listening for it, Aunt Liz was too heated up to notice, I listened to Paul Renfro's pacing, I listened to the rhythmic beat of his pacing and it was as if I had ears in another world, a higher world of advanced thinking and moving history forward. While Aunt Liz chided me, the rhythm of Paul Renfro's pacing, a rhythm enhanced by his use of the board to help keep his balance, carried me away, in my head, to another, more intellectual plane. Aunt Liz discussed the possibility of my beginning to pay rent and the problem of, her words, my Teflon attitude toward personal responsibility, and the difficulties inherent in my so-called adjustment, considering the absurd deprivations of my upbringing, but even as all of those words entered my head, and remained there, to emerge only now, even then I was pursuing, much as I had been at the french fry hopper the day I'd seen that abnormally long french fry, I was pursuing the thinking man's way to empowerment, I would not let Aunt Liz dictate the terms of the situation, I had other things in mind, literally, I had other things in my mind, I was a stronger shield than that. I was imagining, or trying to imagine the kinds of ideas Paul was having, or the kinds of basic questions that might emerge from his advanced thinking, I was trying to deduce from the rhythm of his footsteps and the board the direction in which his thinking was moving, it reminded me of watching the power wires on the side of the road while riding the bus, except that rather than making me sleepy this rhythmic pattern was making me more alert, I was trying to tap into what Maria had called the higher planes, where our spirits were not separate as they were here on earth, when I felt, in my core, an alarm going off, something wasn't right, the rhythm was off. *Pah-dump, pah-dump-dump, pah-dump, pah dump-dump-dump.* An alarm went off inside me and my whole body stiffened, this was automatic, there was no hesitation, it happened in an instant, my body stiffened, and Aunt Liz stopped talking. I don't know if she was responding to my body stiffening or if she'd felt an alarm inside her too, as I said this all happened in an instant. There was an enormous crash in the kitchen, it sounded like a backhoe had come through the wall. Then a patter like hail on the linoleum. We ran in, or I ran in and Aunt Liz followed. We looked up, we couldn't help but look up, the eye was drawn upward to where before there'd been smooth ceiling and now there was plaster spiderwebbed with cracks, and in the middle of it all a hole with a board hanging from it, a two-by-four with socks wrapped around the end, twitching and swinging like a busted windshield wiper. The only thing keeping the board from falling to the floor was an arm, a man's arm, which had followed the board through the hole in the ceiling. Aunt Liz screamed, the board dropped to the floor. I am a slow absorber, I have talked about this before, and one of the disadvantages of being a slow absorber is that I didn't know immediately, as I should have, that this meant everything was coming to an end. I saw Paul Renfro's arm, or most of his arm, scraped and dusty, hanging down through a hole in Aunt Liz's kitchen ceiling, and I saw Aunt Liz's horrified face staring up at it, and I thought, I remember thinking, There's something you don't see every day.

Paul moaned in pain, he was moaning in physical pain from his arm coming through the ceiling, he couldn't seem to pull his arm back up, it hung there and then twitched as he tried and then hung there again, and moaning in physical pain too from his ankle. He was moaning in physical pain, and there was in his moans the sound of another kind of pain, the pain of defeat, of frustration with the fact that his advanced thinking had been interrupted yet again, that every time he seemed on the verge of a breakthrough events and people conspired against him. Aunt Liz dialed 911. She told the operator that there was an intruder in her home, that someone had broken into her home, which they seemed to understand, but when she tried to explain that the hand, the arm, was coming down through the kitchen ceiling they began to ask questions, she told them to send the police, immediately, and maybe the fire department, she didn't know how they were going to extract this arm from the ceiling, no she wasn't on medication, she said, she hadn't been drinking, this was an emergency. I suggested she ask for an ambulance, but she didn't. She hung up the phone and grabbed the biggest kitchen knife she could, she stared at the ceiling, ready to defend herself from the arm, she said she would defend herself, she said she would not hesitate to defend herself, she said she had a knife, she said she was not afraid to put it to use. All of this she said toward the ceiling and in spite of Paul's moans, it was as if she couldn't hear his moans. She reached into the knife block and pulled out the second-biggest knife in the kitchen, she held it out to me, she said that I should follow her lead, she said she'd dealt with this kind of thing before, well, not exactly like this, but the neighborhood wasn't what it used to be, someone had come into the backyard once, she said this loudly, and more at the ceiling than at me, and that intruder had paid the price, that intruder had paid for his crimes long before he went in front of a judge, she said, loudly. I didn't take the knife. Instead I said something that in retrospect seemed like a mistake, but who knows, the unintended consequences are not traceable, there are long patches when everything stays the same, and there are moments when everything changes, this was one of the latter. I said to Aunt Liz that she could put down the knives, that she didn't need to be scared, that even if Paul wasn't stuck, and moaning in pain, and mainly above the ceiling, that even if Paul was standing here in this kitchen, he posed no threat, he had dedicated himself to mankind, to saving mankind from itself, he was a humble servant of mankind.

You never know how people are going to react to knowledge, the knowledge in question here being that the man stuck in the ceiling above us was someone I knew, and that I wasn't shocked to find him there, which meant that I had something to do with his being up there, all of which was bad enough, all of which was making Aunt Liz angry enough, but which was multiplied a hundredfold by the mention of his name, Paul, as if Aunt Liz's anger had been a small fire burning in a metal trash can and the name *Paul* was a gallon of gasoline. She pointed the knives at the ceiling, at the arm, and said, Paul? That man is Paul? I said yes, she kept talking. Was this the man Paul I'd met on the bus from Madera? Was this the man Paul whom she'd expressly declared not welcome in her home? I said yes, and yes, and that he needed help, I repeated that we should call an ambulance. Aunt Liz went silent, she went silent and her eyes went wide, her face got redder and redder, her face became a red bridge between her red hair and red lipstick, and she exploded, she screamed at me, she screamed obscenities, I had never heard Aunt Liz use those words before. I have always understood the need to get feelings out, I have always understood how people use certain words as release valves, so to speak, for their feelings, even if that has never been my particular strategy for dealing with emotions. It had begun to dawn on me, I mean besides seeing and hearing Aunt Liz's anger, it had begun to dawn on me that Aunt Liz had been hurt by my actions, at least in the sense that, her words, she had attempted to make progress where others had not, and that she couldn't help someone who didn't want to be helped, but she guessed that, in the end, no good deed goes unpunished, which was her philosophy, which was not mine, which has never been my philosophy. I felt terrible, but since I had already been disappointing Aunt Liz before Paul, or before Paul's arm, came crashing through the ceiling, since she had already been chronicling the ways in which I had been backsliding, I was more prepared for her harsh words than she was, she seemed shocked at what was coming out of her own mouth.

Paul's moans subsided, his moans decreased in volume and frequency, he was calling for help, he was sobbing and calling for help, I told Aunt Liz I was going to go up to help him. She didn't seem to understand what I was saying, she followed me into my room, still holding the knives. I pulled the chair out from under the desk and rolled it into the closet, where I opened the access panel to the ceiling, the whole time Aunt Liz was telling me I couldn't do this, and the whole time I was telling her that Paul was injured up there, that my friend Paul needed my help. She said that that man Paul was an intruder, he had intruded into her home, he was a criminal, we should let the police handle it, I didn't know what I'd gotten myself into. I asked her something that had been a popular question at the Lighthouse Fellowship, which was What Would Jesus Do? People at the Lighthouse liked to say it, some even wore little bracelets with the initials on them, but I never did, especially after I'd listened to the Bible on tape. You see, Jesus did a limited number of things, he healed the sick, turned water to wine, organized fishermen, overturned tables, gave to Caesar what was Caesar's, walked, told stories, shared meals with prostitutes and tax collectors, washed people's feet, asked God why have you forsaken me, and rose from the dead. So unless you were doing one of those things, asking What Would Jesus Do? was a way of engaging in speculation as to God's mind, and whether you believed or not it seemed wrong to me to try to guess what Jesus would do in other situations, it seemed to go directly against the idea that we couldn't know the mind of God. By the time Paul moved into the ceiling I had gotten past all that, of course, but Aunt Liz remained the good Christian woman she'd always been, and I thought a good way to convince her that Paul should be helped, at least until the authorities arrived, was to appeal, as they say, to her sense of Christian charity, and so I asked her, I asked Aunt Liz what Jesus would do in this situation. You are not Jesus, she said, you are Oppen, you are my nephew, and you are a guest in this house, and I forbid you, she said, to climb into that ceiling, I forbid you, she repeated, to climb up there. I said that I was sincerely sorry for any trouble I might have caused her, I said that I appreciated her hospitality very much, and her point of view, for she had one, a clear one, despite whatever Paul Renfro might say, I said that I understood exactly what she was saying, but despite all that I had to help my friend.

Aunt Liz did not try to follow me. I crossed the beams and ducked through passages to reach Paul, to reach the area over the kitchen where Paul had been pacing and where he had fallen. He was there, he remained there, prone and moaning, his arm stuck into the ceiling below, his injured ankle sticking up at an angle, he looked like he was swimming, like he'd been frozen in the act of swimming.

When he became aware of my arrival he said, Thank God it's you. Help me, he said after that, help me get my arm out. He was stuck, his arm was stuck almost all the way up to his shoulder. I tried to dig away at the plaster and wood surrounding his arm but my fingers alone couldn't do the job. I went back into the crawl space, I dug through Paul's papers, which were no longer hanging everywhere but stacked in a messy pile, and I found a mechanical pencil, Aunt Liz must have heard me, she was still in the closet, she asked me if I'd come to my senses, she asked me to get down, I told her Paul was stuck, she said that was good, he should be stuck, keep him stuck until the police arrive, she said. I returned to Paul. I discovered I could peel away some of the wood above the plaster, I peeled it back in a way Paul couldn't because of how he was stuck, and then I used the mechanical pencil to chip away at the plaster, bit by bit, until the hole was big enough for Paul's arm to come up out of it. The whole time I did this, Paul lamented, his word, he lamented what was happening, he said what was happening was what always happened, he said that there seemed to be no exit from this endless loop, he had inherited it from his parents, who were perversely still alive. Aunt Liz was in the kitchen, I could see her through the hole, she was looking up at me with terror in her eyes, she was still holding the knives. The police took a surprisingly long time to arrive, which Aunt Liz would later say was typical of Panorama City, nobody cared about Panorama City anymore, Panorama City had succumbed to various elements, various human elements that naturally compromised the police's ability to respond in a timely manner, and she wasn't talking about the tax base, or not only about the tax base, but also the lack of motivation, on the part of the police, the understandable lack of motivation to help what she called these people, these people who come here and expect, expect the rest of us to take care of them, Aunt Liz's words.

Now, Juan-George, I have not spent much time in the company of the police, it might seem otherwise based on what I've put onto these tapes, it might seem like I deal with the police on average of once a month, but these two encounters, the first after your grandfather, my father, Aunt Liz's brother, died and the second in Panorama City, the one I'm telling you about, these two encounters pretty much make up all of my involvement with the police, if you don't count further encounters with Madera Community Service Officer Mary, which you shouldn't, she didn't have a gun. And so in terms of advice my knowledge is limited, but I should say, I should mention as I don't think I have already, something that Paul Renfro pointed out to me once, which is that Justice, contrary to public belief, is not blind. Love is blind, but Justice? Look at any statue, at any depiction. She is blindfolded.

As soon as we heard sirens Aunt Liz disappeared from sight, I could hear her telling the police that I was up in the ceiling, too, that she was worried for my safety, that I didn't know what I'd gotten myself into, that I was the tall one, it was the old man who had intruded, the old man was the intruder, not the tall young man, she didn't know if he was armed or not, there was an access in the closet. Paul yelled through the hole in the kitchen ceiling, he yelled down that he was unarmed, that he was surrendering willingly, that no crime had been committed, that he could clear everything up, and that he would happily meet the police in the closet to discuss the situation, it would take him but a moment, his words, his ankle and arm were injured, he needed my help to get there. It would have been reasonable to meet Paul in the closet, but the Panorama City police turned out to be unreasonable types, they had been very slow in coming and now seemed to be in quite a hurry, and so they sent two officers up through the closet access panel and another two officers up through another access panel located toward the front of the house, above the entryway closet, each officer moving forward as quickly as possible despite having a gun in one hand and a flashlight in the other, the bouncing flashlight beams only blinding the officers coming from the other side. Paul and I were halfway to the closet by then, the police bumped me out of the way and tackled Paul with such force the plaster cracked, Aunt Liz's ceiling was cracked by the weight of the police tackling and handcuffing Paul Renfro. At which point Paul screamed, one of the officers told him he had the right to remain silent, Paul kept screaming, he was in pain, they were on his ankle. Once they were off, Paul told the officers that they had no right restraining him in this way, that he was a guest in this house, that he had been invited here to pursue various advanced ideas, ideas they couldn't be expected to understand but would only benefit from unknowingly, he had been invited here to pursue those ideas to their logical conclusions, as a guest he couldn't understand what he had done wrong, he had been expecting medical attention, not a paramilitary force. The officers didn't appear to hear, except one who yelled down to another, I couldn't believe there were more downstairs, who yelled that an ambulance should probably be called, which was what I was trying to tell everyone all along.

They got Paul down, they got him through the access and down into the closet despite the handcuffs, and I tried to explain to them that what Paul had said was true, that I had indeed invited him to stay in the space above the ceiling so that he could pursue his ideas in peace, that he had been an invited guest of mine, but the police were more inclined to believe Aunt Liz's version. At first I thought it was because she could prove she was the owner of the home, I attempted to explain that it didn't matter who owned the home, technically, I had invited Paul in, how could he have known who owned the home, I said, but Aunt Liz had talked to the police when they had first arrived, while I was upstairs giving what she later called aid and comfort to the enemy, she had talked to the police and she had told them that I was someone who was not aware of the dangers inherent in living in the big city, that I had recently lost my father, and furthermore that despite her best efforts she was having some difficulty introducing me to the mainstream, her words, thereby without my knowledge destroying ahead of time whatever credibility I might have otherwise established with the police, meaning it didn't matter what I said on Paul's behalf, the police had come to arrest him and take him away. An argument rendered moot, Aunt Liz's later words, after a visit from Detective Woodward, an argument rendered moot by Detective Woodward notifying us that a warrant was already out for Paul Renfro's arrest, that Paul Renfro had recently escaped from a so-called minimum security facility elsewhere in California, where he had been serving time for various offenses. Lucky, said Detective Woodward, as reported to me by Aunt Liz, lucky his ankle was broken or we might have had a pursuit on our hands. And lucky, too, said Aunt Liz, that the police hadn't arrested me for harboring a fugitive in her home. I tried to explain to Aunt Liz that Justice was not blind but blindfolded, that the right thing to do would be to extract Paul Renfro from this legal bramble so that he could pursue, unfettered, a Paul Renfro word, the advanced ideas he'd been pursuing all these years, but I couldn't convince her on any point.

Detective Woodward and another officer went up into the crawl space and shot photographs for their files, then they took everything that belonged to Paul, all of his papers, all of his ideas, his cardboard briefcase, everything, they took it all away, they wouldn't say what was going to happen to it, they said it was evidence, some of it would be used as evidence, the rest would go into storage somewhere. Aunt Liz couldn't understand why I was so concerned about the illegible scrawlings of a criminal madman, her words, perhaps I should consider instead the fate of the woman who had tried to help me in every way, or consider how much danger I had put her in, how much danger we'd all been in while this creature, this termite, was living under our roof, unbeknownst to her. Which is only one tiny fraction of the extended discussion Aunt Liz and I had at the kitchen table, under the hole in the ceiling, for most of the night and resuming first thing in the morning. As you can imagine, I did not say much, most of the speech came from Aunt Liz's mouth, most of what she said she had already said a few times before, she kept repeating things, she kept saying that she remained in a state of disbelief as to what had happened, and that she was going to have to come to a decision, but every time she began to get close to that decision she retreated, it was clear to me what the decision was, she wanted me to leave, but despite her depending on professionals for everything, despite her adherence to common sense nonsense, despite whatever flaws I might be able to list here, she wanted me to leave but she couldn't say so, every time her giant circles of speech led her back to that inescapable decision point she pulled back, so to speak, she was my protector, she couldn't kick me out.

It was only the next morning, after we'd eaten something, or she'd had coffee, I had oatmeal, it was only with the break of dawn that she stumbled upon a new track, a new piece of speech that wouldn't again lead her to the decision point, something she'd never tried with me, she set down her coffee and looked me straight on, and she said to me, or she asked me, for the first time, What do you want? I said, I want to go home.

The words came out without me even thinking them. Then I told Aunt Liz that I wanted to respect my father's wishes, her brother's wishes, your grandfather's wishes, I wanted to bury him where he belonged, which was next to Ajax and Atlas, which was not in some cemetery next to Kutchinskis and Browns. She took a sip of her coffee, she took a long sip, she looked at me over the rim of her coffee cup, she was assessing, she was considering what I'd said. She put down her coffee cup then, and nodded, and said, her words, That sounds reasonable. She would get me as far as the bus, she said, she would buy my bus ticket back to Madera, of course I could always call her if I needed anything, but for right now she couldn't go with me, she had too much notarizing to do, she had people in need of verification and certification, she needed also to recuperate, she listed many reasons why she couldn't come with me, I didn't need any, I hadn't expected her to come with me, I could take care of myself, I told her so. After which a change came over Aunt Liz, she seemed greatly relieved, she had been trying to force herself to kick me out, she had been battling internally between needing to be rid of me and wanting still to control my every move and thought, and together we had found a third way.

She reminisced about my first day in Panorama City, she talked about the look on my face coming off the bus, and the suit I'd been wearing, and she talked about my first day on the job at the fast-food place, and so on, I had been so promising. Her reminiscing took on a darker tone, there was a dark magnet in Aunt Liz's head, it took her speech and led her where she didn't want to go, she reminisced and then she asked did I know, could I help her figure out where and how and why she'd failed. I told her of course that she had done no such thing. I told her she'd been very hospitable during my stay in Panorama City, I told her that my only regret was that she and Paul Renfro couldn't see eye to eye, it would have made things more pleasant, but east is east, as your grandfather used to say. And besides, I had done what I came to do, or I had stopped doing what I came to do, I had seen the error of my premises. I thought I had come to Panorama City to become a man of the world, while in fact I had come to Panorama City to become a provincial type, thinking that was what it meant to be a man of the world. Had I succeeded, had I never been disabused, as they say, of that notion, I would have indeed become a provincial type, I would be telling you right now that I had become a man of the world, and I would hold up my golf clubs to prove it. Instead, I came to understand that a man of the world is not something you can just kick up your feet and be, a man of the world, a true man of the world, is something you are always becoming. It is a question, not an answer. So I did not mind leaving Panorama City, because although I hadn't achieved my goal I had exposed it, or it had been exposed to me, as a false goal, which is far more valuable than achieving it could ever be, and I had come to understand that I could be a man of the world, or I could keep becoming a man of the world, anywhere, which included Madera, and besides I was eager to find Carmen again, my mind kept turning back to the flowers she brought me when your grandfather died.

# PART SIX

TAPE 9, SIDE B;

TAPE 10, SIDE A

# OPPEN

I departed from the North Hollywood station, everything looked the same as it had forty days earlier. Aunt Liz wished me luck, she hugged me, she told me to call if I needed anything, I thanked her again for her hospitality, I promised updates, I hoped she would visit sometime. I would miss her cooking, I said, which wasn't all I would miss, but I knew how proud she had been to feed me, to feed someone who she called a growing boy, even though I had stopped growing years before. I pulled my leather suitcase out of the Tempo's trunk, the bus driver grabbed it and threw it into the cargo hold, he didn't care how the bags were stacked, he didn't examine my ticket at all, it seemed like he'd rather be elsewhere, though once we got on the road he was excellent, his driving style was fluid and precise. I sat alone in the front row and watched the city get thinner and thinner until we started up through the Grapevine, then some wires bobbed up and down and I fell asleep.

The bus rattled and I awoke in the middle of the Central Valley, golden grasses and farmland on both sides, cars and trucks and buses lined up in two orderly rows to the horizon. I pulled my compact binoculars from your grandfather's old shaving kit, but even through those powerful lenses I couldn't make out why our side of the freeway was clogged. I had expected, Juan-George, or hoped, or somehow felt without thinking that after falling asleep near the Grapevine I would awaken in Madera, but it wasn't meant to be. We lurched forward and stopped, lurched and stopped. The wires on the side of the road kept no rhythm to doze off to. I scanned the shoulder for items of interest but the landscape seemed more suited to being sped past rather than examined in detail. This of course had nothing to do with what was actually on the side of the road but what was in my head, Juan-George, which was Paul Renfro. His papers everywhere, the Christmas lights, his suit inside out. Pouring ketchup packets into his mouth and wolfing down the french fries I'd brought him. The cardboard briefcase, the pushpins, the stuffed socks. I tried to focus on the freeway shoulder, I tried to turn my thoughts to what lay directly in front of my eyes, but sometimes when something is in front of you, even if it's coming right at you, your head, what's in your head, would rather be somewhere else entirely, and my head, for whatever reason, wanted to be hundreds of miles away, surrounded by beams and insulation, in the cranium of Aunt Liz's house. Then the traffic thinned in a strange way, the gaps between cars grew without there seeming to be fewer cars. My attention turned to the road ahead, I wanted to see what had kept us lurching and stopping for almost an hour, but there was nothing. We just lurched one last time, then stopped, then accelerated smoothly to freeway speed. I asked the driver what had happened, maybe I had missed something. He shrugged and said, Random. At which point my mind returned to Paul Renfro, I wished Paul was sitting next to me, making a mess of his papers, Paul would have given the driver a piece of his mind, as they say. The word *random* is a white flag of surrender, Paul's philosophy, for use only by the cowardly and the defeated. To call any phenomenon random is to declare your own ignorance, is to declare pride in your own ignorance, Paul's words, by predicting, falsely, the fruitlessness of further inquiry. But on the other hand, my philosophy, the driver was good at his job, he drove the bus smoothly and precisely, exactly because he was not interested in the fruits of further inquiry. His ignorance, as Paul would have called it, was in fact a tool. We can't all swallow the whole world, Juan-George, some of us need white flags. Even Paul knew this. I remember the police leading him away, Paul going past me in handcuffs, wincing every time his ankle hit the floor. I was still arguing that he was an invited guest in Aunt Liz's ceiling, that he'd been welcome, that they couldn't arrest him. Paul said that I needn't advocate on his behalf anymore, that I was wasting my breath on those people, the police, that small minds could not be changed. He said there was a high probability we wouldn't see each other again, and he wanted to take the moment, before these barbarians dragged him away, to thank me for acting heroically and nobly in aid of a fellow thinker, in service of the struggle to save mankind from its own stupidity. It wasn't fair, I said, it wasn't right what they were doing to him. Paul looked at me with that newly hatched alligator smile of his and said, Oppen, my friend, listen, it's the way of the world, he who laughs last must first endure the laughter of others. Then they took him away.

I was the only passenger getting off in Madera. The driver yanked my bag from the cargo area and dumped it at my feet, then hopped aboard again without a word. I stood on the tree-lined sidewalk, looking down at my leather suitcase on the bricks. The air stank of almonds roasting and grapes fermenting. Through the Dial-a-Ride office's window I could see the same woman I'd seen there when I'd left for Panorama City, sitting in the same position, eating soup while talking on the phone, as if no time had passed at all, as if time had never passed and never would. Then someone called my name. Oppen, not Mayor. Oppen. Above the row of cars parked nose to curb I saw a person, or I should say I saw a person's hair and sunglasses, the hair sticking up all over the place, it was Officer Mary. She came out from between the cars, waving, and gave me a warm hug, her badge hanging from her shirt like she had magnets in her shoes. She told me that Aunt Liz had called her, and that as long as I was back in town, her words, the least she could do was give me a ride home from the bus depot. Madera hadn't been the same without me, she said. What a coincidence, I said, I hadn't been the same without Madera. We got into Mary's police car, I put my bag in the backseat, Madera-style. Leaving for Panorama City had felt like getting on a rocketship to fly to another planet. Coming back to Madera felt more like realizing I'd never left the planet in the first place.

When we pulled up to the house I noticed two things right away. One, there were no longer any tracks cutting across the yard where the mini-excavator and flatbed truck had come through. Nature had reclaimed them. And two, the mailbox, which I had expected to find stuffed, was empty, which was a relief. A momentary relief, I should say. In fact I had gotten massive amounts, all held at the post office, thanks to Wilfredo, and all later sorted through with the invaluable help of Officer Mary. There is a world of paperwork, Juan-George, an alternate universe, Paul Renfro might have called it, where nothing can be done without the right documents, where every human moment is assigned a piece of paper, paper that exists only so that what is evident to everyone involved can become clear to someone who is not. Without Officer Mary's help I would have been lost there forever.

Is it that dust has a way of getting into a house and no way of getting out, or is it that having no people around for a while allows the dust already in the air to settle? A question I cannot answer, Juan-George. Other than the accumulation of dust on everything, the house hadn't changed since I'd walked out the door some forty days earlier. Oh, and the bread, I'd forgotten some bread, it was a fuzzy black ball. I brought my things upstairs, I'm not sure why, but the first thing I did was bring my bag upstairs to my room and put it on the floor. My sheets were messy, I hadn't made my bed before leaving. I sat on the bed a moment, I thought about breathing my own air, but I didn't want to leave Mary alone downstairs wondering. I gathered my strength and stood and walked out of my room again, I had done it so many times, getting out of bed and heading downstairs, it was like every muscle in my body remembered those motions and those views, they'd made a deep trench in my thinking, and my head was slipping into the trench, so that I had this strange feeling, this notion, or suspicion, I don't know what to call it, I mean, I knew it wasn't true, I knew it wasn't fact, but another part of me felt sure I was waking from the dream that had been Panorama City.

Downstairs, I told Mary what I'd always told everyone, which was that I could take care of myself. She wrote down her phone number, said that I should call if I needed anything. Groceries, post office, whatever. I told her I was fine, that I would be fine. She walked over to the phone in the kitchen and picked it up, listening for a moment. You'll need help, she said, getting this reconnected. She flipped a light switch up and down. Nothing happened. And this, she said. I got a flashlight from your grandfather's old toolbox and fetched some matches and candles. Officer Mary left, reluctantly, after offering to stay the night. I took a shower, a cold shower, there was no hot water, and put on the nicest clothes I had in my closet, a white button-up shirt and some plain tan pants. From my window I could see the horizon splitting the sun, clouds turning orange and red, shadows everywhere. I went out to the garage and found my favorite bicycle, the blue-flake three-speed with leather bags. I wiped it down with wet rags, put air in the tires, sprayed WD-40 on the chain. There was something I had to do.

I rode through warm and humid evening air into town, into your mother's old neighborhood, she doesn't want me talking about this, but I don't trust her to tell you, it is important, it is where you come from, Juan-George. It was dark but there were people on the streets, people making the most of the warm night, they were barbecuing and drinking, they were playing loud music. I pulled my bicycle up onto the lawn and leaned it against the house. Carmen's roommate's son Fabio was sitting on the porch in the same place he'd been sitting forty days before, but this time he was asleep with an empty bottle of beer next to him. I knocked, the door opened from me knocking on it. I entered the house, there was garbage everywhere, nobody had cleaned in a long while. Which was odd, from what I had seen before, your mother was a tidy person, this was what they call a disaster zone and it was dark, too, none of the lights were on. I went into your mother's room and saw two bodies on the bed, a man and a woman, doing what men and women do. The man didn't see me, he was facing the other way, but the woman looked up immediately. She was not your mother. I asked her where Carmen was, the man turned around and asked what was going on. The woman said that Carmen had moved out, and the man said to me, Can't you see I'm fucking here? Which was how I learned that your mother had left her house, had left the house she had been renting, I later discovered, because her roommate's habits had become, her words, too risky, which meant drugs, your mother always avoided drugs. I woke Fabio, I asked him if he knew where Carmen had gone, he had no idea. Which was when I found out he hadn't told her I was coming back, which was when I found out Fabio had told Carmen only that I'd come by to say *adiós*, and that I'd been with another woman, instead of telling her that I'd gone away to become a man of the world, instead of telling her that the woman I was with was Officer Mary, instead of telling her that I hoped she would wait for me, that I would keep her in my heart, that I would return for her, the only thing he'd passed on was *adiós*.

Late the next morning I was moving furniture around, I was trying to figure out how I was going to change the house, now that it was mine, I mean, but I was lost, Juan-George, I had no routine. You should know by now, if you've been listening carefully, or even not so carefully, that most problems can be solved by waiting. If I'd been in town, looking for your mother, if I'd been driving around with Officer Mary, asking people questions, trying to find your mother, if I'd taken a day to track down and visit her family somewhere else in the Central Valley I would not have been home when she appeared on my front porch just before noon, peering through the dusty windows, calling my name. She called me, she still calls me, instead of Oppen, she's the only one who calls me Open, like what you do to a door, I decided that day not to correct her. Hello, she said, Open, are you home? I was. Fabio had told her I was back, she said, and looking for her. She came in, I let her in, and together we sat on the sofa in the living room. I asked if she wanted anything to drink, I offered her tap water or warm soda, I apologized and explained that the electricity hadn't been turned on yet, I hadn't gone into town yet to sort that out. She asked how long I'd been back. I told her I'd just arrived the night before. She asked me if I had come looking for her even before going to PG&E. I told her I hadn't come back to Madera to pay an electric bill. And what about the police woman? she asked. She's not your lover? I explained to Carmen that Officer Mary was my friend, only my friend, and that she had helped me a great deal, and that she was still helping me. Carmen squinted at me and then asked if she could have a soda. I opened one for her, even opening it I could tell it had gone flat, she took a sip and put it down on the coffee table. I asked her how it was and she said it was disgusting, which is something I love about your mother, she tells the truth. I asked her where she was living now, she said she'd rather not say, it wasn't a good place. It was safer than with her old roommate, but it wasn't good. She shifted her body side to side on the sofa, I couldn't tell if she was making herself comfortable or getting ready to stand up. My mouth went dry, and my throat felt like I had half-swallowed a pill, and I knew I had reached one of those points in life where any event no matter how small could happen a different way and change everything that follows. I looked at your mother, I tilted my head down to look her directly in the eyes, and she looked up at me, she met my gaze, as they say, and that look, the two of us exchanging that look, neither of us looking away, gave me the courage to mention that there was extra room in the house and that she was welcome to stay if she wished. I told her I'd have the electricity connected again soon, and the telephone, and that I was still in the process of rearranging the furniture to my liking, and that I'd accept any ideas from her, but she was welcome, she would be welcome here. She smiled, her white teeth and gold teeth all showing, and then laughed. I wasn't sure why she was laughing and waited for her to finish. Enough, she said, you don't have to be a salesman about it. Which meant yes, which was her way of saying yes. Later she would say that it was the beginning of her new life. She's staring blades at me now, Juan-George, I wouldn't be surprised if she erased this part of the tape, your mother has always been a very private person, I hope she won't erase this, what could be better than the beginning of a new life?

She helped me fix up the house, she cleaned with me, together we moved things around. And outside, too, she wanted to landscape the yard, she is not as committed as I am to preserving wilderness. She cleared a little rectangle of land, for a vegetable garden, we've eaten cucumbers and tomatoes from it, it's surprisingly satisfying to grow your own food, but the rest of the land remains wild, remains a patch of wilderness. Your mother lost the battle of the wilderness, as she calls it, but she won the battle of your grandfather's room, which wasn't exactly a battle, but I had locked the door to his room and had thereby declared it off limits to any cleaning or rearranging. But once the rest of the house was done, and after the garden was planted, your mother pointed out that we couldn't leave the room locked forever. At that time I was still sleeping on my bed, and your mother was sleeping on the sofa downstairs, which was where she said she felt most comfortable. Emptying your grandfather's bedroom of all his things was like emptying the container that had held him my whole life. I took many breaks to breathe my own air, Juan-George, and your mother let me. She let me, then she'd come find me and tell me to get back to work, she couldn't move everything on her own. Finally one day the room was clean and empty, just some walls and windows and a floor and ceiling, and it seemed as though no one had ever lived in it. Like Tupperware that had just come out of the dishwasher, no sign of leftovers. Which was when Carmen declared that the room could use a bed, a brand-new bed. We went all the way to Fresno, we took her car. At the mattress store, she lay down on mattress after mattress until she found one she liked. I checked to see that it was long enough for me, which it was. She argued with the salesman for a long time about the price, until neither of them seemed happy, and then we paid. The bed was delivered the next day, and we put fresh sheets and pillows on it. That night, we slept in the bed, together, we slept in that room for the first time. We slept in it every night after. We did all this without talking about it, without discussion, which is like when mosquitoes synchronize their wings, which is a symptom of love.

We walked together in town, your mother and I, we liked to take walks around Madera, and I noticed right away that the atmosphere was not the same awkward and lonely atmosphere it had been right after I had buried your grandfather the first time, no, the atmosphere was friendly, and welcoming, everyone said that they had missed having me around. I think your mother had something to do with it, I don't know, she won't talk about it. We must have been quite a sight, Juan-George, I am much taller than your mother, she is much shorter and rounder than I am, I wore my regular T-shirts with Madera businesses on them and she wore the clothing she'd always worn, nothing wrong with showing off her assets, her words, and yet nobody made jokes, I'd expected jokes, but nobody greeted us with anything but warmth. It was strange, I was no longer exactly a shield, I was something else, and your mother was something else too. I wondered, I remember wondering, if that something else was a man of the world, if people looked at me now and saw a man of the world. I had gone, and I had returned. They asked about my travels, I told them about Panorama City. And I realized that despite all the missteps and unintended consequences my plan had come to fruition. The proof was in the fact that everyone called me Oppen, not Mayor. Or almost everyone, the Alvarez brothers were still in the habit of calling me Mayor, as was Greg Yerkovich, but we were such old friends I could understand it.

Then something happened that we hadn't planned, exactly, but not planned against either. By which I mean that we found out your mother was pregnant with you. We laughed at our good fortune, she can tell you about how excited we were to find out you were coming, she had always assumed that she would never be a mother, could never be a mother, maybe she thought she was too old, I don't know, she had her reasons. As soon as we found out, we began the process of converting my old room into your new room. You will be a boy where I was a boy, Juan-George. Which reminds me, in the back of the garage there is a bicycle, I have set it aside, it has training wheels, when you are big enough you can learn to ride it. There are also several acceptable bicycles for when you are older, Carmen knows where they are, and Wilfredo can tell you everything about riding them. Maybe one of those bicycles will become to you like my blue-flake three-speed was to me, not just a mode of transport, not just a way to get from A to B to C, as they say, but an extension of yourself, a tool so familiar and comfortable that it seems almost a part of you, so that its presence goes unnoticed, what they call second nature, when using it becomes so natural you hardly know you're using it at all, like a shoe that fits.

You were present at your grandfather's third burial, you were in your mother's womb, it was still too soon to know whether you'd be a girl or a boy, we hadn't named you yet, but you were there. First, we had to go into Madera. Or actually, first, we had to navigate oceans of paperwork, with the help of Officer Mary, help your mother didn't think we needed but which turned out to be instrumental in getting your grandfather out from the ground between the Kutchinskis and the Browns. The makeshift coffin I'd made for him ended up going straight into the crematorium. The mortuary worker wore a permanent look of sadness and sympathy on his face but couldn't seem to keep the details straight, his mind was elsewhere, it was a mask, he had landed himself in the wrong job. When we were done signing and paying he handed us a cardboard box containing your grandfather's ashes. I opened the box immediately, I don't know why, and looked inside. I'm not sure what I expected to see, I think something about the worker hadn't made me feel confident, and I wanted to make sure it really was your grandfather. Of course, I knew I would only see fine gray powder, like at the bottom of a fireplace that hasn't been cleaned out. There was fine powder, but there were also bits of white stuff, which the mortuary worker said was bone, and some longer narrow blackened pieces, which, he explained, were the nails that had held together the makeshift coffin.

We returned from the crematorium to find Freddy at the house, Freddy my friend from Madera with one leg shorter than the other, he had taken the day off and brought his mini-excavator with him. And Wilfredo was there, too, I recognized his truck as we pulled into the driveway so it wasn't a total surprise. He had made a marker for your grandfather's grave, along with two others, he and Freddy had installed them. In a row, in polished granite: Ajax, Atlas, George Porter. When I saw the markers for your grandfather and his hunting dogs I couldn't contain my feelings, your mother put her arms around me, she wrapped her arms around me and leaned her head against my chest, against the side of my chest, against my ribs, it was better than breathing my own air. Freddy had already dug the grave, he had already made a hole for your grandfather's final resting place, he had made the hole as big as the hole I'd made the day I first buried your grandfather, nobody had told him about the cremation, nobody had told him we wouldn't be burying a coffin but only a small cardboard box.

You were there, Freddy was there, Wilfredo, your mother and I, Officer Mary, a few others. When everyone was ready I went to put the box into your grandfather's grave. But the hole was too deep, I couldn't reach the bottom, and I didn't want to drop it in. I lay the box on the ground and climbed into the hole. Someone gasped but nobody tried to stop me. I took the box and deposited it at my feet, and as I crouched down to do so my eyes came level with the earth and then below it into shadow. Packed dirt, near black and crisscrossed with roots. An earthworm going about his day. Your grandfather would have liked to see that. And then I stood and came back into the light, past the level of the earth, and I was looking at everyone's shoes. I lifted myself out, I took hold of the shovel, the same shovel I'd used to bury your grandfather the first time, and I scooped some dirt into the hole, onto the box. We took turns shoveling the dirt back into your grandfather's grave, it took a long time, but it didn't seem right for Freddy to use the mini-excavator for that. When we were finished, we stood over the disturbed earth and looked at it, nobody talked. It was quiet, what they call a nonevent.

I wanted it that way, this was not fireworks, this was everything finally clicking into place, no more unintended consequences, only peace. And then from some nearby bushes a half dozen birds took off. Everybody looked over, I can't say for sure but I think they were all thinking the same thing, there went your grandfather, there went George Porter, his spirit free now that his wishes had finally been respected, now that he'd been buried where he'd always wanted. Everyone turned their faces to the sky, to follow the birds flying up and away, but my eyes stayed on the bushes, it was like something told me to keep my eyes on the bushes. A moment later a lean gray fox popped out and licked his chops, yolk dripping from his chin.

## REPRIEVE

C: The doctors are doing their rounds.
O: I can hear them.
C: Dr. Singh won't be happy to hear you've been up all night.
O: He'll be stunned I'm still alive.
C: So dramatic.
O: You'll see, *mi amor*, it's a miracle I'm alive, he'll think so too.

There's more to the accident, there's more to what happened. Just before the terminus, before death, I must call it death, on the threshold of death, the scene of the accident is coming back to me, one second at a time, it is like someone is taking the dominoes and standing them back up in my head, I must tell you about it now, before I am gone.

I remember the day more clearly now, I was riding into town, I was riding my blue-flake three-speed Schwinn into Madera for the first time in a long while, I was enjoying being back on my bicycle. You see, Juan-George, your mother and I had been going into town together, we had been doing everything together, making up for lost time, as they say, and so I had spent most of the past months in the passenger seat of her Hyundai, not on the seat of a bicycle. I had talked with her about the possibility of a tandem bicycle, of talking to Wilfredo to see if we could get one, but she has never been a strong cyclist, her words, and it didn't seem safe to start trying now that you were growing inside her. So the other day when your mother was too tired to go into town, and we had run out of milk and a few other necessities, I decided to take my bicycle. The soft burring sound of tires on asphalt, the gentle breeze in my face, the world going by at the ideal speed. I thought, I remember thinking, I am a father-to-be, riding into town to get groceries for the mother of my child, I marveled at how much my life had changed. Then, in the distance, coming toward me down the road, I saw the Alvarez brothers' pickup truck.

As I mentioned, the Alvarez brothers, along with Greg Yerkovich, were the only people in Madera who still called me Mayor. I hadn't thought too much about it, Juan-George, and to tell you the truth it didn't bother me, I figured they just wanted to keep the name going, as a sort of reminder that we'd been friends for so long. But when I saw the Alvarez brothers' pickup truck cross that yellow line into my lane, I experienced the same sensation I'd felt upon rising from my bed that first day back in Madera, a sort of trench appeared in my thinking, we had been here before, the Alvarez brothers and I, we had done this before, many, many times. But while I had gone down to the so-called real world and experienced many experiences, they had not changed at all, they could not change, they would always be the Alvarez brothers, always driving down the same road, always pointing their pickup truck at me. I could see clearly what I had been unable to see before, which was that they were a fixture, a permanent fixture in Madera, the Alvarez brothers were like a statue in the center of town. And, I now saw, they wanted me to remain a fixture, too, so that the two fixtures could be locked in mutual orbit, so that they were always the people who drove at me on the road and I was always the person who rode his bicycle into the ditch.

Unless one of us swerved to the side a head-on collision was imminent, meaning of course unless I rode the bicycle into the ditch. All of this came to me in a flash, and I wondered something I had never wondered before, which was whether riding my bicycle into the ditch was my only choice. I asked myself, these were the words that came back to me this morning, from the accident, that allowed me to unspool and unpack all of these realizations, I asked myself how a man of the world, a true man of the world, should react to the Alvarez brothers' pickup truck speeding at him. I considered the situation from all sides, or from several sides, I imagined what a picture of this scene would look like, I wondered what I could say about this man on this bicycle, about this father-to-be, playing chicken with a pickup truck, I had started to consider the situation from all sides when my thinking was interrupted, or cut off abruptly, I should say, by the truck.

C: As soon as you are out of here, my Oppen, I am going to give Hector and Michael a piece of my mind, those two running you down like that, they're lucky I got rid of my gun.
O: You never told me about a gun.
C: A woman has to protect herself.
O: From what? From who?
C: It was a different life, Oppen, I don't want to talk about it, it's far away now.
[*Tapping on glass.*]
C: It's the doctor.
O: Dr. Singh is here.
C: Good morning, Doctor.
O: Oh, Juan-George, I wish you could see the look on his face right now.
Dr. Singh [*presumably*]: What is this now?
O: He's shocked to see me alive.
[*Shuffling. Tape clicks.*]

O [*distorted*]: Wrong button.
[*Tape clicks.*]

They are gone. I asked Dr. Singh how much longer I could expect to live, I asked him because I wanted to know what I should say to you next, whether I should begin my good-byes or share with you more of my experience, I begged him to be honest with me. He said that the reason he looked surprised when he saw me just now was that he hadn't expected to find me talking into a tape recorder. Then he said that as long as I don't step out in front of any more moving vehicles, he didn't see why I shouldn't expect to live a long and healthy life. I told him he didn't have to spare my feelings, I'd already heard the nurses discussing my case, I could take it, I asked him to please be honest with me, it didn't make it easier not to know the truth. He shrugged and said he was speaking the truth, God's-honest.

I am a slow absorber, Juan-George.

The nurses, when I had heard the nurses talking before, I had attached their words to an idea already in my head, that I was dying, that I wasn't going to make it through the night, an idea that was like a vacuum cleaner in my head, sucking everything toward it, preventing me from seeing what was obvious, what should have been obvious, namely, that they were talking about my next-room neighbor Mr. Pierce, he was eighty-eight years old.

I laughed, my chest felt like it was on fire, but I had to laugh. Your mother shook her head and rolled her eyes. I told Dr. Singh I couldn't believe my luck, and he said he wouldn't go that far. I had come in with a collapsed lung, a broken hip, dozens of lacerations, a fractured forearm, and multiple fractures in my left leg. I had many weeks of immobility to look forward to, and pain management, followed by physical therapy, he wasn't going to lie to me, I was in for a grueling year, I was in for the greatest physical challenge of my life, people with my types of injuries likened it to climbing K2, his words. But you're not going to die, he said, or at least you're not going to die as a result of this accident. Which is the thing about the terminus, Juan-George, it can never be escaped, it can only be postponed, there is no more preposterous expression in the world than *saving lives*, Paul Renfro's words, because every life reaches its terminus eventually. The expression should be, the expression attached to firemen and doctors and other sorts of caregivers should be *postponing death*. I can assure you, Juan-George, that I am confident, that despite my not being able to predict future events I feel confident I will be able to climb K2, whatever that is, and recover fully, and leave this hospital behind, leave the Madera Community Hospital behind completely. Or almost completely, I should say, we'll be back, your mother and I will be coming back soon, not for any terminus but for your arrival. It will be your mother in this bed, and then your mother and you.

Part of my head I didn't know was shut down is coming on again, is coming alive again, I am letting myself imagine something I imagined many times before, I mean something I imagined after I found out you were on the way but before I ended up in this hospital. I imagined, I am imagining again, holding your hand, of course you'll have to learn to walk first, you won't be able to do this right away, I'm imagining holding your hand as we walk together down the dry bed of the Madera River, which is a wide river, you'll see, with hardly any water in it. I can picture clearly in my so-called mind's eye you and me walking together, our footsteps in the shallow sand, coming down one of the banks, down through a narrow opening in the brush, me behind you, me reaching forward over your head to push branches aside, until we reach the riverbed itself, marked with crisscrossing ribbons of tracks from bicycles and motorcycles and ATVs. I'll hold your hand, we'll walk and talk, father and son, you'll have lots of questions, being a relatively new arrival, you'll have questions about the dry bed of the Madera River, and I'll answer them for you, Juan-George, it'll be as simple as that, you and me, walking, talking, questions and answers. I'll show you how and where the water cuts into the land, I'll tell you about the seasons, about when the river is full, about the flowers and grasses and lizards and butterflies and birds, mating and growing, and dying and mating and growing again. Your grandfather used to take me down there, back when he was still going out, back when I was still a little boy. We held hands and we walked, I asked questions and he answered, for a long time I believed he knew all there was to know.

Everything repeats itself eventually, your grandfather used to say, the universe is a giant revolving door. Which reminds me of the bicycle crank, of the turning of the crank, feet on the pedals, the crank going round and round, like thoughts, as I've said before, and the wheels, for their part, going round and round too. Get a rock stuck in your tire and you'll hear the *tick-tick* of it as long as those wheels keep turning. But there is the other motion, too, the bicycle moving forward, covering ground, as they say, the bicycle moving forward over new ground relentlessly, nothing ever repeating exactly the same way, everything always different. Until, of course, you reach the terminus. But my point is that the world isn't either one way or the other, Juan-George, it's both. The crank turns and the bicycle moves forward. Both.

When I picture myself holding your hand, I realize I'm picturing myself holding your grandfather's hand. Only we've traded places, of course, I'm the big one now.

* * *

C: Oppen? Sweetheart?

O: Yes, *amor.*

C: You are alive, you are going to live.

O: Yes.

C: Why are you still talking?

*. . . Gaal saw the people, he said to Zebul, Behold, there come people down from the top of the mountains. And Zebul said unto him, Thou seest the shadow of the mountains as if they were men . . . [Bible reading continues to end of tape.]*

# ACKNOWLEDGMENTS

For their keen eyes and wise words I'm indebted to Eric Bennett, Jack Livings, Brigid Hughes, John Woodward, and Katie Arnoldi. For ushering Oppen through the vicissitudes of rude commerce, Anna Stein and Lauren Wein. For artistic lodestar navigation, James Alan McPherson. For diverting lines, GM Quinte. For everything else and more, I am eternally grateful to Chrissy Levinson Wilson, without whose love and encouragement I surely would have sunk into the mire, never to be heard from again.

CPSIA information can be obtained
at www.ICGtesting.com
Printed in the USA
JSHW080907140123
36154JS00024B/364

9 780544 106277